I0831391

Unusual romances bloom, and fantasy sometimes makes its way to reality in *The Weight of Flowers*. The story is much more than a genre-bending read, it is a psychological and sensual experience. Exuberant, descriptive prose enlivens each page, and complex relationships are deeply explored. Coupled with passionate, incendiary opposite and same sex exploration, amidst its unexpected twists and turns, this debut novel catapults into a category of its own.

—*Stacey Donovan*

New York Times Bestselling Editor, author of *Dive* and *Zalman King's Red Shoe Diaries* book series, book editor, and ghostwriter

D.K. Silver has created a powerful weave of drama in *The Weight of Flowers*, a tale of a fierce young woman's striving to break from an overbearing father in the south of the 1920s. Thoroughly engaging in capturing the deep complexities of family and the destructive brutishness of men.

—*Jeff D. Buchanan*

Author of *The Carnal Education of Miss Vicky*, *The Reader*, *Earthrise*

D.K. Silver's exquisite prose draws you into a lush, vivid tale of intrigue, power and passion. *The Weight of Flowers* transports readers to 1920's Switzerland, where a young American woman has taken a job as a companion, hoping to break free from the schemes and manipulation of her abusive father. But family drama follows her, forcing her to confront her past, claim her independence and explore the true nature of her own desires. Intensely emotional conflicts and sensual descriptions conjure images that will linger in your mind long after you've finished reading this unique, unsettling, beautifully written novel.

—*Claire Haiken*

Award Winning author of the *Sierra Legacy Series*

The Weight of Flowers

The Weight of Flowers

By

D.K. Silver

Heavy Threads Publishing

To request permissions, contact the publisher at dksilverauthor@gmail.com.

Library of Congress Control Number: 2022908126

Hardcover ISBN: 978-0-578-37550-2

First paperback edition October 2022.

Edited by Ange Baker and Stacey Donovan
Cover art by Thomas Darnell
Visit his website at www.thomasdarnell.com
Cover design by Norman Apalis
Interior design by Ange Baker

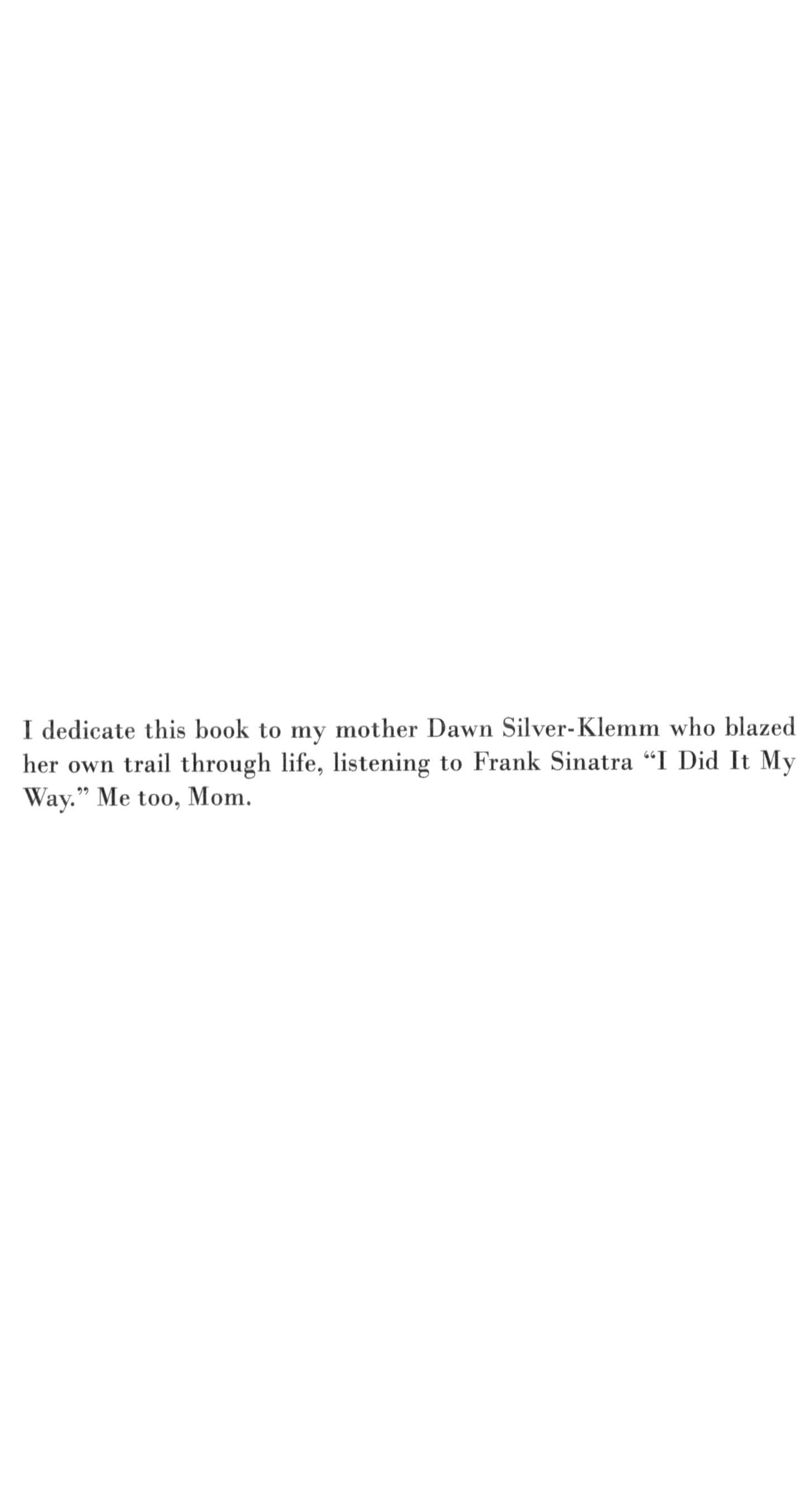

I dedicate this book to my mother Dawn Silver-Klemm who blazed her own trail through life, listening to Frank Sinatra "I Did It My Way." Me too, Mom.

"One life is all we have and we live it as we believe in living it. But to sacrifice what you are and to live without belief, that is a fate more terrible than dying."

Joan of Arc

Section 1: Jamison

1.

A Mourning Dove pitched and ducked, sidling along the naked fingers of a winter beech tree. The wind seeded a flurry of decaying leaves, causing the dove's talons to relinquish, unfurling its wings in bloom. Each stroke of its seraphim wings became kaleidoscopic.

Back on the limb, its body stretched, long tail feathers fanned out like the train of an evening gown. The gray dove's iridescent neck swelled and the velvet of its throaty coo turned over and over like pages of an oversized, well-worn book.

The Colonel flung the drapes shut.

Jamison blinked, and tugged at the sleeves of her woolen traveling suit. She felt the damp touch of sweat along the back of her collar, as she focused on him now sitting behind his massive desk.

The birds fell silent outside.

He tipped back into his creaky chair and blew a thick stream of cigar smoke into the haze that lingered in the room.

Was there ever a time she could have called him her father?

She took a deep breath, quelling her festered stomach, and stared down at the swirling knot in his desk.

With a groan, the Colonel leaned his ruddy palms on the desk to heave his bulk up from the chair, wavering toward a tall glass cabinet across the room to fish out a metronome. He planted it down on his desk.

She glanced up at the neck-mount trophies behind him—their mouths agape, festooned with gray dusty cobwebs; their petrified emotion might have been from something as confusing as this.

The Colonel angled his cigar to the left corner of his mouth, and then he brushed his manicured thumbnail along his lip. He sized her up in that way he did, his eyes meeting hers like a weak handshake.

Jamison kept her hands slack, her eyes centered on his.

"If I write this check," he said, "you will keep up your end of this bargain. Hear me?"

It was the kind of obvious statement that begged an eye roll, but she swallowed hard, trying to hear the song of birds beyond the window.

The Colonel removed the faceplate from the wooden metronome and twisted the winding key, sliding the weight mid-way down the arm. The ticking of it overtook the room.

Unsatisfied, he pushed the pendulum weight to the absolute bottom of the arm to speed up the tempo.

"What are you doing?" she managed to say.

"Shut'n up those annoying little flying rats out there." He gestured at the drapes. From his whiskey glass, he sucked an ice cube into his mouth and then picked up a pen, teasing the cap off and on, keeping to that manic rhythm.

Please for God's sake, she closed her eyes, just let me go.

And then there was the sound of him opening his drawer for the check register.

She opened her eyes to see him spit ice back into his glass. The polished moons of his fingernails whitened as he scribbled the correct amount across the check, and then his name. He ripped the check from the booklet and used it to fan himself, keeping with the metronome.

"You better take it, girl," he said.

When she reached for it, he pulled it away and spoke with a deadpan tone, "Best try harder, Jami*son*, else I'll change my tune."

At that, she straightened up. She had been at college for over three years, and now in these four days being back home the Colonel had treated her no better than trash. "You want me gone as much as I want to be out of here." She gave the check a tug, and his thumb pinched down harder.

Tic, tic, tic.

He laughed, wafting a sweet-sour blanket of bourbon. That same smell always clung to him like mildew on a ripe dish towel.

He let her have it and sat back, propping his boots up on the desk. With no intention of ceremony or adieu, Jamison made her way to the door, folding the check for her jacket pocket.

The ticking was silenced when she touched the door handle. She gave one last look at him.

"I'd pay twice as much to be rid of you," he said, palm smothering the metronome's tic.

Even if she could, she refused to let go of that last encounter with her father. She also remembered soon after, the trill of dove wings that exploded into flight as she opened the front door, stepping down from the porch to the waiting truck. It had taken less than an hour to board the train at Union Station and less than twenty-four before she walked the open decks of the steamer en route to Switzerland.

Now, Jamison watched a thin light seep underneath the heavy hotel drapes, unsure if it was coming or going. Dusk in Switzerland would mean midday in Kentucky. If so, then the Colonel would be occupying the armchair at the head of the dining table, hollering for someone to bring his lunch.

Pins and needles pricked the numb flesh of her backside as she sat on the plum-colored rug. Her fingers gripped the crystal of her necklace as if poised to throw a hatchet. She relaxed her hold, tracing her thumb along the crystal's sharpest edge, the one that led to the arrowhead peak that crowned its smooth face. That perfect smoothness taunted her like a tranquil pond ringed with palm-sized stones.

In Jamison's final year at the University of Cincinnati she'd discovered fellow Sayre School alumna, Miss Gertrude Atherton—a famous feminist writer. She had the freedom to travel the world without a husband, without the tug of any supervisory noose to bind her progress.

Before thinking herself out of it, Jamison wrote a letter saying that she wanted to follow in Miss Atherton's footsteps, and she had the capacity to do so intellectually and financially. To her surprise, Miss Atherton replied almost immediately, consenting to mentor her.

Jamison vowed she would march in *lockstep*, as requested in the letter of intent. She wasn't actually sure how to get into lockstep with anyone; *out* of step was more her style, but she had faith that she'd make sense of it.

Jamison had reviewed Miss Atherton's previous itineraries. She couldn't arrange passage on the same steamer, but she was able to reserve rooms in the same hotels and the same cities prior to their eventual meeting—a trial run to become as simpatico as a shadow. If she'd known the preferred meals of Atherton, Jamison would have gladly tasted them all.

In the three days since she'd arrived in Switzerland, she had been able to identify some of the smells of her hotel room. The bathroom scent was universal, dank and wet with lingering hints of Pears soap and cherry tobacco, as was the sweet almond in the floor polish. And for the linen aroma, she'd simply named: dry.

Everything in her room had been touched by others, worn down, burnished from the oils of many palms. The copper doorknobs, filigree drawer pulls, and even the shimmery silk tassel drop that hung like an earring from the bedside lamp—they were all tarnished and genuine. She couldn't wait to leave her mark.

Jamison walked over to the Victorian lamp on the dresser to flick the slender obelisk crystals, which were reminiscent in shape to her own crystal that hung from her neck—the last gift her childhood friend had given her.

Carrington…

It wasn't as if she needed more tangible items for remembrances, but when time came to leave the farm, she dashed to Carrington's room and willy-nilly grabbed the first thing she laid eyes on—a pair of his pants with the belt still in the loops. Stranger yet was her thoughtless swipe of the Colonel's half-smoked cigars on her way out the door of the main house. What an odd assortment of items to pilfer.

She flopped down onto the hotel bed and stared at Carrington's belt, still threaded through his trousers hanging over the arm of the wooden rocking chair. A simple strip of black leather so old that it had pores and wrinkles like human skin, yet was supple and slightly spongy between her fingers.

Jamison pulled the pants over the seat and rested her cheek on their gray nubby fabric. She inhaled, drinking in the familiar scent of cut stalks of Kentucky bluegrass—vanilla sweet, and earthy, and rich.

She draped her leg over them, sneaked her fingers into the pocket, which always gaped open, stretched out from his fidgety hands always massaging that tatty old rabbit's foot. But then she shook out of her daze.

"You came here for a reason. Focus." Jamison sat up and searched her room for inspiration.

She studied the wall behind the headboard. "In the dim of

evening," she considered, "the walls appear to be a dishonest mint, while in the crisp light of winter's morning, the walls whisper a foamy… celadon."

She collapsed back onto the bed, lying as flat as her words sounded.

She looked down her body toward the bachelor's chest. It was brown and fatly squat with four drawers, each one filled with her clothes; its feet were claws, which looked as though they might collapse from overexertion.

Her dresser back home was plain and empty.

Jamison got off the bed and kneeled before the dresser. When the bottom drawer caught, the metal handles bit into her fingers. The wood scraped and whined when she yanked it open. She pulled a bulky turtleneck over her head and then felt around for the Black Hawk "Chief of the Broadleaves" cigar box. She placed it on her bed.

Jamison slipped on Carrington's pants, securing them tight with his belt.

She always thought that there was something obvious, serious even, about pants. A man could wear a sack on his head and be taken seriously, while a woman was confined to what was above the neck, and even then she hardly garnered the same unquestioned respect.

Jamison turned her attention to the cigar box. Inside was the Colonel's smaller golden Pom Pom cigar tin with a couple of stubs and a matchbox. As soon as she forced open the dented lid, burnt black pepper and oak muddied the Swiss air.

The Ohio safety match caught on the first strike. In the hotel's oval floor mirror, she studied the puckered O shape of her lips around the cigar and thought about how the Colonel's lips looked more like a lazy comma. She let the flame creep closer to her fingers.

Framed by her French doors, she stood like a still-life, *Woman with Cigar* could be the caption—though dressed as she was, she'd wager that folks would have to look closer to recognize that she even was a woman. And once they did, she'd lose their interest and possibly earn their disdain.

Four quick knocks rapped at her door. "Telegram," a voice said.

She gasped and partially swallowed a plume of acrid fumes, doubling over. The cigar fell from her mouth as waves of hot tears flooded her eyes.

Certain the boy had the wrong room, she waited, hunched over for him to realize his mistake. Only her parents knew she was there, and they were not ones to write.

"Telegram," the voice called out again.

She stooped lower to snag the cigar from the rug.

"What?" she asked, flinging the door open. She swiped her hand over her mouth and nose.

The boy looked her up and down, and seemed to take an accidental step back before offering her the telegram and pen.

"Hold this," she said, offering the cigar. When he made no attempt to exchange his pen for it, she cautiously fit it between her lips, struggling to breathe around the cigar. She signed for the telegram and shut the door. With shaking fingers, she tore open the yellow missive.

JOB OFFER RESCINDED STOP LINE OF CREDIT UNTIL END OF BUSINESS TUESDAY STOP HOTEL MANAGEMENT NOTIFIED STOP

The cigar tumbled to the floor.

She was no still-life now. She more resembled a Cubist painting by Picasso. Confusion shoved one eyebrow unnaturally close to her hairline. Disbelief clawed back an eyelid. Disgust slapped her nose to the side of her face.

She crumpled the telegram with one hand, opened the door with the other and then slammed it shut. She slumped down.

Had she actually thought that the Atlantic Ocean would keep the Colonel away?

Her rage felt so potent she'd swear she could make that balled-up telegram hit the wall and crack the plaster.

If her father had his own way, she'd have to say, Goodbye, Switzerland. Goodbye, Hotel Palace Luzern, adieu internship, and au revoir independence. Welcome back to the bluegrass state of Kentucky. Her position was gone. Her dream had shrunk to the size of a crumpled telegram on the Persian rug.

She snatched up the yellow paper and grabbed her purse. Maybe she'd get one more good meal before being thrown out.

2.

Upon entering the dining room a line of tony guests turned toward Jamison like a herd of dull cattle in mid-chew. She briefly wondered why she'd become a spectacle, but she didn't slow to stare them down. Nor did she pause, as she usually had, to gape at the entirety of the room captured by the wall of mirrors.

Instead, she weaved her way to an empty table by the French doors.

Any moment the management could drag her from her chair and toss her out onto the street. She pictured the pathetic snail trail of scuff marks left by her heels and the laughter of guests.

Jamison's imagination was pulled away by a pair of handsomely tailored navy trousers, just inches from her table—and brown oxfords pointing so precisely toward her that there was no doubt of her being the wearer's subject of attention. She focused on the unusual weave and color of his pants, probably something royal, like Prussian Blue, woven from the hair of French aristocracy; meanwhile, her pants were dove gray and…

And her heart sputtered anxiously in her chest, realizing that Carrington's pants was what made her a spectacle. The man in front of her muttered something indistinctly under the pounding of her heart, although the tone was laced with pity.

Before she could even glare back at him, the maître d' scurried into her line of sight, his black morning coat stiff to his ears, a gray Vandyke beard pointing like a hairy arrow below his scowl.

"Mademoiselle, this table is reserved." He stood there with one hand gripping her chair, ready to pull it out from under her.

Jamison saw only one other empty table near the kitchen entrance, crammed against the wall.

"Sir," she said, "I prefer this table." And then she patted the white linen tablecloth with her bare hand.

"But, mademoiselle, this table is *taken*." His ridiculous beard looked as sharp as his enunciation.

"On that," Jamison asserted, "we agree. It *is* taken, by me. And please don't 'but' me again. We Davenports hold on to what's ours—

especially a grudge."

He clicked his heels and stood straighter. "Mademoiselle, this table is reserved for a gentleman, and I *must* insist that you move."

"A *gentleman?*" Jamison looked around the room, sizing up the formal portrait-ready gentlemen. "In Kentucky, a gentleman would never think of removing a lady from her table. If he wants it, he can come right on over here to arm wrestle me for it." She threw her shoulders back, noisily planting her elbow onto the white tablecloth. At that, the room had nearly silenced.

From the other side of the room, the man with the navy trousers gestured for the maître d' to leave. The maître d' then strode back to his station by the entrance.

Jamison lifted her defiant chin and waggled the toe of her silk-heeled oxford.

After that moment passed, all her initial frustrations returned.

She pressed her hands against her face and then splayed her fingers wide. She peered at the view beyond the frosted doors, to an icy veranda and a staircase leading to the carpet of grass and the lake beyond. It was postcard perfect. Soft lights flickered as couples wandered, their breath commingling with the frigid air in small cloudy puffs. Everyone looked to be enjoying the first day of the new year, bundled in love and hope.

Those lucky lovers with sparkling eyes made her feel as gray and cold as the spaces between the stars.

Just the previous night, while watching their celebration below, she had sworn that 1923 was going to be the year she made her mark.

Now, it seemed her time in Switzerland might be coming to an end.

Jamison scratched the word *END* acrostically into her cloth napkin. Was it possible for something to end that had barely begun?

She pulled out her Lady Duofold pen from her bag, ceremoniously uncapping the red top. She traced the etched letters, dotted three periods—and then wrote:

E.volution
N.urture
D.etermination

3.

From across the dining room, Mr. Jon Roe brushed the tablecloth away from his navy pants and slightly angled his chair to enjoy the reflection upon the mirrored wall—that of the lovely invader who stole his spot.

He appreciated the smooth burn of the fine Glenmorangie scotch, and the residual warmth that licked through his body as he watched her stare out the window.

Jon revolved his wrist with the glass in hand, cycling the scotch through the ice—wondering what her story was.

Women had become more daring, participating in activities traditionally enjoyed by men. Many of this new breed fell short—lacking a certain quality that spoke to him on sight—a je ne sais quoi. She had it. She wasn't putting on airs, which made him more curious about her.

He could read her from across the room. Despite those interesting heavy trousers and the turtleneck, she showed blatant anxiety through the tremble of the fabric that draped over her slender frame and the dance of her knee—but there was something more.

He glanced toward the foyer, scoping the possibility of, perhaps, a tardy dining companion of hers.

Her fingers traipsed along the edge of her turtleneck down into the thick fabric, reaching for something. Jon felt his eyelids smooth over as he enjoyed the moment of anticipation.

She revealed a white crystal on a cord. The tip of her tongue lay in wait, resting on the rosy pillow of her lower lip. He could almost feel the rush of her breath escape as an aching sigh when she touched its pyramid point to her tongue.

Jon straightened up.

By the feline roll of her shoulder and the way her tongue teased along the edge of her mouth, Jon was certain she was thinking about a man—most likely the man whose trousers she wore.

Jon was rudely pulled away from his vision by the storm of activity that blew through the lobby's revolving doors.

A couple scuttled into view, framed by the dignified hush of the dining room. The stocky man pitched their bags in the direction of the front desk, as if someone were supposed to catch them. The woman made straight for the maître d's banquette, then rose onto her tiptoes to search the room.

Suddenly, thc young lady who had stolen his table froze solid at the sight of the couple skirting the maître d's station.

A gangly young man trailed somewhat behind. Jon realized that he'd seen that man before.

4.

Jamison pinched herself as her parents approached.

"Colonel, I told you she would be here," Jamison heard from her mother, CeCe, who then proceeded to pull out her own chair. The Colonel sat down heavily at the table. He stretched out his legs and puffed his chest.

CeCe suddenly turned, as if remembering the man behind her. "Jamison, dear, this is Mr. Jennings O'Rourke. We were on the same ship, isn't that remarkable? It's kismet, that's what it is. Kismet. Isn't that right, Mr. O'Rourke?" She plunked down on the seat not waiting for his answer. "And here we are, just in time for dinner!"

None of it made any sense. Jamison's parents were sitting there as if all of it was normal; she couldn't bring herself to acknowledge them.

Then Jennings O'Rourke greeted her. "Miss Davenport," he said with a slight bow, edging into her sightline, "forgive my intrusion into your evening, but I've heard so much about you. I was eager to make your acquaintance."

Jamison squinted at the man; she could see he was speaking, but his words didn't register.

The Colonel already unbuttoned his suit jacket and plugged his thumbs under the straps of his suspenders. Jamison cocked an eyebrow at him before finally addressing the man standing there.

"Well, Mr. O'Rourke," she gripped the edge of the table, "we Davenports are excellent storytellers. I'm on the edge of my seat to know what you've been told about me." She turned to look up at him, attempting a smile that felt as straight as a zipper across her lips.

The Colonel cleared his throat and angled closer to Jamison. "Why don't you invite our young man to sit down?" he asked.

Jamison sat back and dropped her arms across her lap. *Our young man?* She couldn't begin to imagine what any of this had to do with her.

"Okay," Jamison said. "Won't you—won't all of you—join me?" She scooted her own chair closer to her mother's.

Mr. O'Rourke pulled out a seat while glancing around the room.

Jamison mused that he was probably searching for some other place to sit. His fingers took a firm hold against the back of the chair when he seemed to find something more interesting in the dining room. He muttered a quiet "Excuse me," before walking away from them.

Jamison dropped her formalities. She pushed her palms so squarely to the table that she felt ready to leap across it.

"Speak," she said, glaring at her father.

The Colonel was more interested in Jennings' retreat from their table, so Jamison pulled the yellow telegram out from her pocket.

She flattened it before dragging it closer to the Colonel.

"This," she said. "I'm dumbfounded."

CeCe busied herself with the task of creasing her napkin.

The Colonel pulled a cigar from his breast pocket and then bit off the end for the ashtray. His eye was trained on Jamison as he extracted a match from the table holder and then struck it against his boot, stoking the cigar with a few puffs.

"I thought we had an arrangement," Jamison said. She shoved the crinkled letter even closer to her father. "By our mutual agreement, I wasn't going to darken your doorstep, so why in the hell are *you* here?" She leaned forward, lowering her voice. "Thousands of miles away, minding my own business, then here you are."

She glanced at her mother, who reached with a wavering hand for Jamison's water goblet. CeCe shook her head at Jamison in the subtlest way she could manage.

"What's the meaning of this letter?" Jamison asked, jabbing her finger on the paper after each word. "And just who is this Mr. O'Rourke?" She nodded in the direction of Jennings, who seemed finished with his dealings across the room and was now heading to the lobby.

The Colonel mottled red at his escape, before calming at the sight of Jennings' coat still draped on the back of a chair at the table. With the cigar firmly planted between his wet lips, the Colonel scanned the letter with a grin.

"Quite clearly stated here that the internship has been re-scin-ded." He turned the telegram around and used his cigar to point at the word. "Re-scin-ded, Jamison." He held long on each syllable, while ash from his cigar dusted over the yellow paper.

Was it possible that rather than support her, the Colonel withdrew the funds earmarked to endow the Sayre School—a stipulation to her getting a post with their most famous alumna?

"You ask about Mr. O'Rourke? I'll explain this just once." His voice teemed with warning. "You hold the key to our future. I'm planning on getting you with that young man to expand my stud farm to O'Rourke's holdings. You and your mother will be *good* little soldiers and follow my orders."

Jamison searched the craggy terrain of the Colonel's face, looking for a hint of regret, or even shame over what he seemed to be demanding. Instead, she could feel his excitement, as if he were already clearing land to make room for more horses.

CeCe shook out her monogrammed violet handkerchief and then stuffed it beneath the edge of her sleeve at the wrist.

The Colonel then continued. "Go charm Mr. O'Rourke till there's no other option but to ask for your hand." He leaned so hard against the table that Jamison felt it pressing against her ribs. "And, my dear, I do mean that you are to make him feel like he has no other choice. I'm here to cash in, Jami*son*. It's time to pay your debts."

Jamison strained her eyes into a glare as she always had when he would emphasize the *son* in her name. All her life she'd tried to be like the son he wanted, and now he had the gall to offer her redemption for his pain and suffering of her female existence. His success could rot before she gave in.

The Colonel suddenly grabbed Jamison by the forearm and sternly added, "Am I making myself clear?" She flinched and yanked her arm away.

Jamison gripped her crystal in her hand and thumbed along its smooth face. She was certain the Colonel could now taste her mounting fear by the way his lips smirked around his cigar.

"A little bird told me that Mr. O'Rourke was planning this journey," the Colonel said. He looked over at Jennings, standing in the doorway of the dining room and looking as if he'd splashed water on his face and combed his hair. "I saw my chance to bring you two together. Booked a passage on the Mauritania, and here we are, one happy family."

Jamison sat up straight and tugged the sleeve of her sweater closer to her wrist, removing any trace that he'd grabbed her. She wanted to prove that she was immune to his bullying.

"Yes—one happy family," she said.

CeCe immerged from her haze.

"Well, dear," she looked between the Colonel and the ashtray, as if asking permission. "Carrington met Mr. O'Rourke in Ohio while buying equipment for the farm. The young man delivered it himself, if you can believe that, and has ever since been coming round the farm to visit us." CeCe smiled as if his visits were tantamount to those of Woodrow Wilson. She twisted her hankie and then shook it out again before shoving it back into her sleeve.

"Mr. O'Rourke and Carrington are like two peas in beans. They spent scads of time out with one another, doing Lord knows what young men do..." She slowed down before looking at the Colonel. "When Mr. O'Rourke wasn't needed at his factory in Akron, that is..." CeCe canted her head to look under the tablecloth. "Jamison, are you wearing pants?" she asked.

5.

After that whole scene, Jamison rammed open the entrance to the ladies' lounge. She heard a high-pitched shriek in reaction to her sudden entrance; an over-painted bullfrog of a woman frantically swept her things back into her purse.

Jamison shook her head and let go of the door. The lady's eyes bulged above two perfect circles of rouge. Like the line-leader in school, Jamison opened the door for her—and with admirable grace for a heavy-bosomed, tiny-footed top of a lady, she exited the lounge. Jamison waited for her to disappear around the corner and then slammed the door with a vengeance.

She shoved her hands into her pockets and paced along the crimson carpet. The Colonel had to have been planning this all along. All of it was too coincidental.

Throughout her life, many of the Colonel's plans had failed and left a trail of casualties strewn in his wake. Jamison likened the struggles she had with her father to that of a colt outmaneuvering the throw of a lasso. For a long time, she had felt that her hunter-jumper skills were perfect, so now it was something of a shock to find herself hogtied with his boot at her chest.

Jamison flung herself like a ragdoll onto an oversized armchair. "Who does he think he is?" she whispered. "And just who does he think I am? I'm no broodmare to be offered up to the strongest stud."

She studied her reflection. Thick strands of reddish-brown hair had come loose from her bun, framing her face, accentuating the line of her jaw. The cream turtleneck hung loosely around her waist. Her pants bunched like a dirndl skirt, cinched tight by Carrington's belt. "He's delusional if he thinks I'm now going to be a good soldier."

Jamison leaned closer to the mirror. Her heated breath hid her nose and mouth through the fog on its surface.

"He is *not* going to cross me now," she told herself.

Jamison exited the lounge. She stuck her hands into her pockets to hitch up her trousers and then stepped into the middle of the hallway. With a deep breath she walked to the dining room, making sure to hold eye-contact with anyone focused on her return.

A server with an enormous bouquet of flowers neared her table; at his heels was Mr. O'Rourke. She squeezed next to her chair to allow the server room to pass. When he didn't move and was then crowded by Mr. O'Rourke, she had once again become the spectacle of the room.

"Mademoiselle." He presented her the bouquet as if handing over a newborn baby. Jamison held the flowers away like they were stink-weed, certain that the pomade slick man was mistaken and the intended recipient would glide forward to relieve Jamison of her latest burden.

"Well..." Her mother's chin jerked like she had a nervous tic. "Peonies, in the middle of a Swiss winter—those must have cost a small fortune," CeCe said.

The look on the Colonel's face urged her on.

"I assume those are from you, Mr. O'Rourke?" CeCe asked.

Jennings gently pulled out Jamison's chair before motioning her to sit down. He then looked at CeCe. "My dear lady, I'm afraid they are not from me. It appears my opportunity to give Jamison something rare and exotic has been ousted by a fellow admirer here at the hotel—Mr. J.D. Roe, our host for dinner tomorrow night, a traditional Berchtold's Day celebration, should you care to join me at his château." When he paused, Jamison could see an equal amount of elation and anxiety on his face.

The Colonel spat an ice cube back into his glass and then raised it in Jennings' direction. "J.D. Roe, as in Roe Industries of Ohio? So, that's who you've been hiding from me?" The Colonel crowed out in laughter. "Well, of course she accepts the invitation!" He gripped his hand on Jennings' shoulder.

"Well," Jennings raised his hand in a polite pause. "I wouldn't want to force anything upon her."

"Nonsense, my boy!" the Colonel's voice boomed. "She gladly accepts. This is a most exciting prospect for you, Jennings, and we wouldn't dream of getting in your way! But," he raised his finger from the hold on his glass to point at him, "you just remember that this is the little lady who made it possible for you. My..." he looked over at Jamison with a strange happiness, "pretty little Jamison right here."

6.

What had she been thinking? On the spot she should have said no—made up some story. The gleam in the Colonel's eye was telling enough.

Jamison removed her woolen cap from the back pocket of her ski pants and pulled it over her head. She massaged her scalp and then bent down to strap the leather bindings around the toe and heel of her boots. The ski slopes of Engelberg were endless, and worth each penny and every minute it took to get there—a place where her parents would never find her.

Rope tows made it easier to crest the incline without sidestepping the whole way up. Waiting in line, Jamison lost herself in the sounds of the wind swirling every language into one. It invited her to relax because no one was speaking to her. Before she realized, it was her turn to step up to the rope. She gripped the tow. As it dragged her up the slope, she watched some skiers glide while others careened down the hill.

Maybe she'd get lucky enough to crash, lose her memory, and miss the whole fiasco.

At the top of the mountain, she shifted her weight from boot to boot and watched cracks spread in the crisp snow under her skis, leaving what looked like gray webs around her. Dry snowflakes drifted from a cloudless sky, creating a film of fine skeletal shapes. It somehow reminded her of the time she got caught burying her mother's crochet hooks.

The Colonel had just finished berating her mother's latest compulsion to craft white doilies. He held up one that was lopsided, stitched irregular. It was a shape unlike the doilies used to cover an upholstered chair meant to keep a gentleman's hair cream from leaving an oily mark.

He had said she only made ugly, useless, little white things.

At that time, Jamison was nine years old but could still recognize the sheer meanness and disgust in his eyes. He yanked at the crochet threads, and when he couldn't break the strands he simply tossed it into the fireplace.

It was Carrington's father who had found Jamison later digging a hole for the hooks. Her mother never crocheted again; instead, she took up doll-making.

After skiing, Jamison smoothed her hands over her solid, non-broken ankles; she couldn't get hurt on those slopes, even though she'd tried.

She had crossed her skis and toppled over with merely a bruised elbow and a jarred shoulder. She had aimed for a knee-high shrub and skied right through, failing to twist her ankle in the gnarled branches. She even attempted to cross in front of another skier telemarking down the slope, but he had pulled up short of the collision.

A ski accident wouldn't solve her problem, anyway. The Colonel would find a way to get what he wanted, even if he had to piece her back together, himself.

She unlaced her bindings and hoisted her skis and bamboo poles over her shoulder, walked the short distance to the hut where she had rented the gear, and then made her way over to the sleigh that shuttled from the hotel to the slopes.

As the sleigh lurched along the snow, Jamison took off her cap and then closed her eyes, letting the cold air dry her sweat. Cowbells clanged as the four horses pulled the sled back to the portico of the hotel.

Jamison walked directly to the women's spa, checking in early for her appointment to further avoid crossing paths with the Colonel.

She rubbed her calves, attempting to smooth out the distinctive linear weave embossed upon her skin by the thick ski socks. She wrapped the hotel spa robe around her and then rested on the wooden bench outside the steam room. Jamison wiggled her toes, relieved to be free of the scratchy wool and leather lace-up ski boots.

The aroma of moist wool and Lysol hung in the heavy air, an odor that reminded Jamison of her childhood and the hot musty air that wheezed through the attic.

Whenever the Colonel was away on a hunting trip, her mother would drag her up to the sweltering pitched roof space, full of tight angled corners.

"Jamison, my daddy bought me all these clothes in Paris," her mother would say, lifting discolored dresses and petticoats from a misshapen wicker basket—all rotting like a Jack-o-lantern in late November. "I was the prettiest little girl in Lexington."

Jamison couldn't erase the memory of her mother's coquettish posturing each time they were in the attic; her painted-on bow-like lips puckered and strained. Each time her mother batted her eyelashes Jamison could almost hear the clicking sound of a china doll's ceramic eyelids slapping shut.

"The bonnet flowers still look so real!" Her mother had shoved the flowered cap at Jamison's face. At the time Jamison thought that flowers in a hat were a great idea; it was another way, besides the pockets of dungarees, to carry your little wormy friends.

"Looky here," CeCe leaned with the crown of the hat on her fisted hand, "there's even a little green grub trying to eat the flower petal." Jamison remembered putting the worm in her pants pocket.

She now scratched her fingernails along her scalp at the indelible memory of that filthy bonnet—the mites that had scurried through her thick, sweat-dampened hair. Missy, their maid, had stood by in the kitchen ready with the lye soap and the fine comb to sweep them from her head.

Jamison let the memory dissolve right back into the recess of her mind—but she still couldn't forget that her parents were somewhere in the hotel. The Colonel had made a point to categorize her as a mindless pawn—as pliable as her mother's misshapen doilies.

But that was where he was wrong.

Just because she was a woman didn't mean that she was less of a Davenport. Jamison was sovereign to herself, and very capable of changing tact.

She slipped out of the plush cotton robe and wrapped a towel around her torso, before finding her way to a spot on the lower bench, away from two women who sat higher in a darkened corner.

In the light mist she could see the exotic tiling all around her—a watery blur of pale pink, turquoise, lavender, coral, and gold. Altogether, they formed tiny intricate flowers, which surrounded a splendidly pear-shaped body of a peacock, tail flared and spread open over the lower tiled benches. The background was rich gold and looked like a wall of shimmering coins. It was beautiful and exotic, and expertly formed. It looked rather life-like, grand and showy.

Jamison leaned back and closed her eyes, allowing the rising steam to melt away the remaining tension of the night before. She discretely opened her towel to rub the iced hand cloth along her body, and then she took a sip of cucumber water. Her crystal still hung from her neck—the red silk cord darkening, as beads of sweat seeped from her opening pores.

Over the hiss of the steam jets, Jamison heard faint sounds of the women moving about. She peered through the billowing mist. The raven-haired woman had draped her bare leg over her blonde companion's.

As the steam settled, Jamison could see that the dark-haired woman had exquisite white skin, and even in the heat she looked regal—as cool as a marble sculpture. She took a piece of ice from a cup and dragged it across the other woman's bosom. The blonde tilted her neck to one side—openly luxuriating. The raven-haired beauty trailed another piece of ice along the nape, following the same path with her tongue.

Jamison could hardly breathe. She had never seen anything like it, never even imagined a woman's touch—but the sight and sounds of those unrestrained creatures was mesmerizing.

Jamison's legs tensed up, and then that tightness spread up to her face. But she then felt sudden panic about watching them—possibly unwelcome to do so? The ridges and corners of each tile dug into her skin as she pressed her back against the wall. Her eyes swept from the women to the door, and then back again.

The blonde woman's mouth was open, as those silken creamy fingers were exploring between her thighs. The hand moved with assurance and freedom.

They had to know she was there, watching.

Eyes closed, the lovers were deep inside the experience of each other. Jamison inched her own hand to touch herself. By watching them she felt wickedly daring, strangely powerful.

Her head dipped back against the moist tile as her fingers sought her aching center. The hot mist shrouded her perch. Jets of steam grazed over her body in a whoosh as she convulsed forward; the taste of eucalyptus burned at her throat as she gasped for air. A droplet of sweat landed between her feet, and then several other drops. For the long while she listened to the sweat fall, eventually understanding that she was alone.

Jamison eased over to where the pair had been sitting, wondering if they had been watching her at the time.

She trailed her crystal up to her mouth, tasting the salt of her own skin.

Jamison sat before the mirrors of the beauty salon, languid in the afterglow. Floral and eucalyptus scents mixed with the lilting voices of the surrounding women. The longer she sat there she sensed that something had shifted within her. She felt connected to these women in a way she'd never considered possible. What she knew, she couldn't describe; she wasn't sure she wanted to. She didn't want to diminish the feeling by putting words to it.

Jamison closed her eyes and settled into her chair. The hairdresser deftly lifted Jamison's gleaming auburn hair from her shoulders, and then brushed it like a horse's tail. She massaged Jamison's scalp, and then her neck, before artfully arranging her hair so that it was parted on the side. She then drew it back into a loose bun at Jamison's nape.

Feeling the bun rest against her neck, Jamison opened her eyes, reaching for the turquoise feather she had purchased earlier that afternoon in a quaint millinery shop. She was determined to add flair and authenticity to her mission to play the peacock that evening.

A line of goose bumps tickled Jamison's neck as the hairdresser dragged the feather slowly along her hairline. Alarmed, Jamison stiffened and looked at the hairdresser more closely, as the feather was slipped into place along the bun. The hairdresser secured it with small diamond pins that looked like crystallized snowflakes in Jamison's hair.

Before Jamison could say a word, the blonde traced a finger along her collarbone, up to the pulsing artery beside her throat. Jamison felt her pulse quicken. A sweet smile came to the blonde's lips as she leaned down and whispered, "You are beautiful in every way."

7.

As the evening neared, Jamison thumbed through her closet, grateful that ever since she had departed for the university her mother had taken charge of her wardrobe. If it had been up to Jamison, she would have been happy to wear a uniform like she had at the Sayre School; clothes were a practicality to her.

Jamison chose a silver satin dress that was cut on the bias; it draped and hugged her in the right places, making the most of her willowy curves. The dress clung to her sides and her hips—and then at the cleft of her tailbone was a plume of fabric that draped into a train of silver to glide along the floor.

Jamison felt sure that she would draw attention that evening like a preening male peacock would, blatantly on display for all to appreciate.

She paced the length of the dresser. After three steps, she rotated on the heel of her shoe beneath the train of her gown, and then took another three—all the while staring at the washbasin where she had dumped the flowers the night before.

She hadn't really taken a good look at them; at first glance she had considered them baseball-sized, pretty white rose-like flowers with some red here and there.

Now, the flowers made her nervous.

She took a step away from the dresser.

They weren't only pretty—they were voluptuous, affronting, and patient.

Patient? Affronting? Somehow they held her attention, daring her to look away, which she was having a hard time doing.

Yet, they were just flowers.

But a stranger—a man—had selected them. For her.

Thinking of her.

Jamison clasped her hand behind her back, eyeing the bouquet. He obviously didn't know the first thing about her. Because if he did, he would have given her a dozen baseballs, instead—things to strike the scowl clean off the Colonel's fat lips.

She stepped closer and slowly bent to take a sniff. They smelled like roses growing in a citrus grove.

Jamison fluttered her finger over the tips of a flower. The tissue-paper flesh was sturdier and silkier than she had thought.

She backed away, pacing the length of the bureau again, and then kicked her train to land in a perfect fishtail swirl behind her. She slowed to a stop, centered on the basin; planting her elbows on the ledge, she rested her chin in her hands.

And then she blew on the flowers.

Each petal was unique. The white wasn't simply clean picket fence; there were hues of white—innocent blush whites, and you're-hiding-something blue whites, and crunchy chalk whites. Some ruffled lips were edged with drizzles and splotches of scarlet.

No—they were just flowers.

After getting ready, Jamison made her way down to the lobby. She stepped out of the lift to see her parents already waiting. Her father looked her up and down with a critical eye.

"Looks like that getup set me back quite a bit," he said, patting his chest in search of something. "But it *is* pollen, working capital. You be sweet and let him take a sip or two, young lady. Don't care if O'Rourke leaves you wilted—just make sure he leaves a bit of himself with you by night's end. Understand?"

Jamison remembered the tiled peacock in the steam room. Its beak was shut and its gaze imperious. She tucked her chin ever so slightly to watch the Colonel walk toward the hotel bar; he had the springy gait of a child who pulled the legs off frogs for fun. She turned to her mother who stood gaping at the tight clusters of guests in the lobby.

"My, they really know how to put on the dog and pony show here," CeCe declared. "Kentucky has come up in the world, for sure—not as much as you saw in Cincinnati and Akron, with all that rubber industry money, but we don't hold a candle to the finery here. Look there, that's a full sable coat."

Jamison touched her bun to make sure the peacock feather was still in place. "For goodness sake, Mother. You'd think you just fell off the turnip truck, like we live in some back road hick town south of the Alleghenies."

"What would I be doing on a truck, Jamison? And we do live in

Kentucky." CeCe circled around Jamison to see the peacock feather. "Sometimes I have no idea what you're talking about." Jamison could feel her mother remove and reposition the feather in her bun, not once, but twice.

She could tell her mother was on edge. Tonight, the words normally accompanied by CeCe's vacant look were fleshed out and fully dressed—over-dressed. Jamison was used to the ramblings, grown up with her mother's way of scurrying from reality, of making herself inconsequential and worth dismissing. It wasn't until Jamison was older that she began to appreciate the subtle brilliance of her mother's deception. Not that it would work for Jamison. Jamison had the Colonel's blood coursing through her veins; there was no valor in hiding, and no value in second place.

She stared at her mother who continued to gawk at the women with adolescent envy. This was the same person who had told her that she should never put Carrington's birthday gift of a white paper whistle into her mouth, because that's how babies were made. That was third grade, and even in third grade Jamison knew how babies were made.

But now, looking down at her own gown, Jamison felt the weight of her own naiveté.

She turned toward the lift. "Where is Mr. O'Rourke, anyway? I thought he was meeting us here in the lobby." She peeked into the bar and saw her father liberally sipping some of *Kentucky's Finest*. It didn't bode well that her mother seemed to be losing her grip, her father was drinking alone, and her love match was late to escort them to the château where she was to open up like a night-blooming jasmine.

When Mr. O'Rourke alighted from the lift she took a good look at him for the first time. He really was quite sweet looking. He seemed well-built, broad-shouldered, and narrow-hipped. His thick hair was red with hints of blonde, his nose aquiline, long, and graceful. His lips were as full as a woman's. He had a dusting of freckles upon the bridge of his nose and a few on his lower lip. But his eyes were the most striking quality. They were the palest shade of blue violet, with a focus so clear and open. Jamison hoped they truly were the windows to his soul, because she wanted to be honest with him.

While Mr. O'Rourke looked every bit the gentleman in his tuxedo, she had no intention of following the Colonel's order. On principle alone, she would never seduce him or any suitors the Colonel had in mind.

The Colonel stood in the bar quietly observing Jamison. She seemed to be doing everything but kicking the tires as she took inventory of Jennings O'Rourke. He certainly had the right breeding.

Breeding horses was all that the Colonel cared about. If it didn't work out... Well, who was he kidding—it would. His plan was set in motion for Mr. O'Rourke. Sure, the Mr. Roe who would host the evening was no slouch, but he wasn't horses. And horses were more useful to him than rubber tires.

The Colonel threw back a shot, appraising Jennings, remembering back to when that young man and Carrington were a tangle of human arms and legs in a knot of dog paws and tails—the night that storm had brought his demons back.

He remembered how the wind had howled and spears of rain battered the trees against his office window. He'd heard the crack of the front door as it hit the wall, tossing CeCe's ridiculous vase of god-awful daisies crashing to the ground. The whole house stunk of those stupid weeds.

The Colonel was now in a daze, feeling that first taste of bourbon hit his stomach, and the first taste of those memories. He pushed the empty glass closer to the bartender. "Fill it up." The Colonel watched Jamison shake hands with Jennings, and he flashed to the same memory of Carrington reaching for Jennings' hand, both of them laughing on the foyer floor.

At that thought, the Colonel squinted at his distorted reflection in the saloon bar mirror between the bottles of booze shelved in front.

Elbow on the bar, he looked around at the dark and oily wood paneling cover on the walls and the seats, all covered in some sort of yellow, tufty stuff. He liked how close the tables were to each other—good for listening in; if they spoke English, he'd be in good shape.

It certainly was an international crowd at this establishment. He heard some I-talians talking at the end of the bar.

As close as he got to anything I-talian was the full-size replica of a Sioux Indian made by Sebastiano Zappala, an Italian master puppet maker he had met several years ago at the Lexington horse track.

The Colonel closed his eyes considering the definition and expert craftsmanship. That little puppet maker was as knowledgeable as a doctor. The Colonel could imagine a warm breath passing between the Chief's wooden lips, and feel a heartbeat beneath the hard, smooth texture of the Chief's sculptured chest.

He deterred the thought by coughing into his hand and then he turned his attention back to Jamison and Jennings. In the corner of his eye, he saw Jennings crook his elbow, offering to lead Jamison from the room.

Mr. Roe's driver came in to collect the group from the lobby at the Hotel Palace Luzern and then drive them to his château in the Lucerne hills. To Jamison, the night drive was pleasant enough; the Maybach limousine fit them all comfortably; the seal fur throw that Jamison draped over her legs helped to keep the winter chill from seeping into her bones.

They snaked up a narrow mountain road cut into the side of the rugged cliffs above the lake. The view was unlike anything in Kentucky. The journey was lit by a full moon so bright that the roadside snow looked more like diamonds on a white carpet.

Jamison sat next to her mother, facing O'Rourke. She could make out the shape of him leaning away from the Colonel, who sat more to the middle of their shared bench seat than was polite. Even in the dim interior she could tell his eyes were on her while his body was angled toward O'Rourke's corner. She huddled closer to the door and peered through the window.

The glass felt refreshing and cool against her forehead.

There was a one-directional aspect to the conversation between her father and Jennings; it flowed from the Colonel, filling every space of the car.

The events earlier that day crept back into her mind. If she hadn't seen the women with her own eyes she'd never have believed it. On one level, it was how she felt when that man handed her the huge bouquet of flowers; she hadn't asked for that, either. Both experiences demanded something of her.

Her head knocked against the window when the car rolled in and out of a rut in the road—the peacock feather pricked at her neck.

Who was she kidding? Regardless of how she had dressed she was hardly a peacock. And who was she really trying to impress? She knew that her father thought she'd fallen in line with this ensemble... but was it more that the blonde hairdresser had inspired her to wear all of this just to go along with the feather?

The Colonel struck a match to light his cigar, illuminating the car interior. For a moment, Jamison could see her reflection in the window. Her lips were slightly parted. Carrington had drawn her that way. She often caught herself recreating that same look simply to understand what he saw.

She had no idea where Carrington had gone, or why he left the farm. It never occurred to her that he wouldn't always be there, rooted like the catalpa tree at their pond. Everyone had been so vague about him being gone.

She'd riffled through Carrington's dresser in search of anything that might shed light on his disappearance. That's when she found his drawings.

The hairs on her arms now rose as she thought about his detailed renderings of her.

She doubted he'd ever intended for her to find them, especially the way they were hidden in his Sunday trousers neatly rolled in the back of his drawer. The pants were placed with deference protected on two sides by the wooden corner, barricaded in front by a couple of boxes of Cretacolor charcoal.

He saw her as a woman in ways that she hadn't given much thought to. But right now had she decided to wear all of this to be the kind of woman in those drawings? Maybe the woman who is given flowers, maybe the kind of woman who would...

"Isn't that right, Jamison?" the Colonel asked.

Jamison felt her mother's elbow nudging at her side.

"I'm sorry, what?" she asked, turning toward the Colonel.

"I said that you, Jami*son*, are a real demon in the stirrups." The Colonel prodded Jennings, until he nodded his head.

"Well, I don't know if I'd call myself that exactly, but Carrington did teach me to ride." As soon as Carrington's name passed Jamison's lips, she felt the Colonel's glare on her. "You know I grew up with Carrington, right Mr. O'Rourke?" she said.

"Why I did hear..." Jennings started but was silenced by the Colonel gesturing his hand up for Jamison to change the subject.

The Colonel found O'Rourke's knee and started patting it. "Of course he knows Carrington, girl. I told this young man all about you one night, while Carrington sat at our dinner table."

Jennings nodded.

Jamison could already smell the bourbon waft in the Colonel's breath, undoubtedly just the start of his evening drunk. Suddenly, Jamison felt the toe of his boot over top her shoe before he discreetly added more pressure down on her, and then casually returned his foot back over to his space—an unkind reminder of what he could do to her in a more private circumstance. "I told O'Rourke that you were coming back home, and that your mother and I couldn't be happier about the news," he said.

Her body felt like a brick of ice, but her face went hot as she stared across the cab at the Colonel. From her periphery, Jennings and her mother seemed completely unaware as they looked out their windows.

Cold air whooshed between the car windows and the metal framing. The engines whined as they sped up a steep hill. Fat snowflakes began to berm along the windscreen.

Jamison balled up her evening bag in her hands in attempt to fight away the tears that glazed her eyes.

A hand then gently touched her leg. It turned over to display a handkerchief. Jennings' face, now illuminated by moonlight, showed a subtle sympathy in his pale blue eyes. She reluctantly took the handkerchief from him wishing it was doused in chloroform.

8.

As they drove, clouds stole the moonlight into heavy darkness. Jamison could barely see the stars shimmering in the distance from the window of Mr. Roe's car as it pulled up to a lighted gatehouse.

The gatekeeper checked the guest list for their names before waving them onto the property.

In the throw of the car lights Jamison could see Evergreens dusted with snow lining the long drive. Both sides of the cobbled road were blanketed in white, extending to the front roundabout where a fountain waterfall was frozen solid. The mansion was constructed of a gray stone, elegant and masculine—different from the typical chalets closer to town with their whimsical trim and pastel colors.

Upon coming to a stop, Jennings was the first to exit the car. He then turned back to offer Jamison his hand. She in turn circled around to help her mother gather her things. Jamison threaded her arm through her mother's, and then they together followed Jennings and the Colonel to the mansion.

The leaded glass doors opened and Jamison broke into a slight panic, realizing that the person standing in front of her was the very man from whom she stole the reserved table—their host, Mr. Jon Roe.

Tonight, his tuxedo pants were even more exquisitely fit.

Jamison pulled up her fur collar around her ears, slipping out of the light and into the shadow cast by the ample backside of her mother.

Jamison felt a sudden dread and then glanced down the steps behind her, weighing her options. They were steeper than any hill she had skied on earlier that day. An accidental misstep might sufficiently twist her ankle, and then if fortune struck, a concussion would follow. The tip of her shoe tapped farther back, feeling for the edge of the stair. Her chest lifted, while her arm drifted back.

She hopelessly fantasized about it.

But she glanced forward and got trapped in the deadpan stare of the Colonel, who tracked her like a child with a Mason jar in hand.

With a sudden spell of lightheadedness, Jamison focused on the few loose embroidery threads from the shoulder of her mother's red mohair coat. They swayed like flames.

Her thoughts needed to go elsewhere. This evening needed to pass her by like a fever dream. As they stood there, an image popped into her head from some dog-eared English Christmas book, of a well-dressed group huddled in halo-perfection—all basking in the throw of light from one mighty candle, bringing to focus their gleaming faces as they sang for their supper.

She heard footsteps on the landing, and upon looking up she felt as though she were caught like a child hiding a snowball behind her back, captured by the strangely knowing glint of the host's eyes, the suggestive arch of his brow, and the laconic curve of his mouth.

Her strong legs carried her forward until she found herself inches from his black shiny shoes.

Centered in the radiant glow of the gas lamps, it all looked too much like the next page in that Christmas book. Jamison stood there with only a few flakes of snow acting as the barrier between her and her host.

Jennings took a step forward into the lamps' glow. "Mr. Jon Derrick Roe," he started, "may I present Jamison Jones Davenport and—" Before he could finish, Jamison thrust out her gloved hand toward Mr. Roe's belly.

"It's... a pleasure to meet you, Mr. Roe—please let me thank you for the lovely bouquet... and accept my apology for taking your table... I uh..." Jamison rocked back and forth on her heels and then she stopped, realizing how childish she must have looked. She added in a rush, "I've never received flowers before." She felt the color red when his fingers gently slipped over her elbow, forwardly trailing to lift her wrist and kiss her hand.

She leaned in to get a better look at her hand, as if it were privy to something the rest of her was not. She could feel the eyes of her father, but she had to block it all out. None of this, and none of her trip was ever meant to be about him.

"Well, Miss Davenport," Jon said, "I'm glad you like them. Peonies, by the way, signify transformation. And I see," he let go of her hand, giving her an appreciative smile, "I was not wrong in choosing them for you."

Everyone seemed spellbound until the Colonel lurched forward and reached out his meaty hand. "Mr. Roe, I would like to introduce myself. I am Colonel James Duarte Davenport, and this is my wife, CeCe Jones Davenport."

CeCe gushed. "Pleased to meet you, Mr. Roe, and thank you so much for inviting us to your home this evening."

Jon stood as formal as an English butler. "Dear Lady, the pleasure is all mine, I can assure you," he said still staring at Jamison.

Maybe there *was* something to the Swiss air, a lack of particulate matter that magnified the power of this man's insight. It was exhilarating and frightening.

Upon their entrance to the château, Jon led the group into the living room where other guests were immersed in conversation.

At first glance, the living room seemed cavernous and cold, but as Jamison looked closer the cool grayness was magnificently complicated, like the beauty and depth of an iceberg; the entire room was smooth and polished like a mirror, down to the silver travertine marble floors that reflected the gilded furniture. The black marble fireplace was large enough to fit her entire family within its hearth. Above the fireplace hung an enormous rectangular mirror with a gilded frame that seemed to reflect the actions of every guest in the grand salon.

A black baby grand piano was in the far corner, where a string quartet played a classical piece that was both soothing yet oddly violent.

The Colonel, already with a drink in hand, planted himself beside Jamison.

"Don't let that getup you're wearing go to your head, hear me? Mister *Jennings O'Rourke* is our future, young lady," he said, nodding his head in O'Rourke's direction who stood next to their host. "Mr. Roe is *Jennings'* business, and Jennings is *your* business. Yours is to lasso that stud, not parade around like some, some…" Jamison felt the Colonel's hand tighten on her arm as he struggled to finish his thought.

She knew he wasn't afraid to squeeze and twist his instructions into her flesh.

She turned back to face his twinkling yet treacherous eyes, and managed to smile sweetly at him and maintain eye-contact.

"Miss Davenport," called the now familiar voice of their host. "May I introduce you to some of our other guests?" Jon had his eyes trained on the Colonel as he eased behind Jamison, reaching around her to position his hand carefully at her elbow, right below the Colonel's rope-burn grip. One last squeeze, and then the Colonel released her arm. As the Colonel stepped back Jon maintained a calm look.

Jamison glanced at her father to see his contorted face—his upper lip quivering rabidly. She glanced up at where a reflection might've shown the Colonel's grip on her. An uncharacteristic giggle bubbled in her tummy at the thought of Jon observing their private moment, but she bit her tongue to keep it down.

Jon introduced Jamison to various recent expatriates who were calling Switzerland their new home, while their own homes and fortunes were being plundered by insurgencies throughout Europe and Africa. For some reason she didn't feel like she could lump them together with the staid group of diners at her hotel. This collection was unique—individuals, all strangers to her, but each one seemed like an original.

A tiny woman with a severe part down the center of her crimped hair had a snag that cut from the toe of her black silk *peau de soie* shoe and up her silk stocking, disappearing beneath the beaded hem of her dress—yet the smile on her lips was carefree perfection.

Switzerland slowed down her pace; yet, observations rushed at her as opposed to her dashing through them. And now she was caught up in them. She felt herself becoming vulnerable to all of it. But she wanted to control what she saw and to choose what she'd become a part of.

Jamison raised her hand to the crystal hanging around her neck. She turned toward the trio of musicians and asked Jon, "What um, concerto are they playing, do you know?" She tilted her head, raising her ear as if the music was being poured into her mind.

"Chopin. Number one in E minor." Jon turned toward the musicians, his hands clasped behind his back.

Jamison took on the same posture and listened for a few moments, while pretending to be interested in the smooth ceiling. "It's um... powerful and... delicately haunting, at the same time." Jamison thought her words sounded appropriate, but she wasn't so sure when Mr. Roe didn't respond. She leaned against the casing that framed the entry to the music room and then drummed her fingers along the cool wood, wondering if he had actually heard her and was just ignoring her. Maybe she was trying too hard to be like any of the guests. She truly must have come off as a fake. Jamison slumped back upon the casing, feeling the feather in her bun tickling her scalp. She rubbed the back of her head on the molding.

In mid scratch she noticed something familiar about the pianist. It was in the long column of her neck and the way her eyelashes shadowed her cheeks, as her porcelain fingers traveled along the keys. Jamison leaned off the wall and took a step toward the piano.

Jon leaned close to her ear and whispered, "Miss Davenport, I believe you are a lover of music?" His tone seemed thick with innuendo. It was as if he could see every bit of her clamming up at the sight of the familiar pianist. Jamison felt the heat rise in her cheeks, as she recognized the lady as the same raven-haired woman from the steam room.

The music ended and the guests clapped, as the musicians took a slight bow and moved away from their instruments. The pianist stayed seated, who then turned to smile at Jon.

Jamison could feel him bow ever so slightly, while she, herself, remained focused on the pianist's dark almond eyes. Jamison was captivated by her smile; it switched from a gracious thank you to an evocative hello. The pianist swept forward, her burgundy *Boué Soeurs* frock swishing like a bell around her silk-clad calves. Her shoulders swayed with the delicate edging of her fine claret-colored filigree lace strap.

"Miss Davenport, may I introduce you to the Countess Veronika Boganovich Cherlina, my hostess for the evening." Jon stepped back so that Jamison was standing in front of the Countess. "Countess, Miss Jamison Jones Davenport," he said.

The Countess enfolded Jamison's hand between both of hers, holding it a bit longer than necessary. "Miss Davenport, it is a pleasure to share this evening's festivities with you," she said with a heavy Russian accent. "Did you enjoy watching us perform?" A sly smile crept across her lips. Jamison's body flushed, as the Countess's hands continued holding hers. She could only think of those talented fingers, and how they elicited moans from her steam room lover.

"It—it was an inspiring performance," Jamison managed. "I had no idea that people could perform with such passion." When the word passion slipped from Jamison's mouth, she froze and shut her eyes—and then a list of more appropriate words flashed before her mind, less provocative, better in general—words like skill, joy, and expertise. When she opened her eyes the two of them continued to stare at her, as she was unknowingly rubbing her crystal along her lips.

"Touché, *ma chérie*." The Countess moved toward the bar. "May I offer you a glass of champagne, Miss Davenport?" The Countess selected a champagne flute from the tray of glasses, and then expertly filled it so that a half-inch of froth would tickle the nose. Jamison held the flute to her mouth; the bubbles fizzled along her lips, making her nose itch. The Countess picked pieces of ice from the bucket with her bare fingers, and then dropped them piece-by-piece into her own crystal glass.

A strange hot chill spread across Jamison's chest as the Countess then splashed scotch over the cubes.

The Countess smiled and licked her lips. "Anything else I can do for you at the moment, chérie?"

Jamison stared at the damp corner of the Countess's mouth before noticing the quill of her feather needling the skin at the nape of her own neck. She could feel moisture that dampened the delicate fabric along the lower curves of her breasts. She felt as though she was unraveling; the cool imperious peacock that she wanted to portray was molting, and she needed to reconsider herself in private. "Would you know where the powder room is?" she asked.

The Countess dabbed the edge of her index finger to the corner of her own lips. "Please, please allow me to show you, Miss Davenport. Excuse us, Jon Derrick." She led Jamison away from the party and then up the stairs.

If she hadn't seen this woman make love to another woman, Jamison could have followed her without thought. She would have felt each solid stair beneath her.

The Countess had to know full well that Jamison at the time was watching every brush of the Countess's fingers against her lover, and that she had strained to hear every sigh and murmur from each intimate caress.

Jamison's legs felt rubbery and boneless—yet she couldn't stop herself from following the Countess. Part of her hoped that they were truly going to the powder room, while another part wanted to know what it felt like to be the focus of the Countess's talented hands.

Jamison darted her eyes between the staircase and the formal portraits hanging along the walls, and then at the Countess's back and buttocks swathed in burgundy silk. She felt as if the eyes of each oily dower face mounted on the wall were following her, exasperated by her clumsy ascent through their well-arranged domain.

9.

Jennings O'Rourke had been standing in the cross hall with a view of the music room to his left and the grand salon to his right.

He was keenly aware of the length of his arms, the clasp of his hands, and the curvature of his spine—the way he stood countless times in seminary, waiting for the body of Christ. He knew the blessing that awaited him, as long as Jon Roe was the man he'd believed him to be.

Jennings had kept his eyes trained on Jon, Jamison, and their hostess in the music room. He had willed their conversation to be over, before cursing at himself about his impertinence; he struggled to remind himself that he was simply a guest and would need to wait on his host. Each time that his impatience got the better of him and he wished Jamison and the Countess would leave, he'd recite the Lord's Prayer in Latin as penitence.

And then he'd catch himself speeding through the prayer, which raised his ire, knowing that the Lord deserved his true attention. But then he reminded himself that God saw all, that He knew what was in Jennings' heart and on his mind—and if God knew everything already, why did Jennings have to bother with penitence?

He was only human.

All the while, Jennings managed to keep a peripheral eye on the Colonel, who had walked through the foyer three times, then three times more retracing his tracks. Eventually, he then approached Jennings with an acknowledging nod.

"This is some hoity toity soirée, eh Jennings?" the Colonel said, swinging his glass back and forth. A bit of his drink sloshed over the rim and he lifted his hand to lick the dribbles from his wrist.

Jennings peeked around the Colonel at the guests and saw the Countess leading Jamison from the music room. He cleared his throat. "It is indeed a jovial group, sir," he said, crossing his arms over his chest.

"You know, Jennings, we have plenty of parties at Davenport Holdings. Jamison is quite the uh, party thrower. But you don't seem much in a soirée mood, if you don't mind me saying, son. Go ahead, tell me what you got on your mind." The Colonel took a step right in front of Jennings. Jennings stepped around so as to not feel hemmed in and could keep an eye on his host.

"Well, Colonel, you are right. I do have business in mind. As I mentioned, I came all this way to speak with Mr. Roe face-to-face, and I'm quite anxious to do so. You see, it has to do with the Rubber Board and their…"

"Say no more, son." The Colonel waved his glass in front of Jennings' face. "I understand. They're holding all the cards, right? They have all the aces and you're trying to draw to an inside straight."

Jennings stared at the floor and shook his head. "I don't play cards, sir, but I believe what you're saying is…"

The Colonel placed his hand on Jennings' shoulder and squeezed. He then hunched down, so he could look up at Jennings' downcast face. "What I'm *saying*, son, is that you need to make a plan. I'm *the* Colonel 'cause I'm a strategist." The Colonel straightened up, shook the cubes of ice in his drink and then took a sip.

Jennings watched the Colonel tilt the glass at such an angle that an ice cube tumbled out and hit himself in the nose; he then rattled his glass around, before lifting it to his mouth again and again, greeted by ice cubes at every tilt.

Jennings politely extricated himself to find Jon Roe, who by then had left the music room.

Jennings stopped short. Before him in the shadow of the curtains stood a remarkable-looking man whose skin was a rich caramel brown. His forehead was broad, his dark piercing eyes framed by arching black brows. A white turban covered his head, the tail draping down over the back of his neck. His long white tunic hugged his lean frame and hung below his knees. It was cinched at the waist with a white sash that held a bejeweled dagger, the hilt shone smooth from years of handling. His narrow white trousers reached down to his ankles. There Jennings saw cuffs of a golden gild with locks hooked through loops. The turbaned man met Jennings' stare.

A mustachioed violinist approached Jennings' side. "We are a collection of misfits and nomads here tonight." The man seemed to answer Jennings' mystified look. "That unusual gentleman is Mr. Roe's butler, Ishmael," he said. "A Bedouin nomad from Arabia.

They call him 'The Ghost of the Desert.'"

"'Ghost of the Desert,' you say? How remarkable. I've never seen an Arab before."

The short violinist took a step back and tilted his head, looking from the tip of the turbaned man's head to the cuffs at his ankles, as if he were appreciating a sculpture.

"He is remarkable," the violinist said. "I've never heard him speak, not a sound. Rumor has it that Mr. Roe bought him from a slave trader in Africa when he saw the slaver searing the nomad across the chest with a red-hot branding iron. The story goes that the Bedouin didn't even scream, he stood there taking it."

"That's barbaric. Branded—my God..." Jennings whispered, bowing his head in prayer.

In the next moment Jennings finally spotted Mr. Roe turning to leave with a serious and distracted look on his face.

"Ishmael has been his butler and guard since that day," the violinist said, before turning on his heels to walk away. He carried his violin as if it were a newborn.

Jennings looked again toward The Ghost of the Desert, whose eyes were fixed on Jon Roe as he strode from the room.

10.

Jon quietly walked up the stairs, passing the Countess's quarters. He opened a concealed door just beyond, stepped into a narrow room, and then settled down onto a well-worn upholstered chair. He poured himself three fingers of scotch from a crystal decanter. The room was set up to his specifications so that from this anteroom he could see the sink, the shower, and, of course, a woman from head-to-toe should she be on the other side of the two-way mirror. The anticipation of Jamison entering the room made it difficult for Jon to breathe.

By the time the Countess led Jamison to her suite, Jamison stopped wondering whether powder rooms were typically found on upper floors or in private suites. She forgot her concern as the Countess told her the story behind every piece of art and furniture.

The parlor was spacious with French doors leading out to the landing, a view of Lake Lucerne. Between one set of French doors stood a small delicate black piano and bench. The pale-yellow walls had hints of pink, and it made the room look as though it were fashioned from a wedding cake. The drapes were pink and yellow striped, tied back with black tasseled bands. The sleigh bed positioned in the middle of the room was light gray wood, and the bedding was pale yellow and voluminous. It was angled toward the ornate fireplace of carved black marble. From the ceiling above the bed hung a canopy of cascading yellow silk. In the center of it was a mirror, and from the middle of the mirror hung a chandelier made of colored crystal flowers.

It was obvious that the Countess had a permanent place in Jon Roe's world. His earlier innuendo must have been in reference to second-hand knowledge of what had transpired in the steam room.

She seemed to know everything about his château, praising Jon for his thoughtful and ingenious designs that allowed dozens of devoted servants to move around the house undetected. That was not a quality that Davenport Holdings could claim.

"My powder room is through those doors, Miss Davenport," the Countess said. Jamison glanced at the door and hesitated. "Let me know if you need anything else, chérie. I'll wait right here." The taffeta of the Countess's gown swished and rustled as she took a seat on the bed.

Upon entering the bathroom, Jamison barely recognized herself in the mirror. A red blush crept up her chest and neck. Her stomach was tight and her mouth was dry. If she didn't know better, she'd think she was getting sick.

But she knew this was how she felt whenever she learned something—before she was ready to.

The very first time it had happened was when Carrington showed her why she wouldn't grow up to be a boy. She'd had the distinct feeling that she lost track of time, got caught in a disconnect where her mind wandered and then fizzled out.

That feeling of disjointedness had increased ever since watching the Countess make love to that woman in the steam room. A hot and cold sort of tension oscillated within her; she was aware of a verge, another boundary as sharp as the edge of a cliff, yet unable to reason herself through it.

She reached for the glass on the counter to get a drink of water, but misjudged its dainty weight and ended up smashing it into the faucet. Shards of paper-thin glass sailed about, scattering everywhere in what then looked like the white paper whistles that Carrington used to make. Jamison didn't even know where they came from; she didn't remember them being there on the counter—but the idea of Carrington's white paper whistles stuck in her mind, to the point of being more real than the glass that shattered.

The door flew open and the Countess rushed in.

"Oh, my darling child, let me help you!" The Countess swept from the sink's ledge all of the white whistles splattered in blood, before grabbing another towel to wrap around Jamison's bloodied hand. "Hold that there while I wet another to wash your cut."

Jamison's head pounded with every heartbeat. Her eyes were fixed on the now red paper whistles collected in the towel that the Countess had used to sweep them.

All of them reminded her of her past, of her innocence and Carrington—crisp pristine folds sullied with her blood. At that sight, Jamison wasn't sure she wanted to continue looking at herself.

The Countess returned and carefully set aside the bunched towel, before easing Jamison onto a small buttery yellow velvet settee in front of the bathroom's French doors. She then knelt at Jamison's feet to check her wound.

The blood ceased to flow. The Countess brought Jamison's hand to her own mouth.

Jamison pulled her hand away, covering the tears of embarrassment that she then realized had been streaming down her face.

"Don't cry, don't cry, my darling." The Countess tugged at a swath of fabric that matched the wallpaper. "Take off your dress, so I may have it cleaned. Come, my dear—stand up." She gently pulled Jamison to her feet, helping her to lift the dress overhead.

Jamison caught her own reflection in the tall mirror, as her dress was whisked to waiting hands outside the door.

One moment she was reaching for a glass, and now she was standing there before her hostess more nude than not. She covered her nakedness the best she could.

She swallowed what little moisture was left in her mouth, and then glanced at the Countess, who watched her by the closed door.

Jamison looked away at her own reflection in the mirror. Besides her stockings and shoes, the crystal around her neck was the only item still on her. She brought it to her lip and found it was surprisingly cool against her skin. Jamison heard the Countess's breath catch while Jamison licked the smooth face of her crystal with the tip of her tongue.

Jamison used that smooth face to trail a line from her own lip, down her chin and then along her throat. When she reached her chest she felt her heart beat against her wrist, as she paused to look at the Countess in the mirror. The Countess didn't look like marble as she had before—she looked of fire; desire billowed out from Jamison in waves. She desired to feel the heated touch of the Countess's hand. She wanted to smell the Countess's perfume mixed with her own sweat.

Jamison turned her back on the mirror, and then eased her body upon the little yellow velvet stool.

The Countess moved closer. She removed Jamison's turquoise feather from her bun, and then held it in front of Jamison's face. She touched it to the bow of Jamison's mouth and slowly drew it over her bottom lip, along her chin, and down the long column of her neck. She paused at Jamison's collar bones.

The Countess then crouched down and placed her hands on Jamison's knees, delicately parting her thighs. Jamison sat up, leaned back, and looked down at her own nakedness. She was nervous, yet she felt neither shame nor judgment when the Countess looked at her.

The feather tickled as the Countess traced designs on her bare thigh. She could feel the Countess breathe on her skin. When the Countess glanced up and put down the feather, Jamison stared at the feline arch of her perfect eyebrow and how the blue flecks sparkled in her dark-brown eyes. It all had an intoxicating effect on Jamison's curiosity.

Those eyes told Jamison everything without a single word. Rightness flared within her, giving her the opportunity to get what she really wanted.

She wanted to *know*. She wanted to find herself—define herself as she wished, and not be a phony in her own life.

The Countess rubbed her nose and cheek along the smooth skin of Jamison's knee, to the gentle swell of her inner thigh. The Countess then paused to deeply inhale. Jamison's heart fluttered in her chest. She stiffened, her brow furrowed, waiting for the Countess to continue—hoping she would continue. Jamison felt brazen when she brought forward her hips, silently urging the Countess on. The Countess traced the same sensuous path with her tongue; Jamison felt as though her whole being existed only where the tongue met her flesh.

She teetered on the mysterious edge of ecstasy, a place she had only visited alone. She wanted to touch the Countess's hair, to see if it felt like satin ribbons, rich and decadently heavy between her fingers.

But she continued to wait.

The Countess reached up to Jamison's face, and Jamison swayed like caramel onto a spoon. Her cheek turned and then she smoothed a kiss over the Countess's hand. The Countess moved her thumb across Jamison's lips.

She remembered Carrington's drawing of her, of his thumb upon her lip.

Would his touch feel the same as this?

She thought of him as she felt her touch, and wished he was with her—with them.

Jamison began licking, sucking, and nipping at the Countess's delicate fingertips, moaning above the turbulence of their shared breath. She became rooted by the heaviness of her own need. The Countess brought her mouth to Jamison's nether lips and then began to torture her with every slow and quiet lap of her tongue.

Jamison tensed and arched; the tendrils of her damp hair fell loose, tickling her back and shoulders. Her head lolled from one side to the other.

The Countess reached for the feather on the floor.

The downy hair-like barbs felt like a gentle breeze upon Jamison's nipples. Jamison arched forward, aching to feel something firmer. The Countess then swirled her tongue around Jamison's sensitive bud.

Jamison gripped her chair, trembling as the orgasm hummed through her. The Countess snaked her hand around to the small of Jamison's back, pulling her closer—her mouth sucking in the swollen folds, as Jamison bucked out her climax. The Countess put her lips to Jamison's and then probed her mouth, bringing to Jamison the taste and smell of her own sex. Rather than draw away, Jamison sealed her lips over the Countess's, wanting to savor the flavors of earth, salty sea, and an interesting slightly sweet caramel. She pulled away, light-headed. The shudder rippled down her body, leaving her to feel like flesh without bones, a brain empty of thought.

The Countess smiled and brushed her fingers along Jamison's jaw.

"You are so very lovely, chérie." The Countess swiped the moisture from the corners of her own mouth with her ring finger. "I enjoyed our tryst very, very much." She cocked her head, glancing over Jamison's serene face. "You don't have to say anything; I can see that you enjoyed it, too. That is all that matters."

A light tap at the door startled Jamison.

The Countess rose to answer it and retrieved a small bundle. She handed it to Jamison and then moved to the large mirror to reposition her own dress. She spoke to the reflection of Jamison, who sat on the velvet seat nude, flushed, and delightfully tousled. "And next time," she said, arching her eyebrow, "I shall look forward to *your* touch, chérie."

She kissed Jamison's cheek and then left.

Jamison slipped her cleaned dress over her head and then smoothed it along her chest. Her nipples reacted immediately, tightening, sending a ripple of heat down her belly. She grabbed for the sink with her head curled down to her chest, shuddering as another sudden orgasm rolled through her. She grabbed from the sink bowl a whistle doused in red, as her breath shuddered against her ribs.

11.

After Jamison clicked the door behind her, she had to prop her hand against the nearest wall. With every forward step she didn't know if she was closer to bubbling up into giddy humor or crumpling over and crying out onto the floor. But she stood there listening to the muffled voices of the guests below, working to contain herself.

What just happened? What actually just happened? She almost had to chant that out in her mind to make it sink in. And yet, something in her actually had changed. That was all she could recognize. She walked along the Persian runner, smiling. She actually had opened up like a night-blooming jasmine.

Before stepping from the hallway to the staircase landing she heard the unmistakable labored breath of an inebriated Colonel loitering in the foyer.

She managed to see him there with his glass in hand, his tie too slack for this early in the evening. The back of his shirt collar was oily with sweat and hair cream.

Was he waiting to finish his drink before going to dinner? More likely gulping it down for a fresh refill.

She backed against the wall, uncurled her fingers to lay her palms flat on its surface. Right then she dreamt of becoming a chameleon. She would stay there for so long. Days, even weeks could pass—and she'd blend into that wall long enough for him to find another scheme, and to forget he ever had a daughter in the first place.

"Why couldn't he just leave?" she whispered, pleading to the wall.

When she peeked again, he had moved to the bottom stair; his hand was on the banister finial and he seemed to focus his eyes on the landing where she was.

She couldn't determine whether he'd actually seen her when looking up or was maybe too drunk to grasp if she was real, the drinks playing their normal games with his mind. He seemed that kind of drunk right then—on the heels of the ugliest kind of aggression.

He held the banister to keep upright. His whole body listed toward the hand that held his glass of bourbon, and to keep from falling he slotted his thigh between the two balusters. Moored, he tried again to bring his tumbler to his mouth, his tongue outstretched and seeking. As he did so, a few ice cubes skittered across the marble floor.

She could imagine his accusatory glare as he pitched unsteadily, sighting each cube on the ground.

"Don't need ya watering down my whiskey…" she heard him say as he ventured toward the staircase again.

Jamison took a backward step, and when she heard his unsteady footfalls she turned into an anxious sprint.

It was her only answer to that situation. The fear came back as it always inevitably had—scalding, searing reality into place; that man would only ever be able to hurt her, and she'd only ever be able to run.

It was all a blur how fast and mindless she acted. Was there another way to the dining room from up there? The slim hope she had was in how the servants always managed to move around unseen.

Jamison tried the door opposite the Countess's suite and it opened to a closet. She was already half-willing to stuff herself in there, but she kept moving. The next revealed a tiny room with a chair and table. And then behind the third door she found a narrow stone stairwell. She nearly fell in her scramble to reach the ground floor. It led to another reasonably wide hallway where she could hear the rattle of pots and the chatter of hurried voices.

She placed a hand to her chest and caught her breath while heading toward the kitchen sounds.

"Excuse me," Jamison said stepping into the bright and bustling room. She cleared her throat. "I seem… to have taken a wrong turn." She spoke to a server who was in the midst of rushing over to grab an empty serving platter. "Which way to the dining room?" she asked.

The server turned to her and composed himself.

"…And is there a route that avoids the foyer?" she added with a hopeful lilt in her voice.

He let out a deep exhale and smiled. "Miss, you may follow me."

Upon exiting, the server opened one of the swinging doors with his left hand and presented her a back entrance to the dining room. Before she could say her thanks, he closed the door and returned to the kitchen.

Jamison paused before stepping into full view of the guests.

There were two seats available at the long table—the farthest was next to her mother, while the other directly in front of her was beside her host, Jon Roe.

After her scramble to get there, she considered that a more charitable take on her father climbing the stairs would've been that he merely intended to announce that it was dinner time. She wanly smirked at the thought, rubbing her finger over the area where he'd grabbed her at the start of the party. Of course it still hurt. That was the point.

After managing to sit down, she cordially turned toward Jon Roe. He didn't acknowledge her. Once again, she wasn't sure if he did so on purpose. Maybe she was being overly sensitive.

At the other end of the table, her father's chair remained empty. Her mother's eyes grew large as she looked from Jamison to the empty chair, pressing her scented kerchief to her nose and mouth.

Jamison shrugged to feign nonchalance.

She managed to slow her breathing. She uncurled her fingers to lay them flat over her lap. She inevitably though found herself searching the table for the Countess, who was brushing her finger along her red lips, deep in conversation with a heavyset gentleman with remarkably delicate hands.

Beyond the Countess, Jamison caught sight of the Colonel as he herringboned his way into the dining room. Her mouth went dry as she watched him collapse into his seat.

The Colonel cleared his throat as if to punctuate his graceless arrival. There was not even a stutter in the dinner conversation, and then his eyes squinted at her in a way that might've said *this is your fault.*

But then his eyes glazed back over as he loosened his tie and unbuttoned the bottom of his suit vest, the same way he'd act when sitting at his own table. He picked up a glass and raised it above his head, pointing to it as he pivoted in his seat, looking around the room. "What ya gotta do around here for a drink?"

Before the Colonel had a chance to lower his arm, a uniformed waiter appeared holding a tray with a fresh tumbler of whiskey. The young man took the empty glass directly from the Colonel's hand and fit a new one into his grasping fingers. The Colonel only scoffed in place of his thanks.

Jamison focused on his new glass, knowing it was the one that would take him over the edge.

She glanced at their host who still maintained a silent, albeit likely more than cursory, awareness about the goings on. With that, though, she couldn't help but think that maybe not sitting next to Jennings was the real mistake here. Maybe if she got up and spoke to him the Colonel would ease off his cocktail.

Jennings had on what looked like the same mask of fear and anticipation, as if wanting to heed warning to Jon of the Colonel's temperament.

Jamison stole another glance at the Countess, who was then busy talking to a regal-looking blonde woman. Were they huddled together whispering about her father?

A man on the other end stared at Jamison. He had a thicket of silver hair falling over his eyes like a Schnauzer's eyebrows. The tiny bird-like woman seated to his left leaned close to his ear. Jamison peered at the guest sitting to her right. His chin was buried in the curve of his own shoulder, looking like a sleeping duck as he tried to hear the hushed comments of the cravat-wearing guest a couple of seats farther up the table.

She had to stare down at the tablecloth to silence it all.

At the sound of a boisterous laugh from the Countess's companion Jamison suddenly felt ill, imagining that they were talking about her, or about the Colonel. Then she looked up and caught the Colonel saying something to her mother, as laughter continued spreading through the other guests like a rash down the table.

How odd that their host could be holding court like a king, appearing to miss nothing and remain calm while the Colonel raised his empty glass in the air once again. She had a hard time imagining this host was doing anything other than studiously avoiding all things Davenport, including her.

He appeared wholly captivated by a nasal-sounding English dowager, who reminisced about her poorly trained hounds getting caught under the hooves her late husband's mount. But his golden-brown eyes would then land on another guest, and then another. She could almost imagine him as a great cat, as invisible as a panther on a moonless night; he stalked, and he paused. There was a slight tightening at the corner of his eye, a tiny twitch at his cheek, as if through the air he caught all of their emotional scent, and without them being aware he gleaned both the essential and the relevant.

But she was experiencing this much differently, and could only wonder what he grasped from her right then. Jamison while sitting closest to him must have imposed an acrid aroma—her distress swelling and dripping from her skin like the taint of a wounded animal.

Jon Roe was undeniably handsome in a solid and serious way. A few thin wrinkles fanned out from the corners of his eyes, yet the skin around his mouth was smooth as if he seldom smiled—or if he did, he would only show it through his eyes. At that, she then saw his eyes smiling at her.

Jon leaned in. "Miss Davenport, I see that you've cut your hand." She could feel the rumble of his voice as if he was pressed against her with his lips at her throat. "Did you know that each slice in the skin of the rubber tree makes it stronger?"

Jamison glanced down at her hand.

Another red paper whistle?

She gazed at it, inexplicably positioned between her index and middle finger; she drew her eyes back to Jon. His irises had darkened and the flecks of green became more vibrant, provocatively shimmering in such a way that she became entranced. Her breath hitched in her throat as he looked down her body, taking in every detail. She placed the whistle behind her ear like a flower, wondering if anyone else could see it.

Jamison looked at his mouth and wondered what it would take to make him smile with those lips. Would he smile like the Countess had if he were kneeling between Jamison's legs?

Chasing that thought from her mind, she blushed, musing that his lips might form the outline of a bird gliding on the wind. When she peeked again and the image in her mind took life, she realized that he was indeed smiling at her. She tucked her chin and tilted her head away, hoping he hadn't noticed her attention.

The conversation from the other end of the table had risen in volume—bits and pieces about Berchtold's Day. While the man with delicate hands passed a plate of butter, he mentioned something about sharing food with strangers regardless of country.

Jamison immediately tuned in to the voluptuous throaty roll of the Countess's voice.

"I don't have a country anymore, chérie." The Countess fingered the emerald drop of her earring. "I am, I am—how you say?—liberated." She placed her hand upon a matching emerald necklace, pressing her neck with her palm. "I was a Russian Countess with responsibilities that I didn't ask for but accepted because I was born into my role. I had responsibilities of my station and my family. I had no free choice. I was no better than a… peasant. Yes, I had money and comfort, but no free will." She angled her body to take full possession of her chair. "I have no country, yet I have never felt freer, more liberated in my life. *I* reap the benefit of my effort, no one else. I reap what I sow."

"Tic, tic, tic, tic, tic…" the Colonel annunciated louder until it was clear everyone heard him.

The Countess raised an eyebrow. "Perhaps you have something to say, but have forgotten your words?"

The Colonel slid his elbow on the table with his drink in hand. "Tic," he said shifting the glass to the left. "Tic," he repeated shifting it to the right.

The Countess kept her eyebrows raised as if wondering if he'd actually say something, or was just lost in some kind of mania.

"Well, Countess, that's very interesting and cos-mo-politan of you to say." The Colonel used his glass as a pointer. "Things run better… with one person." He raised a finger. "When *one* is in charge. Decisions… are up to me." He knocked his tumbler against his chest. "Who sows and who reaps? I don't open my door to just anyone who knocks. I don't share with anyone just because," he said. "Tic, tic, tic, tic…" he muttered. "They have to deserve it—and to deserve it, they have to work for it. My farm—it *is* a dictatorship." He felt his pockets and removed a cigar. He bit off the end and spit it onto the table. Striking a match, he lit it up, puffing each time he looked at a person at the table. He tossed the match on his butter dish. "Whoever doesn't like it can move on, 'cause I can find plenty of replacements to toe the line." He sat back in his chair and took a satisfied drag.

The Countess took a sip of her wine. The Colonel held his cigar in one hand and raised his glass to her with the other.

She seemed to hold her tongue as the Colonel then rattled his glass in the air. The waiter once again refilled his bourbon. The Countess placed down her wine goblet before resting her hands over the lion head fronts of her armchair.

Her eyes met Jon's before she gave him a little smile and nod. Jon sat back, crossed his legs, and began to rub the face of his watch with a linen napkin. Jamison pushed herself against the corner of her chair to watch the other end of the table.

"Mr. Davenport," the Countess started, "I've heard you are a man from a small town in Kentucky, in a pubescent country. Yes? What is successful for you on your little farm is not in the least relevant to the bigger picture of global political struggles. Remember what happened to Marie Antoinette and her King Louis XVI when they told their people what they could reap?" The Countess made a cutting motion across her neck before dismissively turning to converse with someone else.

Whatever conversation she'd started with the person next to her was drowned out by an uproarious "Here-here!" by the man with the bushy eyebrows. All the other guests raised their glasses—some cordially laughing while doing so and others quite serious about it—but all sharing the same spirit of the Countess's words: we are all liberated.

The Colonel scraped his chair along the stone floor and lurched to his feet. He threw his napkin on the table and then crushed his cigar into the remains of the trout on his plate. He glared first at Jamison and then at his wife. "We're leaving." He turned to Jon Roe, who already had his hands on Jamison's chair. She looked from her father to Jon, knowing her mouth was gaping open.

Jennings rounded the table to stand next to Jon. "I am sorry that…" Jennings started, as Jamison abruptly stood and put her hand up to stop Jennings.

"Th-thank you. We must go now," Jamison said, hurrying toward her mother.

"Indeed, you must," Jon replied and then nodded at the door. "Jennings," Jon acknowledged.

The Countess stood as Jamison and her mother neared. "Good night, chérie, Jennings." She offered her hand to Jennings, who then raised it to his lips as the Countess made eye contact with Jamison. Jamison stole a glance at the guests, attempting to grasp their reaction, readying herself to defend her family's hasty retreat.

But the Colonel was already gone, and what could she possibly say?

The calming lilt of the Countess's voice pulled her back. "Chérie," she said with trifling shrug, "we shall see each other again, soon."

On the way back to the hotel the only sound in the car was the hiss of frigid air slipping through the seal around the windows. As the Colonel stared out the window, Jamison only once dared to look at his eyes; they shuddered in their sockets as if some invisible hand inside his skull was shaking them like dice. The alcohol made him a monster, but it was the first time Jamison ever saw a kind of fragility on his face. All of this resulting from the confident words of a powerful woman.

When they arrived at the hotel, the Colonel exited the car first. "Don't wait up," he said to the night air, as he lumbered from the car to the reception, directly to the bar.

Jamison and Jennings helped her mother through the quiet lobby to the lift.

"Goodnight, Miss CeCe, Jamison." Jennings bowed. "If I can be of any service…" his voice trailed off.

"I'm sure that won't be necessary. Thank you," Jamison said, giving her mother's shoulder a hug.

While the ladies waited for the elevator to open, Jennings took to the stairs.

12.

Late the next morning, Jamison was startled awake by a knock at her door. She pulled the pillow over her head and then curled into a ball.

After the night's fiasco she only wanted to stay cocooned in the security of her comforter, and not venture out where she might be recognized as that man's daughter.

The knock got louder. She groaned, before bolting up-right and throwing her pillow to the floor.

"Yes?" she asked, squinting through the dim light at the door. Something was slipped beneath the crack.

"Oh, for Pete's sake, not another telegram." No doubt because of the Davenport Berchtold's Day debacle she was now being thrown out of the country. Jamison kept her eye on the telegram as she moved to the edge of the bed, and then tiptoed to the door.

It wasn't a telegram but a heavy white envelope sealed with black wax and stamped with a bold cursive R.

Jamison leaned against the dresser, and then carefully fit her finger beneath the envelope's flap and seal. The script was male, the words an invitation to return along with Jennings to the château. She tapped the card to her mouth; it smelled faintly of some kind of masculine fragrance.

She propped the note against the washbasin and then stepped away.

It made a provocative composition: the strict white card, the black handwriting with long sweeping strokes. She happened to have placed the card in the shadow below the palm-sized peonies.

Jamison exited her room bag in hand. She was shocked to be invited back by them, and honestly a bit mortified. She, herself, felt the slightest bit unreal in how quickly she accepted to return to his château. The Countess and Mr. Roe had certain enchanting qualities that seemed to move her—perhaps not totally against her own will—but she did feel that same kind of boldness that continued to exhilarate her.

To her surprise, Jennings was already in the lobby. It gave her a strange feeling to have him go with her; she supposed he was the perfect means for her to return to the château without overtly playing defiance against the Colonel.

Maybe if she was forward with Jennings about what the Colonel wanted of her...

No chance. She didn't really even know what kind of man Jennings was, though he seemed pleasant enough.

The easiest choice was to go with the motions. She could just lie to the Colonel, bide her time until she found an out that actually made sense. And then, if Jennings did start to show interest in her...

It occurred to her once again that none of this was tidy; she was partly lucky that the Colonel was too drunk in the night to question why she sat next to Jon Roe instead of Jennings. If she'd have to lie to her father in one way, she'd also have to lie about that, too—and if he actually did see her run away from him she'd have to lie about that, as well. She made herself sick thinking about how that conversation would go, because she knew that the lies were as meaningless to him as the gospel truth. Regardless, she could hardly wait for the car to pull away.

She tried her best to massage the Colonel out of her mind and focused on the Countess and Mr. Roe. They actually, truly, appreciated her, didn't they? She felt a smile creeping, the same quiet kind of smile that happened to be on Jennings' lips as she approached him. Considering the possible read he might've had, she adjusted herself to be tight-lipped.

"Good day, Miss Davenport," Jennings said. "Let me take your bag. Mine is already in the back."

"Well, thank you Mr. O'Rourke, I think I can..." Jamison's unfinished sentence pressed to the roof of her mouth as Jennings grabbed her bag, ushering her out to the portico. She swallowed it down as he handed her bag to the driver. Jennings then rushed around to the opened car door.

He wasn't bold or rude enough to tap his foot, but his posture reeked of the Colonel's standard line: *We're burning daylight, here.*

She glanced up at her parents' empty balcony above the car park and then back to Jennings, who now had one hand on the door and the other on the door handle. Perhaps Jennings was as tired as she was of being dogged by the Colonel.

She looked back at her parents' balcony as the car slowly motored down the drive. The Colonel had appeared, solid as the flint balustrade. Even though she couldn't see his eyes through the hazy cloud of cigar smoke, his message was clear.

With a huff, she crossed her arms and settled against the cool buttery leather of the upholstery.

"Are you chilly, Miss Davenport? May I hand you the fur?" Jennings asked, reaching for the blanket on the opposite seat.

Jamison draped it over her lap, tucking it behind her legs.

"Hm... Thank you, Mr. O'Rourke." She looked out the window and then back to Jennings, who sat as measured as a Skowhegan folding ruler. The thought was potent enough to have her suppressed laughter ache through her whole body.

"Is there something funny?" he asked. She dropped the hand that was covering her mouth.

"No, no—I'm sorry. It's just that you seem so anxious, and, well... stiff." Jamison bent her elbow and pantomimed hands in mittens. "I'm sorry."

He gave a slight nod and a charitably humored look. What might've first come across as him being nervous around her then seemed redirected toward his upcoming meeting with Jon. There perhaps wasn't one thing that told her this... Well, the smile maybe. Maybe, too, the way his eyes so often stared at nothing at all; much like what Jamison would do when trying to leave a place through her mind. She just as well could have made fun of herself.

Jamison crossed her arms again, rubbing her knuckles back and forth along her lips. "Did you happen to see the Colonel this morning?" she asked.

Jennings brushed his hand over the knee of his trouser. "For a moment, only. He surprised me, actually. When I walked out of the bath on our floor, there he was standing outside the door. He said he'd like to have a drink before we left, but then the car arrived, and... I didn't want to keep our host waiting." Jennings clasped his hand in his lap.

His pause seemed a polite change in course.

"I see," she said. "And you're right, of course. It would be rude if we were late." Jamison stretched her legs and turned to face Jennings, who sat on the other end of the bench seat. She rested her arm along the seat back. Jennings continued staring straight ahead through the chauffeur's cabin to the oncoming road.

"May I call you Jennings?" Jamison asked. "Mr. O'Rourke just seems so formal, when we are nearly the same age."

Jennings leaned his shoulder against the door and then he turned to face her. He looked a little wary as he thought about it. Jamison wondered if he had many friends. She then remembered her mother stating that Carrington was also his friend.

"Yes, please do," he said. "Jennings would be better—at least when we're alone, and in each other's company."

"Yes, of course. Like now." Jamison fanned her hand between them. When he didn't respond, she thought he might have felt coerced and was only being polite. It also occurred to her that this was probably the exact thing the Colonel wanted her to do. She felt sickened by the specter of him urging her on to do more. *That's it,* he'd say, *first show him what he can have, then gradually pull him on over. Make it a dance, but then you gotta make him yours.* She rolled her eyes and then rubbed her forehead against the glass, glancing out the window as they drove past shops in town.

The narrow street was lined with shoppers, mainly women. They passed one gentleman who was holding a package wrapped with a bright yellow ribbon.

Make him yours, make him yours…

Jamison closed her eyes and let the sun warm her face. She lifted her crystal to her cheek, focused on it; it was as cool as the window at her temple. Jamison thought back to her nineteenth birthday, when Carrington presented her with the crystal necklace.

On that day, she had risen before the sun peeked through the round windows of her bedroom—even though she knew there would be no party, cake, or games, and certainly no table of gifts.

Up until Carrington had moved onto the farm, her birth had never been a celebration. He brought change by marking each event with a little hand-made gift.

She kept them all in the Chief of the Broadleaves box; it held the collection of items she treasured. The things that he had created for her made her feel useful. She felt valuable as his inspiration.

Jamison now pressed the tip of the crystal to her lower lip, remembering the shame that prickled her armpits when she threw the tiara that he'd woven from grass back in his face. She'd shouted that boys didn't wear tiaras, so neither would she.

The crickets and fireflies were the only ones to see her sneak out in the middle of the night to retrieve it.

She remembered placing it next to the miniature ship mast, with the paper-thin butterfly and dragonfly wing sails which Carrington had made six summers back. She still remembered holding her breath and her arms tight to her body, just dying to see it out on the water—but she also itched to snatch it back up for safe-keeping; with that in mind, their pond had looked as treacherous as the Port of Louisville.

She remembered kissing the paper whistle that he created for her ninth birthday—the tip discolored and thin from all the times she'd held it between her lips.

Now, back in the Maybach limousine she glanced over at Jennings, wondering if Carrington had ever told him anything about her.

Truth on the farm might as well have been a disguised party crasher, impossible to recognize. The bucolic setting belied the deception and deceit that lay shallowly beneath the surface of the bluegrass. One false move, like an overturned planter of gardenias, would reveal a mass of slugs. The only reality that was supposed to matter was what the Colonel deemed valuable.

She hadn't been honest in her charade claiming to be a boy, but she wanted to be accepted and was willing to do what she thought would result in being loved.

A childhood fantasy.

Now, she wanted to reclaim what she had denied herself—and that meant she needed to start taking control, little-by-little.

"Mm, Jennings?" Jamison finally said. "My father mentioned that you met Carrington through business?" She wanted to make it sound innocent enough.

Jennings crossed his arms over his chest. "Indeed, yes, I did. He came to my factory for replacement banding for your bailing machines, and then I ended up delivering them once they were ready." Jennings' face had an ease to it as he said this. "We became friends. I made the trip a few times." But then he turned away as if he didn't want to talk about it. The sudden change in attitude was perplexing. She wanted to push Jennings a little harder. She wanted to ask, 'Is that all? What happened to him? Where is he for Pete's sake?' But of course Carrington *had* made the choice to leave, maybe even told Jennings not to say anything to her should they ever meet...

She found herself letting it go. Jennings might know nothing at all, and if she started asking him questions she wasn't certain she'd ever know how to stop.

She moved on for her education, so Carrington would move on too. It was a mistake to hope he'd be there in Kentucky forever—making it an actual home for her to go back to.

"I see." Jamison clasped her hands in her lap. "I'm glad that all worked out then."

The car slowed as they rounded the final bend. They both leaned forward to once again see the elegant house through the limousine windows. Jamison looked over at Jennings—his eyes were closed and he was mouthing words. When Jennings crossed himself, she quickly looked away feeling like an intruder.

"Are you ready?" he asked, reaching for the door.

"To be honest... it's a bit surreal. Just like last night." She ducked down to see Mr. Roe and the Countess stepping onto the landing. When the car stopped Jennings reached for the door. Jamison placed her hand on Jennings' shoulder. "Jennings, wait."

He kept his hand on the door lever and looked over at her. When he saw her eyes he let go of the door to face her squarely. Jamison bit her lip and then took a deep breath.

"Say a little prayer for me too?" she asked. "I'm nervous."

"Of course, Jamison," he said, placing his hand over hers. She watched his lips move inaudibly. She preferred not hearing how his words reflected her.

He then opened his eyes and smiled. "We're all set. Shall I come around and open your door?" he asked before opening his own.

"No, don't bother. I've got it," she said moving her hand toward the door lever. She puffed all of the nervousness out from her lungs, leaned her shoulder on the side of the door, prepared to proudly walk back up those stairs to save face from the mess that was left in her father's wake; however, the door opened from the outside by that ever courteous chauffeur, causing Jamison to spill shoulder-first out onto the packed down powder of snow.

While shooing away the gloved hand of the chauffeur, Jamison felt hopelessly situated on the losing side in her war against gravity. She lurched upward as if she could will herself into an upright position, but the heel of one shoe diagonally dented down into the snow, while the other flopped around the ample leg-room within the Maybach.

Jennings walked around to her side of the car and offered her his arm.

"Miss Davenport," he said with a face that looked as embarrassed for her as she felt about herself.

"I uh... yeah, okay," she mumbled.

She took a deeper breath before threading her arm around his. "Mr. O'Rourke," she acknowledged, doing all she could to correct her balance.

13.

Jennings straightened his blue and gold striped Notre Dame tie—a calculated choice, invoking Salve Regina to assist him with his plan. He'd prayed and he'd planned, and now he was walking toward the man, circling the moment where his future rested; either Jon agreed with him and voted in favor of Jennings' patent, or Jennings would be railroaded by the rubber board.

"Welcome! Welcome back," called out the Countess as she clapped her hands in front of her chest. Jamison gave a timid wave, before clasping hold of her crystal.

Jennings bound up the staircase ahead of her. "Thank you for inviting us back," he said with a tone hefty with conviction. Jennings shook Mr. Roe's hand and then bowed to the Countess.

He paused and then silently waited for Jamison to catch up. He looked back at her fitting one shoe on one step, repeating the process to the next. Surely she had to understand that any past transgressions were forgiven upon receiving the second invitation. Her nervousness compared to his own was a curiosity.

He considered going down to help her along, but he reconsidered after looking back at his hosts; their faces shone with joy, akin to parents who were seeing their child take those tentative first steps.

Jennings recited the Lord's prayer again as penitence for wishing she'd hurry up.

When she got on their level, clutching her necklace in hand, she appeared unsure about how to greet them. They seemed willing to wait for her to decide. She hid her other hand in her pocket as she looked from the Countess to Mr. Roe. "Yes," Jamison finally said, nodding without making eye-contact. "Thank you for your invitation. It was most unexpected."

"I did say we'd see each other again," Jon replied. He stepped aside, allowing the Countess to usher them in.

"Jamison and Jennings… might I ask, will you be together tonight, or separate rooms?"

At that, Jennings felt caught off balance, but then it really wasn't too unexpected given the spirited effort the Colonel had in talking her up, and Jennings' own constant pairing with the lady. What he didn't immediately know was how to handle the possible interest Jamison might have had in him. After all, it was because of her that...

"Separate rooms," she said.

"Yes. Separate," Jennings agreed.

The Countess looked over with a smile at the stoic Mr. Roe, as if they now solved an on-going mystery. "Perfect," she said. "We didn't want to assume one way or the other, but we do have two rooms made up for you both. Please, please, let me show them to you." The Countess led them to the staircase. "I believe Jon Derrick has some work to finish before we take a stroll on the grounds."

Jennings tried to put out of mind whether the work Mr. Roe had to complete had anything to do with him. He truly hoped, though, that their meeting wouldn't be put off, or fit between activities that included the four of them together. Walking on the grounds was the last thing on his mind.

The Countess sounded slightly out of breath when they reached the third floor. "There's a dusting of snow, but I believe you will still find the formal gardens quite breathtaking and amusing."

The Countess opened a bedroom door, and then Jamison just stood there.

Jennings peeked around her.

Everything connected to J.D. Roe was ordered, understated, yet opulent and powerful—from the fancy cars to the château. Jennings envied that structure, and Jon's power, as well as how understated it all was. He wondered if it was that way because Jon had incredible command of himself. Nothing was superfluous.

They left upon seeing the whimsy etched across Jamison's face when she stepped over to the four-post bed and ran her fingers along the lush lavender fabric draping down from the canopy.

The Countess placed her hand on Jennings' elbow, and then led him up another flight of stairs. They passed one bedroom that had the drapes closed, so there wasn't much in it for Jennings to see. They passed another that was a lighter tone. He slowed and glanced inside. He then found himself in the middle of it, with his mouth agape.

He turned slowly to see it all.

The walls were a shade of creamy gray. He supposed its

reminiscence was of the mist that rose from Lake Lucerne in early morning. On one wall hung a huge painting featuring a white-clad exotic man standing next to a mammoth gray horse; the white background made the figure fade seamlessly into the distance. Along the other wall stood a copper desk inlaid with tile. And thus, the real prize: books of all shapes and sizes, all piled upon the floor.

The Countess joined Jennings in the room. "You seem quite taken by this one, Mr. O'Rourke. I had another room in mind for you, but if you would prefer this..." she said, picking up a book from one of the stacks on the floor.

"Well... my needs have always been little," Jennings said. "A cot, a chair, and a table had sufficed while I was in seminary school." He walked to the French doors and then looked out. "I have tried to keep my world simple since then—so that God could fill all spaces as He chose, and not be relegated to a particular spot." Jennings walked past a stool and then sat down on it. "But if it makes no difference, I *would* like to stay in this room. I'm not sure what it is, but this feels like it's right to me." He stood up and then leaned back against the tabletop. "I hope it will not inconvenience you or Mr. Roe."

Jennings found himself pressing his hand to the copper table ahead of him. Upon lifting it from the surface, he was oddly pleased to see a handprint left behind.

He looked back at the Countess and saw what appeared to be the same look on her face that she had when Jamison was walking up the stairs.

"It will be an honor to have you stay here, Mr. O'Rourke," she said. "Make yourself at home."

When Jennings' bag arrived a few minutes later, he unpacked his satchel and gave thanks to God for his good fortune. He placed his homemade candle on the bedside table, evoking memories of his time in the seminary—reminding him to continue to burn with a pure flame.

14.

Jon looked up from his desk at the sound of the Countess's traditional triple staccato tap on his office door. He placed his fountain pen in the mini megaphone-shaped holder, affixed atop a mat rubber brick. Jon could barely see her eyes over what could be misconstrued as a pack of black bear cubs tousling in her arms. She dropped furs onto the sofa to the left of his desk.

He pursed his lips and blew over the wet ink of his ledgers, as she took a seat on the arm of a leather high-back chair in front of his desk.

"Jon Derrick, you know, you look like a little boy when you do that," she teased.

He blew then smiled, blinking prettily at her. She twisted her emerald rings around her baby finger.

He tested the ink with the tip of his finger. "Bepa, I assume our guests are as anxious as you are to enjoy the fresh air?" He opened the lowest file cabinet in his desk before pushing back his chair. He thumbed through the folders and made space for the file he had just reviewed, and then closed and locked the drawer. He pulled out the narrow center drawer and slipped the ledger book inside.

"I know you, Jon Derrick," the Countess spoke up, "and I know that you're as anxious to be with her again, as I—so don't pretend otherwise. You cannot hide from me, Mr. Roe."

Jon rubbed his thumb along the face of his watch and then looked up at the Countess. "No, Bepa, you're right. I will never hide from you." Jon stood and rounded his desk to where the Countess sat. "Let's go and find our guests. I could use a little fresh air, myself." Jon gathered up the coats and followed the Countess.

The extra coats came in handy; the day had become colder and the wind picked up, as a snow shower loomed. They, at first, walked along as a group before splitting into pairs—the Countess beside Jamison, while Jennings paired off with Jon. Jon stepped aside so that the Countess and Jamison could walk ahead.

"Countess, Miss Davenport." Jennings tipped his hat as they

ventured by, following the path lined with box hedge. Jon stared at the tiny prints their shoes made in the snow. He looked up when he saw their tracks get closer together; the Countess had taken Jamison's arm and placed it on hers.

"Shall we?" Jon asked, waving Jennings onto the path. The tentative smile on Jennings' face looked scrawled-on by a nervous child. Jon understood the gravitas of Jennings' issue without explanation.

Jon was the biggest player in American rubber; he knew how the industry worked. Jennings actually had the nerve to make the trip and force a meeting. He said it was faith that had brought them together, but Jon saw it as gumption.

"Mr. Roe," Jennings started, "the government wants to dictate our production, spreading orders around as they see fit. I'm concerned that this is like the British Rubber Growers Association scheme to limit rubber exports."

Jon listened, slowing his pace enough behind the ladies to appreciate the view framed by his garden.

"Government is trying to tamper with our business," Jennings continued. "The British government is meddling in our ability to import what we need, while the US is trying to dictate which orders we fill. Right now they're holding patent approvals over my head..." Jennings turned and began scissor-stepping, as if he was carrying on a conversation with someone leaning out of the window of a departing train. "...which I need in order to protect the process that I created. Unless I vote to spread the wealth as they see fit to their cronies, they'll deny my patent requests and I'll lose my business." Jennings then halted their pace.

Poor man, Jon thought, noting that the nervous energy that propelled Jennings forward left him stranded in mid-thought. Jon then stared up at the white gray clouds, tracking a seabird overhead.

In Jon's periphery, he could see the ladies kneel down to look at a cluster of blue forget-me-not flowers poking out from a layer of ice.

"You have a great deal of power, Mr. Roe. My guess is you wouldn't want Washington to dictate anything to you. So, I'm... begging you—please vote alongside me to protect our livelihoods, and our integrity."

"You make a good point." Jon waved Jennings back onto the path. He then slowed to maintain the original distance. "I knew the vote was imminent," he said. "That's one reason why I'm in Europe." Jon looked down at the blue flowers, and at the ladies' footprints as he passed them. "I've met with Belgian scientists who are working on what's called synthetic rubber." Jon once again held back as the ladies stopped.

Jamison, even though she was tall, was swimming in the fur coat he gave her.

Jon imagined her heat warming the satin lining, and her scent lingering upon the fur.

Jon continued. "Which would mean that someday we could produce product at home, in our own factories, without interference from foreign governments. I believe it will be the wave of the future."

Jennings nodded vigorously. "Ah yes, synthetic rubber. One of my professors at Notre Dame was doing research, experimenting with acetylene as a basis for a type of synthetic rubber."

Jon nodded to him before stopping to watch Jamison make a snowball. The Countess was pointing at a tree in the distance.

"I'm familiar with Reverend Nieuwland's research," Jon said. "He's brilliant."

Jamison pushed the fur sleeve up her arm and then took aim.

"So, you'll stand with me?" Jennings asked in a rush of breath.

Jon didn't want to miss Jamison take her shot.

She stepped her right leg back and then arched her body, cocking her right arm as her left hand pointed at the tree twenty feet beyond the path.

It was a mistake to give her such an oversized coat; she was delightfully unconventional. He imagined under the coat was the graceful arch of her rib cage and the swell of her breasts, as she leaned back and then, quick as a whip, heaved the snowball toward the mark. It arced like a fastball to home base and exploded on impact, sending white flakes to shimmer around the trunk.

Jon's laughter mixed with Jamison's hollering, the Countess's clapping, and the crunch of the ladies' boots as they danced upon the snowy path.

"Brava!" Jon yelled out to her.

Jamison curtsied and then waved goodbye as the Countess pulled her ahead.

Jennings was still staring at the tree when Jon turned back to him. With a sudden nod Jon said, "Without question. I'll back you up with my vote," and then he clinched his promise with a handshake.

15.

Dinner that night for Jamison was quite a different affair than the formal dinner of the previous evening. The four ate in the library at an intimate table set before the fireplace. The trays of food arrived, filling the air with the aroma of saffron and cinnamon, along with the earthy smell of basmati rice imported from the Middle East.

A spit turned in the fireplace, dripping fat from the succulent lamb leg, which made the fire sputter and wheeze.

Jamison felt transported to another land—a place where her worries seemed to disappear. Maybe in his prayer, Jennings asked God to help her refrain from over-analyzing, so that she could experience herself in the moment rather than from the viewpoint of others.

Dining with the Countess and Jon seemed so easy that night. She even found herself laughing and sharing stories of her childhood on the farm.

Jamison tore a piece from the communal flatbread. "You may not believe this, but I am an expert with a hatchet," she said, scooping tender lamb and rice with a piece of bread. She eased over her dish as lamb fat dripped down her index finger. She licked it off, and then continued chewing.

The Countess cleared her throat. "Chérie," she said, wiping her own mouth, "but why would you want or need to learn that?"

"Obviously, Countess, you've never had a hatchet in your hand." Jamison cocked her arm with an imaginary axe and pretended to throw it. "I'm very competitive, and when Carrin... this boy said he could do it better, I said he couldn't—so it was on. Sure enough, he did beat me in that contest, but I'll tell you what I did." Jamison planted her hands on her thighs. She leaned forward. "I didn't throw a hatchet when he was around, until I *knew* I'd beat him. I practiced while he was working with his daddy. I even set up a little secret practice arena in my closet. I threw that hatchet until I could pin a rabbit down by its hind leg." Jamison shuffled her palms together and then turned to their host. "Do you hunt, Mr. Roe?"

Jon put down his glass and then slipped his tongue over his bottom lip. The moment his eyes raised to hers shifted the mood in a strange way that stunted her heart from beating.

"I do. Although, I enjoy pursuing bigger game than bunny rabbits."

"Oh." She dragged out the *O*, imagining bears, lions, and gazelles—and then she guessed that he could've meant women. She took a gulp from her wine glass.

The Countess nudged Jon with her elbow. "Jamison, you've changed my mind. I think it's wonderful that you throw an axe." Her eyebrows raised in a spriteful manner. "It might come in handy someday."

Jamison looked over at her, half wondering if there was any sarcasm in her words as she said them—but she saw nothing but a kind, soulful feature about her face. It actually made Jamison feel quite wonderful.

"I think so, too," she said. "I think that a woman should know how to do everything. She should be able to take care of herself. I mean, we have two arms, don't we?" she asked raising hers, "and two legs, and a brain, and eyes that see. Why should we be taken care of?"

Jennings cleared his throat. "Well, Miss Davenport, I have to say that I agree with your progressive attitude. God made us all in his likeness, and I believe God can do anything; therefore, each of us has the ability to do it all—if we choose to, that is."

Jamison heard Jon shift to lean his elbow on the ottoman. She looked at his face; his eyes were narrowed, and for a moment he looked exhausted as he stroked his thumb along the face of his watch.

"Regardless of one's faith," Jon said, "I'm in agreement that anything is possible—except going back in time."

The Countess put her hand on Jon's shoe; it seemed so inconsequential, but the way Jon stared at her hand made Jamison wish she could read his mind.

Going back in time… Jamison would go back to the last moment she spoke to Carrington, after he'd given her the necklace.

She wouldn't be so stupid, so prideful this time. She'd tell him to visit her, to court her—instead of needling him, inferring that he'd just get lost in the big city.

Why did she tease him like that when it was maybe the last time she'd ever see him?

Jamison's thoughts had taken priority over Jon Roe's conversation; she shifted her focus back to them.

"...my faith lies with me," Jon said, "it's my creation, and, therefore, my responsibility." Jon looked from Jennings to Jamison. He continued speaking as if every word had weight to it. "I think a person, man or woman, should be able to choose their own path—but they first need to know who they are, and that takes, not only time, but freedom, strength, an open-mind—and astute teachers."

Freedom and strength. Jamison agreed with that. It's how *she* had figured she'd find her way; as long as she had her freedom and wherewithal, she could make a go of anything.

"The largest caveat," Jon added, "is that a child needs to be raised in a safe home, and in a community that believes in individuality."

Jamison nodded her head, wondering if he was considering her when mentioning a safe home, perhaps talking out of concern over the Colonel's behavior last night?

"I see what you're saying, Mr. Roe," Jennings said, "and this is precisely where the concept of *us*, as children of God comes into practice. We are a reflection of Him; therefore, we should celebrate the expression of ourselves and find joy and respect in others, as they are reflections of God, too."

"Mr. O'Rourke, that is so profound," Jamison said, "but I would expect that from you, being a priest and all." She squinted up at the ceiling and then at the others, who continued looking at her as if they expected her to say more. She cleared her throat. "Um, but, I think what you've said is that we all deserve a chance to find ourselves, and once we do we need to be ourselves, because... if we didn't, we'd be, in a way, *denying* God's existence."

Jennings pressed his palms together and nodded. "That *is* what I'm saying, Miss Davenport. We are all perfect, but we lose a bit of our perfection when we aren't honest. And, by the way, I am not an ordained priest." Jennings' face was still, but a little flush crept up his neck.

"You're not? Are you sure? You seem so good at it. I mean, you're so pious and gentle and honest, and perfect in your way," she said.

Jamison heard the Colonel's whisper again buzzing in the back of her mind, urging her on. *That's it, girl. Lock—him—in.* It caused her to pinch her leg as hard as she could. The voice was utter nonsense. She was purely genuine with the words she spoke to Jennings, and she refused to believe that *any* of her words came from a place that acquiesced to the Colonel.

But the slight whisper made a point, too. She could merely tell the Colonel that she appealed to Jennings' religious nature, that she'd found a way in on him.

Wasn't that what he wanted? Reassurance that she fell in line? It would at least keep him from being that… monster.

The thoughts made her feel gross; but as well the idea was at least there, catalogued in the back of her mind of things to say when words were all that she had left.

Jennings sighed and let his hands drop to his lap. "Miss Davenport, I assure you, that I am not perfect, although," he smiled warmly at her, "thank you. I do strive to be honest with myself and others."

The Countess patted Jon's shoe. "As do we all," she said quietly. A contemplative lull seemed to hit everyone.

Jamison wanted to be honest, but honesty was a component of a communal reality—at least on the farm it was—and if that reality was not on the up-and-up in God's pure world, then did that mean she was an imposter to Him, too? Even though, as Jennings had said, she actually was part of Him.

But, one man created reality on the farm.

She was tempted to ask Jennings about bad men and God—how they could exist if God was perfect.

Jamison looked over at her host. Jon looked perfect, terribly handsome in his tuxedo, with his hair slicked back and curling at will over the crisp edge of his starched standing collar.

The Countess looked elegant, in another burgundy taffeta gown with a complicated geometric pattern of jet beads—undoubtedly stitched together by nimble and knowing hands.

They fit well together. Jon looked regal, while the Countess *was* regal.

Jamison stretched and smoothed her hands over the crisscross of silver and lavender crystals sewn under her bust. The bright yellow satin of her dress hugged her sleek frame, but her sleeves draped like movie-house curtains, exposing her slender arms.

It was all *working capital* according to the Colonel. Except for the crystal necklace hanging around her neck; she had won that just for being her.

Was Carrington sitting somewhere, too, wondering where *she* was?

16.

After dinner, the entire table, still crowded with the remnants of their meal, was removed with precision by staff—and with equal facility was replaced by a large round copper tray laden with coffee, brandy, and dessert.

Like bohemian gypsies, the party reclined on the floor near the fireplace, propped up on layers and layers of oversized cushions.

"Voilà," Jon removed a silver dome. "My favorite choice for dessert… the Oreo cookie." He announced it with a boyish smile, revealing the cookies. "To my mind, the Oreo cookie is a perfect representation of my business. I see the creamy white center as the sap from the rubber trees, the life blood if you will that makes my business possible." Mimicking a tire, Jon rolled a cookie along the tray. "It's fascinating when you think about it." He plucked the cookie between his fingers and twisted the two dark pieces apart. "This half represents the vision of the products I foresee from the sweet creamy sap of the tree. The other half is the reality of what I make possible, because of the vision. It's all inspired by this lovely—" he paused to lick the white center from one side of the cookie, "—creamy center." With a licentious smile on his lips, he then popped the cookie into his mouth.

"Bravo, Jon Derrick. I love your little speech," the Countess said before taking a dainty bite of her Oreo.

Jennings brushed the cookie crumbs from his mouth. "Yes, that would definitely make an interesting presentation for the meeting of the Rubber Board!" Jennings said.

Jennings rested his back against the sofa skirt, gazing at the sleeping fire. It popped once, and then again as if bidding adieu.

The room seemed to be caught in some expectant inhale; even the folds of the drapes had sucked back against the open space between the French doors.

The Countess's hand rested atop of Jamison's fingers. Jamison didn't want to break the mood, but she wished she could take a step back without disrupting the scene, to get some distance just to see if it looked right. She used to do that all the time at home when she was little—spy on the workers, on Carrington, and keep an eye on the Colonel from the round window in her closet.

She peeked up at Jon, who seemed to be eyeing her necklace. She peered over at Jennings who was looking toward the staircase beyond the hall, while the Countess's soft stare had landed on where both her hand and Jamison's touched.

Jennings cleared his throat, and then looked at his watch. "If you'll excuse me, I'm going to turn in early this evening."

Jamison took a shuddering breath, before sitting up a little straighter.

Jennings looked at her, and then to Jon. "I have some letters to write—now that we have a plan of action." Jennings unfolded his tall frame from the floor, brushing at stray crumbs and a few imaginary wrinkles on his suit. "Mr. Roe, I cannot thank you enough for your kindness, your hospitality, and your vote of confidence in me. I am honored to have shared time with you, and I look forward to seeing you again when you return stateside." He bowed in Jamison's direction, and then she raised her hand from her lap figuring that he was going to help her up. He merely turned and left the room.

Jamison rubbed the back of her neck before resting her hand on her lap.

She blushed, inspecting her own fingers as the sweat collected under her breasts.

The grandfather clock chimed in the entry hall, the fire crackled, and the drapes billowed away from the French doors. The melting ice in the crystal bucket tumbled down the container.

That's when the Countess got close enough for Jamison to smell the tuberose scent in her perfume.

Jamison stared at Jon Roe's fingers wrapped around his glass.

If Carrington was the one watching Jamison, would she lean as easily into the caress of the Countess's hands that stroked the back of her neck?

Jon took a sip of his scotch, stood up from the floor, and then settled back against the worn leather club chair as the Countess dragged her fingers down Jamison's arms. Jamison closed her eyes and Jon disappeared from view. She tilted her head as the Countess's knowing fingers caressed her.

Jamison's body was heating up; she could smell on herself the lavender oil she had earlier applied. As if the Countess was now aware of that very thing, she deeply breathed in the scent of that oil. The sheer acknowledgment that the Countess gave Jamison by accepting her scent as one that's beautiful—it made Jamison moan. A delicious heat spread down her belly as the Countess kissed her shoulder and then reached for Jamison's breasts, cupping them under the smooth layer of silk.

Jamison's eyelids fluttered open, though her focus was inward. Her eyes traced the movement of the Countess's fingers on her skin—soft against smooth, gentle on warm, curious without a demand.

Jamison was both lulled and energized. She wanted to be more than just an object of adoration—she wanted to touch, as she was being touched. And she wanted to use her lips to taste the Countess's velvety skin; she wanted to mold her warmth to the Countess's voluptuous curves.

Jamison's eyes focused on the red tint painted over the Countess's lips. She slicked her tongue over her own lip wondering if the red tint tasted of berries, or of wax, or if the Countess had a flavor all her own. Jamison glanced up at the Countess, whose dark almond eyes continued their encouraging stare. Emboldened, Jamison leaned closer and then lightly traced the tip of her tongue along the slope of the Countess's lip.

She explored the taste and textures. She watched the Countess's eyes, gauging from her what to do next. The Countess raised her chin and then her eyes softened even more. Jamison went deeper, traipsing her tongue along the Countess's sharply ridged teeth, and moist satiny cheeks.

Jamison stroked the Countess's hair, feeling the gilded hairpins. She removed the hairpins to let the black mane tumble past the Countess's shoulders. Jamison recreated what the Countess had done to her the prior night; she kissed the Countess's neck and dragged her own tongue along the Countess's collarbone. Jamison then laid her head upon the Countess's chest to listen to her rapid heartbeat. How perfect it was, the deep flutter of a heart, the blemish-less flesh, and the knowledge that her, Jamison, was who made the Countess's heart race. *She* made the Countess's body tremble.

Just by being Jamison.

Jamison eased the Countess down upon the silk cushions. Then when the Countess gave her an approving, encouraging smile, Jamison undid the tiny jet buttons on the Countess's bodice.

When the hallway clock chimed out the half-hour, Jamison caught Jon's hungry eyes staring at her. From that look she felt within herself a surge of heat which she hadn't felt from the Countess; his eyes were demanding. It excited her, but it also made her want to hold back, and deny him.

Because that excited her more.

She closed her eyes and thought of Carrington as she drew her crystal along her parted lips.

The Countess's breasts heaved beneath her black corset. Jamison unlaced the rose-colored ribbons that held it in place.

The Countess moaned and ran her hands through Jamison's hair, loosening the bun at the nape of her neck. Jamison's hair cascaded over the Countess's face and shoulders. The Countess softly placed both palms on Jamison's collarbone, and through her bodyweight she eased Jamison's back down onto the cushion before swaying her ample breasts in slow and slight movement just above Jamison's face.

To Jamison they looked so ripe and enticing, she wanted to taste them. Jamison glanced over at Jon, whose quiet smile had since disappeared.

The Countess dipped her nipple closer to Jamison's mouth. She took it in, swirling her tongue along the firm breast toward the darker hue of the nipple, fondling the voluminous globes over her face.

It was overwhelming—the Countess offering herself, while Jon watched them both. It was all so new to her, but perhaps not new for them. The Countess never once looked at Jon. This apparently was *her* time.

Jon shifted in his chair as she continued to tease her own nose, lips, and the side of her face along the Countess's skin.

She wanted him to come closer. A flash of that very first meeting of Jon Roe strangely made an appearance to her mind. Pants. Just a pair of Navy pants was what she saw, and that right now—that silly first meeting—made her stir.

The Countess embraced Jamison and then sat up. She looked pointedly at the gold filigree button at the precipice of Jamison's arm. Jamison raised her shoulder. The decision was hers.

She lifted her crystal to her lips and then looked from the Countess to Jon, who hadn't moved. She continued to hold the crystal between her lips, the red cord draping over the curves of her collarbones.

Jamison released the buttons, letting her dress fall free from her shoulders.

The two women were now on their knees, bare-chested, hair loose along their shoulders, skirts hanging from their hips. The Countess still looked as elegant as a Francois Boucher painting, while she felt as naked and earthy as a Vermeer.

"*Ty tokay milyy*," the Countess whispered. Her foreign words curled around Jamison's ear like the caress of a beckoning finger. Jamison tightened her pelvic muscles, and then ground herself deeper against the Countess. "*Tak milo*," the Countess whispered almost cat-like. Jamison's skin flushed as she bucked into an orgasm, looking directly into the eyes of Jon Roe.

The Countess followed closely behind, pulling Jamison down onto the cushions. Side-by-side they lay, Jamison's long lean body arched over a silken pillow, languid and warm next to the Countess, who lazily stroked her fingernail along the smooth plane of Jamison's belly.

Jamison opened her eyes at the sound of retreating footsteps. She tilted her head back, stretching the column of her neck to look at the empty chair where he had sat.

She threaded her free hand through the Countess's hair. The Countess had given Jamison an experience that she would never forget.

She suddenly felt deprived.

Even though he hadn't touched either one of them, Jon's withdraw removed something that Jamison hadn't even been aware of.

17.

After Jennings retired to his room, he lit his special candle before changing into his nightclothes. He knelt by the bed to say his prayers, thanking God for allowing him to journey to Lucerne and speak with J.D. Roe, and for having Mr. Roe listen to his plea.

Jennings reached for the book that he had earlier chosen from those piled on the floor and began to read *Arabian Nights.* He fell asleep just as Scheherazade started her first story to the cuckolded king.

Jennings' candle had gone out, but the moonlight shone through the open curtains he'd forgotten to close. Something woke him. He blinked as the clouds in the sky played tricks with the moonlight, making it appear and disappear throughout the room.

As his senses became more aware, he noticed the pleasant aroma of charred sandalwood and clove before he looked deeper into the shadows.

He thought he saw a white robed figure near the drapes.

Jennings surreptitiously walked his fingers along the spread, searching for the book. He held it in such a way that the corner of the soft worn binding pointed away from him; it was perhaps the silliest excuse of a weapon, but there was nothing else immediately in reach. His heart was pounding, certain that there was an intruder in his room. At least if the book was thrown at the figure in just the right way, Jennings might then be able to make it to the door.

A gust of wind blew the curtains into the room, revealing the shape of a turbaned man.

There he was, the man he remembered as The Ghost of the Desert standing just outside the threshold of the open French doors. He was dressed as he had been earlier, but now he truly did look like an apparition. His sleeves and the skirt of his tunic wafted in the breeze, while his eyes shone like full moons.

Despite the unmoving eyes of this man, Jennings recognized that the countenance wasn't overtly trying to intimidate or strike fear. Jennings put the book back on the spread. "Please... Come closer," he managed. The Ghost neared the bed. "This is your room, isn't it—

Ishmael?" he asked.

Ishmael kept his head bowed as he answered. "It is my room, *Habibty*, but it can be yours for as long as you wish to stay." The Ghost stood at the foot of the bed, his whole presence disorienting—how little noise he made with his movement, and how mystical his voice had sounded.

"*Habibty*? What does it mean?" Jennings sat up higher against the headboard, resting his cupped hands on his lap.

"It means 'my love' in Arabic." Ishmael stared deeply into Jennings' eyes.

Jennings pulled his arms to his chest and tightly laced his fingers together—shaking from the sudden ease through which Ishmael had spoken those words. Surely one deserved a small amount of relief, a validation for being born—and being good, and earnest. Jennings had never asked for much, but at this moment he wanted as much as he knew others were daily given. Yes, he wanted to be accepted and loved, and wouldn't be bold or boisterous about it—but would be pious, grateful, and if it was to be, he would be perfect, as this: an honest reflection of God. He silently pleaded with God as he leaned over to relight the candle next to his bed.

"I..." Jennings gave a soft, uncertain laugh—one that had no smile at all behind it. "I thought I was dreaming." He spoke in a hushed tone as he picked up *Arabian Nights* from his side.

Jennings had been telling stories his whole life, stories that kept him alive, just as Scheherazade had night after night. He didn't want to tell any more tales; he just wanted to live his own life within the truth. Jennings stared past Ishmael into the blue haze of moonlit dark and wondered if this would finally be the night for him to share his true self.

"I'm... glad that this is not a dream," he said, hoping that Ishmael's truth reflected his own. Ishmael didn't move or speak. Jennings seized up in a shiver of embarrassment. "You *are* showing yourself to me by coming here—by waiting for me to show myself." Jennings shifted onto his heels, determined to not miss his chance and make sure Ishmael understood him. "I was drawn to you from the moment I saw you in the grand salon." He stared at the striking face of Ishmael. "From that moment, I prayed for you." Jennings hung his head. "I prayed that you saw me."

Ishmael moved around the bed, offering his hand. Jennings clasped it and stood before him.

Taking Jennings' face in his large hands, Ishmael leaned down to place a tender kiss upon his brow, upon the tip of his nose, then to his lips.

Jennings felt lightheaded, as if swaying—flickering like the candle flame with every breath that Ishmael took. He felt bonded by Ishmael's hands and lips on his face, yet he feared this union as much as he desired to surrender himself to it.

Ishmael walked Jennings over to the standing mirror and then stopped behind him so that they could look into it together. He unbuttoned Jennings' nightshirt, which fell to the ground leaving Jennings standing with his loose drawstring pants slung around his hips. Ishmael trailed kisses along Jennings' neck and collarbone, and then back to his lips again.

Without thought Jennings reciprocated. The feeling of Ishmael's lips beneath his own was everything he had dreamt it to be—curiously firm, smooth, yet demanding.

Ishmael reached his hand to Jennings' drawstring and then loosened it, reaching in to embrace his heat. A sigh rushed out of Jennings' mouth, as he felt Ishmael squeeze his hard cock.

He felt Ishmael drag his fingers from the base of his cock up to the tip before going down and up again, each time firmer, each time slower, until a bead of pre-cum elicited from its tip. Ishmael began pumping his hand faster, leaning his head on Jennings' shoulder.

Jennings pulled away and then dropped to his knees. He loosened the front flap of Ishmael's pants, revealing his manhood. Jennings brushed his face up and down his firm length. He bowed even more, bringing the nape of his neck to Ishmael's heavy balls, and then dipped his head down to the balls, back up to the broad head, licking the pulsing twitching cock.

Jennings' sun-kissed head rubbed reverently beneath the dark curls. Ishmael's fingers trailed along Jennings' shoulders. Jennings placed his hands on Ishmael's thighs before wrapping his mouth around the engorged head, circling his tongue around the firm ridge, eliciting a low growl of pleasure.

Ishmael motioned for him to stand then led him over to the bed where Ishmael removed his turban. He placed it atop the tufted pillow on the nightstand.

"Please remove my clothing, Rourke."

Jennings unbuttoned Ishmael's tunic allowing it to fall to the ground, revealing Ishmael's broad chest. A startled groan of pain came from Jennings as he saw the shiny, angry, raised medallion-shaped brand just above Ishmael's left nipple.

"Do not be sad for me, Rourke. It is but a little scar. The real pain I carry with every beat of my heart is the memory of my family who died that day in the desert." Jennings placed his hands on both sides of Ishmael's face and then began to place soft delicate kisses along the raised edges of the scar.

When the first light of dawn began to make its appearance in Jennings' guestroom, he rose from the bed and then packed his satchel. He looked back at Ishmael, who lingered in their bed watching Jennings' every movement. Ishmael patted the rumpled sheets beside him.

"*Habibty*—Rourke, I shall miss you like the earth misses the sun when it is hidden amongst the clouds." Ishmael reached for *Arabian Nights* on the nightstand. "Take this to remember our first night."

Jennings picked up his handmade candle and then offered it to Ishmael. "I don't have much to give, but I would like for you to have this candle that I made." Jennings dropped his hand to his lap and then hung his head. "Each night that you light it... I pray that you will look into the flame and remember me." Ishmael embraced Jennings, cradling him in his arms. He kissed Jennings' forehead again, and then smoothed his palm over Jennings' face as if memorizing his features with the touch of his hand.

Ishmael pressed his cheek against Jennings' and then said, "*Habibty*, I put something very dear to me in your bag. I shall see you again when we return to America; what you do with it will tell me what I need to know."

Jennings left the room understanding that Ishmael wanted him to find the gift on his own without audience.

He felt sheepish trying to find Mr. Roe or the Countess in the large property. It had become uncharacteristically quiet—not totally lifeless, but it was as though even the château needed its rest. Upon spotting a maid, Jennings asked, "Is Mr. Roe around? I just wanted to give him a last bit of thanks and bid him farewell."

"Need car?" she asked. "You leave?"

"No, I… Well…" But then Jennings smiled. "Yes—car. Thank you."

"You are welcome!" she sang out showing a brilliant smile, all teeth.

Before the car pulled away, Jennings looked up at the balcony eager to see if Ishmael would watch him leave, possibly give him another sign that they would again be together. They had declared their feelings, but now that he was in the car about to leave that majestic place, away from Ishmael, he wondered if it could all be that simple.

He waited, and his heart quickened as the car idled. The exhaust clouded his view before he motioned for the driver to proceed. He kept his vigil, staring out of the back window until he could no longer see the château in the distance.

18.

Jamison lingered in bed the morning after her intimate dinner with Jon and the Countess. The linen sheets felt like satin against her body. Her skin was like the subtle velvet of a rose petal—slick, yet dense and slightly grippy. The ivory sheets, the trapped warm air, and the scents of the previous evening had clung to her, willing her to stay in bed and reminisce.

But there was another voice sneaking in, as the light drifted under the curtains toward her bed.

Her mind woke up and struck a raw discordant key—lilting murmurs, foreign echoes, and explicit images all drowning out the earlier serenade. She sat up and leaned against the headboard, now fully awake.

Jamison recollected the moments of the previous day every time her sexual desires sprouted up, seemingly out of nowhere, taking shape through her childhood friend, then lusting for a woman, and then further aroused by the man, nearly a stranger, who watched her do it all… She wondered most about one thing—was she a harlot?

Had she become ruined?

She pictured the goddess Libra in her mind, with her golden scales balancing a half-naked harlot against a sign-touting suffragette.

In her mind she could see the two images cast against each other. One looked daring yet demure, while the other looked defiant and determined. She wondered if they were mutually exclusive. Couldn't she be daring, while also demure and determined?

Though, demure was foreign to her.

She cocked her head, trying to see if those two could merge in her mind. She smiled, watching them waltz closer.

Demure was a stubborn bitch, refusing to take part.

Jamison faced the mirror. On the wall, hanging beside it, was a painting of a nude woman stepping into a pond. The woman angled her body with a dropped shoulder, pointing a toe like a willowy goddess testing the water.

Jamison crouched lower and angled tighter, trying to master the woman's position.

She felt more like a horny toad bobbing up and down. Her hands felt ridiculously large, like hams pressed against her chest and mouth.

Why had she been cursed with the Colonel's hands?

The difficulty of playing at demure certainly gave her something to work on. Jamison lifted her chin to the painting—before sticking out her tongue.

It was hopeless.

She marched to the balcony, threw back the drapes and flung open the French doors. Frigid air made her eyes blurry and her throat so cold that it ached. The sound of her barking cough set a tree full of Starlings clattering out into the air. Her eyelids stuttered over her eyes to clear the blindness.

She followed the flock—watching them all fly together like a swath of gray, swooping down over the large lawn that lined the property before funneling higher, fanning out over the lake.

Down there stood Jon, alone, staring up at her. He was as still as a column—a solitary, elegant, well-carved column—physically imposing, and possibly… fragile and out of place?

She spread her fingers and gripped the handrail. It was freezing. She thought that if it were Carrington standing out there this would surely become a contest to see who could remain still longer than the other.

Her fingers began to burn with cold as she willed herself to stand her ground.

This man didn't know the cadre of childish games they had played, just seeing who could best the other. Yet, he stood there just the same.

Something about how very still he was made her think that he was lost in his own mind—staring at her, sure, but seeing more than the nightgown fluttering against her body; he seemed to have a *need* to look.

It made her feel powerful. For some reason he couldn't look away, and that made her feel… invincible. She wanted to *know* what he saw in her. What fascination did he recognize that she failed to see in herself?

The skin along the rim of her fingernails turned numb, as she continued mulling over how intense those eyes were. Whatever it was, he instilled her with need—a need greater than her desire to control; it was a need to captivate just by being herself.

19.

The ride back to the hotel was quiet. Jennings truly must have gotten what he was looking for, to have left the château so early.

During the ride, Jamison might have taken the time to think things through. She might have even heard the Colonel's voice and then sparred out some excuses, listing out every moment she was friendly to Jennings—construing it in her mind as actually playing the coquette.

But as the Maybach continued shifting gears, accelerating up and down, smoothly closing the distance toward the Hotel Palace Luzern… Jamison chose to let her mind be still.

Upon entering her hotel room, Jamison spotted her mother huddled in the wing chair. She pulled the key from the lock, and then peeked around the door to see if the Colonel was there. Jamison then closed it, satisfied that they were alone.

"Mother," she quietly said placing her carpetbag on the ground in front of the dresser.

Her mother looked vacant, as empty as a dry bowl. The needle and thread poised between her fingers were forgotten, just like the strips of fabric and soldier dolls that were strewn over her lap.

Jamison whispered out to her again before kneeling at her feet.

Her mother looked tired. She had always been careful with her makeup; now it looked heavy-handed, garish.

Jamison rested her head on her mother's lap, squeezing her own eyes shut, trying to block out the guilt rising inside. She realized that maybe if she'd been a better daughter her mother wouldn't be so fragile now, so lost and worn out. She'd sided with the Colonel, the seat of power on the farm—but what did that get her? She was now merely a bargaining chip in his latest scheme.

As a Davenport, Jamison was neither a boy, nor a girl—unsuitable, unassigned, and undefined. But that's what she wanted to find out, why she had wanted to assist her suffragette idol, and now why it mattered so much to know what Jon valued.

She felt her mother's dimpled hand stroke her hair. Jamison kissed her mother's skirt.

"Jamison, I came to your room. The light's better. It's so hard for me to see my sewing." CeCe bounced a figure of fabric in front of Jamison's face. "I'm making a new battalion."

Jamison flattened her hand over her mother's and then over the little soldier. She knew that a militia wouldn't change a damn thing for the Davenport women.

"I'm making us an army, even have some women." Her mother scrounged around the seat cushions and pulled out a limp pink ribbon bow. She extracted a pin from the arm of the chair and then carefully skewered the bow; even then, it drooped off center just above the black button eye of the soft-sided soldier. "See? Suffragettes, like us."

Jamison ground her teeth, exhaling until her chest felt like a stone. She realized that, somehow, that girly bow transformed the tiny soldier into a target.

Jamison hadn't been a soldier, she'd been a coward—always running, leaving her pink bow of a mother behind.

She watched her mother pin more bows above other buttoned eyes, and then picked up one of the decorated soldiers. Jamison unpinned the doll's bow before repinning it onto her own blouse.

The room was so quiet that Jamison heard what sounded like the calls of Kentucky birds—warblers, even cuckoos.

Jamison breathed in heavily before letting it all go.

Because her mother really did need her.

The swaggering gait of the Colonel's boots stumbled outside beyond the door. She could feel her mother tense up.

Jamison kissed the skirt of her mother's dress before standing.

The Colonel entered the room and narrowed his eyes at the two women. "Didn't think you'd be here, CeCe. Well, no matter. You just stay sitt'n there." He shut the door and turned to inspect Jamison. He took his unlit cigar from his mouth and then pointed it at her. "I got business with the girl."

To Jamison's recollection the Colonel had never called her that.

"So," he said, "how did it go with our Mr. O'Rourke? Were you a good soldier, Jami?"

Jamison ground her teeth more harshly. She moved in front of the wingchair, stepping her feet wider.

Go ahead, she thought—do it, Jamison.

"He… left before dawn this morning," she said. "Apparently said he needed to return to America." She placed her hands on her hips and then jutted out her chin. "I guess he concluded his work with Mr. Roe."

Jamison felt her mother stiffen up in the same instance the Colonel's face tweaked at her words.

He reached up and rubbed his head so hard that strands of hair came out in the grasp of his fingers. He staggered over to Jamison. "You are nuth'n if not a soldier—doing what *I* want!"

Jamison leaned close enough to see the broken trails of red veins across his nose. She felt the little hairs raise on her arm. Her cheeks felt like they were on fire and her throat threatened to close up—but her voice broke through it all.

"I've *always* been nothing to you, father. So, no, to your orders! You… you wanted me to seduce Mr. O'Rourke? Are you crazy?" The command in her voice had somehow undone the previous gamut of feelings—those potent visceral signals that always had blared out the one defeating word: *Run! Run! Run!*

No, the command in her voice yelled louder than the lifetime of conditioned fear, and it now told her: *Stand!*

Jamison barely registered his straight-arm cutting through the air until the back of his clinched fist smashed against her cheek. It sounded like an ice-block splintering into pieces behind her eye. Her head turned on her shoulders. She saw a stinging red and then a thick black, before falling to the floor. She felt as though she had no bones, no body, nothing to weigh her down but the throbbing rumbling through her skull—and the truth that she would get up again and again to fight back, even if it killed her.

"You stupid little bitch! You let him go like that?" The Colonel pulled Jamison to her feet and then held her by the front of her blouse, slapping her repeatedly. Her collar cut into the back of her neck. Some blows landed hard and flat, swiveling her head on her shoulders; others missed, but in the missing, he still marked her, slicing her skin with his manicured nails.

But every punch spurred her on. The strikes became muffled by the ringing in her ears, and she finally threw back her fists at the blurry figure in front of her.

Her eyes refocused just enough to see the battalion of half-made dolls bouncing off of the Colonel's chest, and the quirky look on his face in reaction to the harmless, weightless soldiers, which apparently her mother had thrown at him. His high-pitched laugh was absurdity clashing against the moment: everything she currently felt.

Jamison's vision was once again shoved aside by a shot of black; she then smelled the strange scent of ammonia and rose. She stumbled against the dresser, knocking her head into its edge. Her capacity to see returned to a dim slit.

She slipped to her knees, only able to make out her mother's tiny white hand jabbing miniscule scissors into the Colonel's meaty shoulder. But she was relentless, poking it in and out as if her needlepoint thread was snarled up on the backside of a canvas.

Jamison wanted to yell but her tongue wouldn't cooperate. Mute, and panicked, she watched him rear up. Jamison pulled herself from the ground, using each drawer handle like the rung of a ladder to lean heavily over the dresser. She wrapped her arms around the water basin and hurled it at the Colonel, sending the flowers, water, and herself spiraling closer to him. As Jamison collapsed to the ground the Colonel hefted her mother like a sack of flour over his shoulder. From that movement, the Colonel groaned and then buckled, reeling to the side like something in his gut gave way. Still, he had the momentum to toss her mother against the wall where she smacked her head upon the baseboard.

Jamison only had the smallest tingling awareness of the rug's woolen threads underneath her palms, prickling the skin of her knees as she moved closer toward a heap of black silk.

The Colonel's hands soon clamped around her throat, his fingers like spoons hollowing her out. She choked and sputtered, her tongue swelled and her breath seized in her chest. Her neck stretched as he lifted her to her feet, and then hurled her over like a bully swinging a cat.

At this point, she couldn't see him but she could smell and feel his breath near her face. "Always kick'm when they're down, Jamison. Remember that!"

She was so down that she felt as though she was seeping into the rug. He then kicked her with the force of a Henry Repeating rifle; she knew she hadn't slipped down far enough. A rib buckled, and then another. She folded into the new crease, exposing the other side of her rib cage to another assault.

Her mouth was open. Her breath stalled, stuck between her back teeth and her collarbones.

The Colonel oddly lurched back, hopping and shaking out his ankle as if he had sprained it. Maybe she didn't see it, just felt his movement through the floor; maybe she dreamt it—as she puddled even thinner.

She strained to open an eye.

"Say you're sorry, bitch, and maybe I'll stop," he said. "But then again, maybe I won't. You failure, you worthless little nothing. Maybe I'll just grind you down."

Jamison could no longer focus. Instead of seeing him, her mind saw the image of the demure woman in the painting. Jamison smiled at her, now knowing why that woman's smile was so unforgettable.

Jamison rose up from the floor.

With her broken ribs the demure drop of the shoulder was easier than ever, but then she did see the Colonel; her inner Davenport gave her the strength to rear up, curl her tongue, and then spit. It rolled down his cheek, before he grunted at her in disgust.

To Jamison he seemed like a wounded animal. He brought his fist down against her face. She went down deeper than before, spread so thin that she fell between the fingers of wool, seeping below the crude burlap canvas that held those fibers up.

Unraveled, she disappeared.

20.

The quiet was what CeCe Davenport first noticed. Her upper lip was thick and twitching to a pulse. Her eyes felt sewn shut with scratchy yarn. Her head throbbed and her body ached worse than childbirth.

She struggled onto her back. The ceiling looked unfamiliar. Her head lolled to the other side, before noticing her daughter's motionless body crumpled on the floor.

Through tears she saw that the rocking chair was knocked over on its side, a lamp lay shattered on the rug, and her stuffed soldiers were scattered all over the room—and no signs of the Colonel. She dragged herself along the floor to where Jamison was sprawled out in a mess. Shaking and out of breath, CeCe collapsed over Jamison's legs.

She tried to reach upward, but the fire coursing down her arm grew hotter with every movement. She dragged her right arm closer to her face. Her fingers clawed at the cuff of her sleeve, to free her hankie so she could plaster her nose in the smell of ammonia.

Her eyes watered at two whiffs.

She forced her other arm to reach out, and then pressed her hand to Jamison's chest. "Please God," she whispered, "let her be alive."

In her state, CeCe wasn't even sure if she felt a pulse from Jamison's heart. With that uncertainty, CeCe convulsed into a sobbing mess. She hobbled over to the bathroom to retrieve a towel and a bowl of water.

She dabbed the wet cloth to Jamison's busted lip, before looking around at the scattered soldiers on the floor.

"Jamison," CeCe croaked, carefully wrapping a wet towel around the angry red lash circling Jamison's neck. "I'm going to get help." CeCe nuzzled her face against her daughter's.

She glanced at the door. She needed a chair to keep him out.

CeCe crawled over to the rocking chair that was toppled against the bed. She tugged it closer to the door and then fixed it upright. She then pulled herself onto the seat to catch her breath.

Her eyes darted from Jamison to other numerous objects in the room—the lamp, to the bed, back to Jamison, and then over the scattered soldiers, back to the lamp again. "Don't worry, honey…

mamma is going to fix this," she said, stumbling over to the lamp.

She reached for it before falling back to the ground. Tears streamed in warm trails down her cheeks, hearing the Colonel's voice in her head, *You can't even get up, can ya, you fat cow?* She scooted her way back to the chair with the lamp clutched to her chest, and then froze at the sound of approaching footsteps.

She turned the lamp over in her hand, ready to use the bottom mass of it.

The steps outside continued with a steady rhythm leading up to the door—and then with the same steady pace, they passed the door toward somewhere else.

CeCe heaved herself back down onto the seat, curling her body around the lamp on her lap.

She looked at the phone. She needed to get help before the Colonel came back; she couldn't know where he'd have gone, but she hoped he was down there drowning his cares in whiskey. Her first thoughts were that he'd return to admire what he did here, look down at them as he would upon carcasses from the hunt. No, he'd likely return in panic, wouldn't he? To make sure he finished them off?

CeCe balanced the lamp on the teetering chair before walking over to the table.

She lifted the receiver to her ear and then clicked the cradle.

An operator answered.

"Palace Luzern." The voice seemed small, distant.

"Hello, hello, yes," she managed, struggling to keep the receiver up to her ear. Both of her arms dropped to her sides, and she dizzily angled over toward Jamison. She then continued to speak, "Hello, I need to get my hair done." She stood the phone upright on the bureau—the receiver rolled against the long cord.

"Ah yes, and will it be for yourself only?"

"My… self," she answered, pressing her fingers to her face, easing the skin back. "My hair… the skin…" CeCe's voice trailed off.

"Hello ma'am? Are you there?"

CeCe leaned against the bureau. "Operator," she said, pushing her hair from her face. "I need to get my hair done. I want that… hairdresser I had before, Irena—that nice girl. Room 281, please."

CeCe walked back to the door, losing grasp of the voice. She stood next to the chair with her back to the door and her arms spread wide, as if holding back the weight of whole darned world.

Several moments later there was a knock.

"Madame, it is Irena from the salon." CeCe cocked her head, listening for any other sounds in the hallway. She thrust the door handle down and then pressed herself flush against the wall again.

Irena pushed the door open, which made the chair rock and tip over the lamp. She squeezed through the opening before shutting the door behind her. "*Govno, bozhe moi!* What happened?" She looked over to where Jamison still lay unconscious on the floor. "I call the front desk. This is... This is too much!"

"It was the Colonel, my... husband." CeCe gasped sullenly. "I need your help."

Irena fit her hand under CeCe's arm and led her over to the seat. "Better I call someone else."

21.

Jon sat at his usual table in the hotel restaurant watching the gears move on his golden Bréguet Skeleton watch. The fine tourbillon movement defied gravity by mounting the escapement and balance wheel in a rotating cage. It took centuries to develop that ordered precision. He valued order, beauty, and history—and the effort taken to maintain them.

It had been a little over forty minutes since Irena had called the Countess, subsequently leading Jon to have his driver rush to the hotel and pick up Jamison to return her back to his château. While those preparations were on course, he had the maître d' request upon the Colonel at the bar to meet Jon in the dining area.

That man was undoubtedly sponging up every bottle of bourbon he could from their ample stock. This behavior wasn't totally unrelatable to Jon. Perhaps the man did it to dampen his conscience—or maybe the binge for him was simple routine, as regular as any dietary habit. In whole, though, it made more sense to think of the Colonel as a real life monster, who didn't at all care about what he did to his beautiful daughter.

The damage inflicted upon Jamison couldn't have been more than five measured tics of his watch.

That thought had tested Jon's grip on order.

He feared that the rage within himself might oscillate into frenzy, a reminder of what tied him to Switzerland in the first place.

He believed that he knew rage like his own face in the mirror. The rage would compound, build, become more focused, more saturated, until it became a line of pure hatred.

The Colonel picked a path through the dining room, drink in hand.

Experience had taught Jon that the vilest reprobates didn't stick out in a crowd; at least, not in a way that was off-putting. The most dangerous weren't the insalubrious vagrants littered on sidewalks and doorways. They had charm and savoir-faire, and the need to blend in.

His parents had been as charismatic and enchanting as tiny bubbles in champagne—but when alone they were as flat as a strap, and as rapacious as wild dogs.

Upon noticing Jon, the Colonel had an uncertain stare. Whatever could have existed of the man's charm was tarnished and dulled by the broken capillaries and the unsteady gait of a boozehound. Despite his puffed-out chest, the Colonel's eyebrows had a slight tremble, and with closed eyelids his eyes gave a sudden roll and then darted back and forth—most certainly arguing with himself.

A few feet before reaching Jon's table the Colonel offered a handshake, which Jon promptly ignored.

"Well, that's a hell of a way to greet another American, Mr. Roe." The Colonel made a show of reaching for his gray suede gloves. "Why, I should take out my glove and slap your face."

"Sit down, Mr. Davenport." Jon's voice was intent to cut through the man's foolishness.

The Colonel's forehead wrinkled with disdain, but he did sit down.

Behind Jon stood Ishmael, motionless against the wall.

Jon took a measured sip of his tea before contemplating the pitiful sight before him, the shell of a man who had sweat stains at the armpits of his jacket, and the stench of an alcoholic.

Jon recognized the Colonel as nothing but a pathetic husk of a man who turned into a vicious monster when he didn't get his way.

Jon placed his teacup on the table and then folded his hands onto his lap. "Should you ever touch Jamison again, I will kill you with my bare hands."

The Colonel stammered before smacking his glass to the table.

Jon held up a halting palm and then the Colonel went lax, as the angry cast of red stormed up his face.

"I have rebooked your departure," Jon said, "and you are now leaving this evening on the 9 PM train from Lucerne, which will transport you and Mrs. CeCe Davenport to the ship you will board—never to return to Switzerland again." Jon sat relaxed yet ramrod straight, drawing no attention to himself nor to the guest in front of him. There was no mistaking the precision of his tone, nor his words. Nor the glint in his eyes.

The Colonel sat still. His face would have been perfectly stoic, if not for the quiver of his bottom lip.

"If I find out that you have ever left that little travesty you call

Davenport Holdings of Kentucky, I will track you down and shoot you." Jon cocked one eyebrow before leaning an inch forward.

The Colonel then leaned his back against his chair.

"Do I make myself clear?" Jon asked. He rose and then shoved his own chair aside, striding off while his bodyguard stood poised against the wall, ready to react should the Colonel make a move.

22.

CeCe jolted awake, knocking her head against the wooden back of the rocking chair. Her high collar tugged at her throat. All that CeCe heard and felt in that moment was her heart flopping like a frog stuck in pond sludge.

She slowly opened one eye. Near her knee was a potbelly stove. She strained to look farther into the room. Bits of memory entered into her mind, as she felt that painful burning sensation race up and down her arm. She curled over, trying to get her nose to the hankie in the cuff of her sleeve.

Then she recalled that the hairdresser and the turbaned man had shown up.

CeCe took a deep breath before opening both eyes. The Colonel's bag was near the door. She was back in her own room but had no recollection of getting there. She then realized that she had on her gray travel suit.

Something bumped against her chair, giving her a startle. Her carpetbag then tumbled off of her lap. Its contents spilled out: a book on equine surgery, colorful scraps of fabric, needles and thread, and a number of small handmade fabric soldiers, all looking like they were in various stages of mutilation.

The Colonel had before told her that they looked more like voodoo dolls.

She wished that they were.

She counted two, four, five, six… and then CeCe's heart stumbled in her chest when a boot kicked the seventh doll, sprawling at her feet. Her hand flew to her mouth and then she bit down, unable to silence the scream that tore from her belly.

The Colonel grabbed the back of the rocker with one hand, and then with the other smashed the side of her head into the wooden rungs. "You shut-it, you fat cow."

The rocker creaked as she squirmed.

CeCe yanked her head from under his palm and then snapped her mouth shut, pinning the length of his pointer finger between her teeth. CeCe followed the sweeping arch of his body as he cocked his arm to smack her; her tear-stricken eyes then glanced over to the turbaned man who was suddenly standing there at the doorway. The Colonel turned to see what she was looking at, before his arm fell against his side.

Ishmael retrieved the dolls around her feet before repacking her carpetbag. He handed it over to her with a bow, and then turned to look at the Colonel before turning back to her, offering her his arm.

CeCe smoothed her gloves over her hands, sitting up straighter. She threw her shoulders back, and then looked from one corner of the room to the others. She stood, and then raised her chin. She looked over at the Colonel and then down at her feet, before allowing herself to be taken from the room.

The turbaned man escorted them to Jon who waited near the boot of the car. Jon placed one arm around her shoulder and then reached for her hand with the other.

His voice brooked no discussion. "Mrs. Davenport, Ishmael will join you on your return voyage home. Please, don't hesitate to call on him." Jon looked over her head at the Colonel, and then at CeCe once again. "He is at *your* service, madam."

She sagged with relief.

Jon lifted her chin up before saying, "We will take care of Jamison. She will have all of her needs met."

"How..." CeCe started, and Jon stared at her questioningly. "How did that sweet hairdresser know to contact you?"

Jon smiled. "Irena is close to the Countess. She also met your daughter."

He stepped back, indicating that it was time for her to leave.

23.

Back at the château, Jon paced outside of the room where Jamison rested, waiting for the doctor's slower ascent up the winding staircase. Every echoed step pushed Jon's anger close to boiling over, damning his own stupidity at his inaction. Why hadn't Jon confronted her father the very first moment he had grabbed her arm in the dining hall?

Was he so entrenched, titillated with his need to watch that he lost sight of humanity? Why hadn't he the other night ordered her to stay put at his château after the Colonel's tantrum? He had seen that look in her eyes, a moment of terror. So why didn't he...

But Jon knew the truth, of course.

His interest in Jamison was very much there; she invoked within him an intense lust, but he had come to know his own truth: passions are fickle. And before now he had zero intention to break the comfortable, safe system he had constructed for himself. He'd go through the motions as he had before and then move on to someone else when the flame was burned out. However, while waiting for the doctor he was surprisingly relieved to have broken the tidiness of his perfect life. It was not the correct time to consider what he might lose.

Jon glanced down the hallway toward the landing when he heard the doctor take a steadying breath at the top of the stairs. Proper decorum dictated that he should wait for the doctor before entering Jamison's room. He hadn't any idea what damage she was going through, and that perhaps was what aggravated him the most.

The tremble of his hand made him grip harder upon the door handle. The sake of proper decorum could indeed result in him tearing the door off its hinges.

He knew the layout of the room—where the bed was, where the sitting area was, and how the light during different times of the day traversed those intimate settings; he'd seen it all from the secluded anteroom next door.

But ever since Jamison was placed in that bed, he hadn't stepped into the anteroom to watch. Whatever was happening in her room was more intimate a moment than sex had ever been; Jamison was fighting for her life.

As the doctor neared, Jon opened the door.

There was stillness in the room. Not even the fire crackled in the hearth. The Countess sat next to the bed, one arm wrapped at her own waist, her other rested near Jamison's shoulder.

The doctor walked past Jon without a word. The Countess rose from her seat and then moved over to the end of the bed.

Jon crowded behind the doctor, who was inspecting Jamison's face. Jon felt each of his muscles lock around his bones as he bent to brace himself on the nightstand. He groaned at the sight of the half-moon, bluish-red bruises on Jamison's side, indicative of the tip of a man's boot. Jon rubbed the face of his watch along his pant leg.

The Countess walked over to Jon. She pressed her hand gently against his. She leaned closer, and then spoke with slow and careful words. "Jon Derrick, go downstairs to your gym, and take out your anger there." She led Jon to the door. "Jamison needs to be surrounded by calmness; you are anything but tranquil. Go." She then shooed him out of the room.

Jon managed one step before noticing the door at his back, and the silence, and the dust motes drifting in the light that streamed through the window. He felt the overwhelming sense of something being taken away from him—just as he had that time before. He leaned against the door.

She needed him. With his guidance and support, she could thrive in his world.

Now, at Bepa's order, he found himself in his gymnasium squaring off on his sparring bag.

His punches became automatic and his mind went elsewhere, picturing Jamison with Bepa. Bepa had first sheltered him, and now he sheltered her. She brought women into their world; he watched them until he saw the look of hunger in their eyes, and then they became his—and then he took them until he was bored, before another would take their place.

The system had become immutable. Jamison wasn't ever supposed to be more than a working piece in it—even though, by some strange course of events, he had found it so difficult to see her as just another in that same collection.

He realized that it wasn't merely his sympathy for her now; it was an itch in the back of his mind that festered in him after that second time she was with the Countess. That look in her eyes when she stared at him, when she came—it was as though she never had intention beforehand to be aroused by him, but then it suddenly happened, like a mistake. The mystery in that look she gave, he had no way of learning the reason of it without first getting to know her more than any of the others.

Silly as it was, he could have just pinned her as being sapphic and then moved on, but…

He perhaps more needed her to be around to understand his own feelings on all of this. It truly hadn't been about her at all, had it? What was changing in him?

Why was she changing him?

The doctor entered the gymnasium and stood at the door, watching Jon relentlessly pound his bare fists into the bag. "I already have one broken patient upstairs," he spoke up. "I don't need to patch up another down here." The doctor walked around the swinging bag.

Jon stopped, arms limp at his sides.

The doctor continued. "Jamison is going to need a great deal of attention over the next few weeks, and this week will be the most challenging for her; we'll need to keep a close eye. Perhaps you and the Countess can create a schedule, so that one of you is with her at all times. She has four broken ribs and some swelling around her trachea. She won't be able to do the most basic things without assistance." Like a father, the doctor put his hand on Jon's shoulder. "You are a man, Mr. Roe, and Jamison will have certain requirements which might be better handled by another *woman*."

Jon looked at the doctor's hand before shucking it off of his shoulder. The gist of the doctor's declaration wasn't lost on Jon, even in his rattled state.

"I am prepared and perfectly capable of attending to her, with or without the Countess's assistance," Jon said, still out of breath. "I'll let you know if there's anything that we require."

The doctor shrugged and sighed. He fiddled with the lock on his medical bag, and then he looked up at Jon. "I've spoken with the Countess, voiced my concerns." He walked to the door. "I'll be back later to check on her."

Jon rested his head on the cool leather of the punching bag, and then dug his fingernails into the seams. He heard the Countess's signature triple knock on the door. "Come in, Bepa," he said.

The Countess opened the door. Jon stood with his back to the bag while the Countess leaned against the doorframe. Without speaking, they both knew that they were thinking the same thing; the delicate balance of the world they had created and shared was in the midst of being thrown off by what he had dragged in.

Bepa pinched her lower lip between her bejeweled index finger and thumb, a cue that she was deep in thought.

She eventually sighed, stepping into the room and then closed the door behind her. "You look terrible, chérie. Can I get you a drink?" The Countess plucked Jon's shirt from the floor before handing it to him. She then walked over to the bar.

"A drink would help." Jon slipped his dress shirt back on. "He wasn't at all concerned about his daughter—or his wife, for that matter. He *should* be incarcerated."

"It would not be wise to alert the authorities, in this case," the Countess said, taking a sip of her brandy. "They would make sure that the Davenports stayed and were tried—and that would be a long process, best avoided." The Countess held her snifter to her lips.

The wrinkles at the corners of her eyes went taut.

"It would be in the papers," she said. "If an investigation were to take place, we'd be vulnerable. This one," she pointed up at the ceiling, "she will be okay. She is young and strong." The Countess handed Jon his brandy. "I just wonder how her mental state will be, once she wakes up," she said.

With both of Jon's hands he clasped her fingers gripped over the drink.

So many years had passed, and so many secrets kept safe between them.

Jon said, "Bepa, thank you for all of your help."

The Countess dipped her finger in the glass of sherry, and then held it to her tongue. "Is it the case, that you are feeling love for Jamison? I have not seen you like this before."

Jon looked away, unwilling.

"Be patient with her," the Countess said. "She is very young, naïve, yes; she could be willing to learn—perhaps on her *own* terms, though. You cannot ask for more than that." She stared down at the spots of sweat on the gymnasium floor. "And, maybe… you'll learn, too."

"Learn? Learn what?" Jon furrowed his brow.

She gave the tiniest smirk. "Neither are you very old, Jon Derrick. Your system works for you, but there's always more to learn. Yeah?"

24.

Jon slept fitfully that night, and for many days and nights following. The Countess and Jon traded places, taking care of Jamison while she remained semiconscious. Each time she jerked, twitched, or moaned it took all of his strength to stay calm and rational, and to not cable Ishmael to use his Bichaq dagger to make chum out of the Colonel.

Sitting next to Jamison's bed, Jon had plenty of time to think about what the Countess had told him in his gymnasium.

Love Jamison?

He was only sure that he wanted to have her; he'd wanted women before, and Bepa had been... a generous purveyor. The women he'd selected were always unencumbered, whereas Jamison was surrounded by complication.

Ever since Jon was old enough to manage his own affairs, he never allowed any of these women to linger in his life, except for Bepa. Had she not appeared when she did, he couldn't begin to imagine where he'd be now. But with her guidance and the help of Madame Raisa, the Countess's companion, he'd been able to construct a world where they could thrive.

He had needs and Bepa had hers, and often their needs intersected.

She knew that he would keep his distance until he was ready, if ever, to step from behind the two-way mirror.

Section 2: Carrington

25.

Before Jamison had the luxury of solitude in her Swiss retreat, a boy named Carrington was the only person to ever make her feel loved. Upon every birthday he'd give her a special gift. He had done so, each time, trying to make one that would outdo the previous—and he was to make his greatest gift for Jamison's nineteenth birthday, before her planned trip to begin college in Cincinnati.

He woke up that morning with a little seed of uneasiness in the pit of his stomach; now, walking to the main house, that seed had bloomed and laid down roots that wrapped all around his insides.

He had to make her day special. No one else, not even her mother, had ever paid her any notice. The gift, before she left to college, had to say more. It had to say, *remember my face*, when one of those college boys offered to carry her books to class; *think of my strong hands*, when he's guiding you along the dance floor; *hear my laugh*, when you get caught in a spring shower, walking with him in the moonlight.

Carrington felt sicker just thinking about what other men had to offer her.

He was stuck there on the farm. He knew horses, crops, and how to craft things, but none of those skills seemed to be enough for Jamison.

She was funny that way. It wasn't that she ever acted better than him, but she didn't act any less than him, either.

He watched her when no one else was looking—which was most of the time.

She was skittish and jumpy. He reckoned she was only moving for the sake of moving. Moving too fast to think straight. Running with blinders to an unfamiliar place—tall buildings for shade, motorcar exhaust for breeze, and men roaming the streets like wild turkeys.

He didn't want her to forget this world of theirs, so this time he made up a story to go along with his gift. Usually, he told her stories off the top of his head, but today's tale was written out and memorized.

It was about the sounds that live underground, deep in the forest floor, underneath what they believed to be the largest and oldest white catalpa tree in Kentucky—their tree.

Birds called and screeched, insects buzzed. Lizards scurried from the shade of the taller grass and then stopped, their finger pads plump, arms jerking down and up, as if they were looking high and low through rays of hazy sunlight, reaching through the dense foliage.

Carrington lagged slightly behind Jamison as they made their way to the pond. He drank in the scent of lilacs that rose from her hair. Her feet left perfect outlines in the powdery red dirt.

Carrington and Jamison's every breath, and every step, was the sound of their communion, a whispered hush below the continuous whistling, warbling, and rustling of the morning, which hung in the damp fragrant air like a nostalgic hymn.

Jamison stood at the edge of the water, her arms long at her sides. She lifted her chin, draping her hair below her shoulders.

Carrington imagined that even with her eyes closed she could perfectly see their pond, and play back the memories they had built together.

He watched the soft cotton of her dress become heavier with dew and cling to the gentle swells of her body.

She wasn't a little girl anymore, he thought. And he was glad that she wasn't; although, at times, he still wanted to shake her like a rag doll when he caught her glaring at him—like he was the lucky one, just because he got to be the boy.

He'd never forget when *that* scowl first landed on her face.

They'd been swimming after finishing chores. It was an unremarkable afternoon, except for that.

He remembered it started out as it usually had, with her asking what he wanted to be when he grew up. She'd just lost a tooth and was able to spit an arc of water clear across the pond through the new gap.

Carrington swung back and forth on the rope swing, his feet gripping both sides of the slippery knot. "Heck, Jamison, I already told you what I'm gonna be."

"I know, but tell me again. I like to hear you say it," she said, sweeping an armful of water at him. He kicked at the spray.

"I'm gonna be an artist. I'm gonna make things, special things—magic things."

"Then what?" Jamison asked, punctuated by another armful of water in his direction.

"Then I'm gonna sell 'em." Carrington pumped his body, tipping back and forth to get the rope to swing higher. "Then I'm gonna have enough money to build you and me a house, in this here tree, right by this pond." He let go of the rope and fell back into the water.

"But, why would you do that?" She treaded closer to him.

"Because we're always gonna be together, that's why—just like this." They were so close their knees banged accidently. Then they banged on purpose. And then their feet took up the fight, until the pond water flew like a fountain, lifted up by their giggles. Jamison stopped her kicking to tread water, lifting higher than Carrington. She sized him up.

"I'm gonna be a boy when I'm all growed up," she said. "Maybe build a house next to yours here on the pond."

He looked at her like she was crazy. "But *I'm* gonna build the house," he said, "so you can live with me." The water rippled as he treaded through it, trying to rise higher than her.

"Two boys can't live in the same house, silly. I'll build my own, next to yours. Maybe over there," she said, pointing at a tulip poplar.

"Jamison, you're not gonna grow up and be a boy, so knock it off."

That's when she gave that glare for the first time, making him wonder if he could be wrong—that maybe she would become a boy, someday. He remembered screaming at her, "You're not like me!" And then they got into a shoving match. Even now, he still had a scar on the bottom of his foot from a thorny rose branch that had caught him between rocks.

She riled him up like no one else could. He got crazy when she smacked him in the chest, taunting him to prove it. He would never forget how the sick feeling in his stomach made his legs ache.

When she shoved him again he couldn't think straight, but he remembered watching the chucklefish slither between his feet, as he waded to the shallow water; Carrington yanked his pants to his slim white hips, and showed her the incontestable difference between them.

Carrington let that memory drift away at the sight of Jamison, now in front of him lying on the plush grass—like he imagined she would if getting into bed after a day filled with Miss CeCe and the Colonel. He wanted to believe that visual every time before their walks, of her letting go of whatever burden she'd carried.

He wondered if his own burden would slip away so easily.

Carrington stared at her reclined on the low grass dotted with wildflowers in the shade of the catalpa—and for a moment he forgot his prepared story.

He followed a single white flower separated from a bridal-white cluster. It drifted down to send a ripple across the still pond. Jamison was just as still; the only ripple was the rise and fall of her chest, and the dance of her heartbeat along her neck.

The tree and the crystal were his inspirations, and she was his muse.

"The story starts here, under this catalpa with its huge canopy of leaves—so heavy that the boughs shake when the wind blows, sending white flowers to swirl like a blanket of summer snow, covering the spaces between its long, sinewy roots. The roots unfurl, and a tiny root bud sprouts every time the tree shakes."

He looked up through the branches, wondering if the tree was listening for the truth of his words, having stood witness to all that they'd shared in its shade.

"One stormy night, the catalpa shook hard in the wind, and the rain battered the leaves—and the tree twisted to and fro. And, all of a sudden, a finger of lightning came down and zapped it, lighting the whole tree up, like it was full of fireflies. The electricity zinged down the branches to the trunk, all the way to the roots. Then a baby shoot sprouted up. The shoot formed a crystal—an amazing crystal—as strong as the tree trunk, and as white as the electricity that made it. In the center of the crystal was a vein that glowed red—something nobody had ever seen before."

Carrington broke away from his tale to look at Jamison. The curves of her body were as lush as their surroundings, subtle shadows below peaks of light, like a painting of dawn—purity waking up, stretching innocence.

Jamison abruptly sat up. "What happened next?" she asked. She perked her eyebrows at his hesitation.

He gathered his wits and then pulled her gift from his pocket, wondering if he should have kneeled in front of her.

The cotton pouch felt insignificant, yet huge in the palm of his hand. Would he ever see her wear it, or would it go the way of all the other little things he had made her?

He watched her clutch the red silk to her chest, her eyes looking bright, but the hopeful curl at her mouth drooped enough that the knotted vine encircling his guts had once again sprouted talons, shredding his fragile ego. At that moment, he wasn't sure he wanted to breathe again.

Never before had he given her something so lasting—and, to him—so personal.

When he'd found the crystal, he knew it was right.

Carrington had searched for the perfect piece of mahogany to fashion the crown, and he had polished it until it had shone reddish brown like the richest Kentucky soil. The red of the wood was the same red as the vein, which traveled down the middle of the crystal, miraculously forming the letter J.

She lifted it up, reaching to a shaft of light that broke through the mottled shade—almost looking like Lady Liberty, but seated and much less serene.

Jamison lowered the crystal to her lips.

His heart took to a frenetic beating, so fast that the vibration alone was shaking those talon-sharp thorns within him, clawing, eviscerating. And he looked away from her.

It turned quiet again.

A little yellow butterfly flitted over his shoulder. He followed its bouncing flight over an invisible breeze before he finally looked to Jamison. There were tears welling in her eyes, but her hands were balled up.

Carrington then pulled her to her feet. She was so close that he could feel her breath on his neck. His mind went as blank as dirt.

A bead of sweat slid down Jamison's neck into the collar of her white cotton dress.

She pulled away.

"I like it," she said. "I like everything you've ever given me, Carrington."

Her smile looked like it was held up with straight pins. She had to know this gift was different from the others.

"Would you… like to wear it? It's a necklace." Carrington grabbed the crystal and his fingers grazed her breast. His eyes then grew wide and he dropped the crystal. It seemed as if the argument she was having in her head was so consuming that she didn't even notice he'd accidentally touched her.

"Listen, Carrington," Jamison said, holding up one hand. "I love the necklace. It's beautiful. You're so sweet to remember my birthday."

He watched her walk down to the water. She then turned to face him, got closer. He thought that maybe then he had a chance. Sweat trickled down the center of his back as she stared at his shirt. Her mouth opened. He opened his mouth and she leaned in.

But then she stopped short. "I…" she swallowed, "I hate that I'm leaving, but I am," she said. Her words hung in the empty space as she swung back around, and then trudged toward the shore. "I'm leaving this place. Going to make something of myself."

She talked as though she had all the angles figured out, using him as a pivot point.

He watched her move like she was competing against herself, trying to make her argument.

"And, Carrington, you don't have to visit me. It's all right." It didn't matter what she was saying, because he already got the gist. "I'll be back for Christmas, I'll see you then." She smiled.

Before she could turn around again, he grabbed her shoulders and pulled her close. He swept his lips along the warmth of hers—so soft.

He then pulled back and then lifted her chin. "I'll come visit you in the big city?" he quickly added, hoping she didn't hear the little twang of a question in his voice.

She only stared at him with wide eyes.

"Carrington," she said, managing to fully compose herself, "you've never even been on a train."

His hands dropped from her body and he shifted away, staring at the bushes.

"No, I haven't been… but I've ridden a horse since before I could talk, so I imagine I'll be able to handle a train just fine."

"Yah, yah, well—well, I'm going to be really busy with my new friends, you know?"

"I guess you got it all figured out, Jamison," he said. "You're a real planner, just like the Colonel." He didn't need to see her face to know that his words hit hard.

He started back to the ranch, and she followed stride-by-stride.

The breeze still touched them, and as they walked their feet still made imprints in the dry soil. Both of them stole curious glances when they thought the other wasn't looking.

Carrington heard the Colonel's voice before seeing him. "Stop lollygagging with my daughter and get to work, boy!"

26.

It was a hot day even in the shade, and Carrington couldn't stop the sweat from streaming down his back. He looked up at the house; normally, Jamison would be sitting next to him, razzing him about one thing or another. He missed everything about her, even when she needled him like that.

He sat on the whitewashed fence chewing on a blade of grass, watching a new foal scamper a slight distance from her mother, and then turn back to face her again as if teasing, *come get me.* When the foal whinnied, Carrington's prized black Morgan swung his head around to look at the mare. Carrington had been helping to bring that little beauty into the world.

Carrington looked to his horse and asked, "Cole, what do you suppose Jamison's doing now?" He absentmindedly stroked Cole's silky mane. "She's quite the filly and she is far, far away from her mama—not that Miss CeCe was ever much of a mama."

Carrington hooked his boots behind a fence rail and then he sagged forward, leaning his elbows on his knees. "You think she thinks of me, boy? Dad said the Colonel loaded them up real quick, soon as I was off the farm, drove 'em right up to Ohio. Why do you think they left while I was gone?" Cole had his head down while nibbling the grass. He then snorted in reply. "You're such a smart boy, and here I'm feeling stupid. And you know why I didn't ask my father about it? He'd look at me like I sprouted another ear, telling him about my feelings for her. He doesn't say it, but I know he thinks it—we're hired, not family—so I shouldn't be reaching beyond myself."

Carrington crossed his arm over his chest. "Do you think she got any of my letters yet? Maybe that's why she hasn't written me back—or more likely she got a couple, and she's playing the staring game with me… waiting to see how many she'll get before I make a move and call her, or something. Maybe it's all her schoolwork." Carrington sat up and massaged his lower back. "Nod if that's it—no? Then why you think she isn't answering my letters?"

A thick breeze rolled over the green pasture, rustling the coffee trees that lined the fence.

Carrington swatted an errant gnat and then he slumped forward again, staring at the carpenter ants that scurried over the dirt and grass. A waft as calm as his breath encircled him. He felt too similar to the air around him, as if he was the same temperature, suspended, unforced, invisible. He wasn't sure how much time had passed before Cole nosed his shoulder. Cole seemed to urge him on to forget about her.

When Carrington's mind started to drift it usually led him astray, down a path to either frustration or embarrassment.

He slipped down from the fence onto Cole's back.

Carrington envisioned Jamison and himself running beside the horses, jumping on and off as if they were acrobatic bareback riders.

He pictured her legs hugging her horse, her long red-brown hair whipping in the wind. He'd grab her and pull her over to sit between his legs, and then lose himself in her hair. He'd inhale the scent of her moist skin and taste the sweat along her nape.

Carrington leaned forward and then buried his face into Cole's mane, his arms wrapped around the horse's sleek, muscled neck. Carrington rode over the low hills, his fingers tracing Cole's soft coat, imagining the creamy skin of Jamison's inner thighs.

He had never done more than hug and kiss Jamison the day he gave her the necklace—but, geez, what that one kiss had done to him.

27.

Carrington kept busy taking on the manual jobs at the ranch, usually performed by the laborers hired by Mr. Moses.

He needed to get those feelings out of himself.

There was no task too difficult—and if it caused him pain, all the better.

She had left Kentucky when he had been called to assist with a difficult foaling on a neighboring farm. She didn't even leave a note.

"Turner, give me that damn axe. I can finish this." Carrington thrust out his arm.

When Turner hesitated, Carrington reached for it.

At that, Turner grabbed Carrington's wrist and flatly said, "Carrington, you ain't finishin nothin. Look at your hand, boy, you blind?" Fresh, pink calluses on Carrington's hand had been torn open and raw. "You go anymore, and the damn thing's gonna fall off. Your mamma ever tell you 'bout stopping things before things fall off?"

Carrington's mamma had been dead for years. Carrington yanked his arm free. "Give me the goddamned axe!"

Mr. Moses hurried out from the barn at their scuffling. "That's enough, boys," he warned, pulling Carrington away.

Carrington could barely make out over the ringing in his own ears what Mr. Moses was droning on about. It sounded like a swarm of cicadas nesting in his hair. He scraped at his head, his heart pounding against his ribs as he staggered like a drunk into the barn.

Normally, he'd stop and trace the shafts of light cutting through the dusty gray air of the paddock, and he'd chuckle at the buzzing horseflies that only circled in one direction—while giving each impatient mare a little nuzzle as they eased their noses through the stall bars, and warbled their lips.

But, ever since Jamison had left, he felt reduced and acutely primal. He was like an inverted triangle of points—hard and hot, forged of needs so primitive that his brain didn't register. From his groin to his chest, to the sinuous muscles of his triceps, he twitched and pulsed like a sexual bellow.

Mr. Moses caught up with Carrington, who had already started to muck out an empty stall. Carrington ignored him while cleaning, feeling irked that Mr. Moses was still there, silently waiting.

Carrington shook his head. "Now why'd you go and do that, Mr. Moses? I could split wood all day long." Mr. Moses handed him a handkerchief. Carrington leaned the shovel against his chest and then wrapped the cloth around his hand. "Just a little cut, is all. No big deal about it." Carrington maneuvered a wheelbarrow to the next stall.

Mr. Moses leaned against the barn wall, listening to the sound of metal scraping across the stone floor. "Carrington, you've got nothing at all to prove around here. This ain't your job, son."

Carrington kept shoveling, talking over his shoulder. "I know that, but I can't stay inside doing the books no more. I'm all tied up. I..." Carrington dumped a load of manure into the barrow. He knocked the shovel against the metal edge. Before he could turn around to continue shoveling, Mr. Moses grabbed the handle. Carrington let go and crossed his arms over his chest and then looked everywhere except at the overseer.

Mr. Moses laid the shovel on the barrow. "I know, son, I know. No need to explain. But, you go now—see Missy in the house. She'll put you to rights in no time." Mr. Moses gestured for Carrington to leave the stall. "Till she fixes that hand, you'll likely make the ledgers a mess, anyway."

Carrington trudged to the main house. If he hadn't been ordered to find Missy, then he would have kept his distance; stepping through the front door was like getting punched on a bruise. At the foot of the staircase he hopelessly listened for the unique creaks and groans of Jamison walking around on the hickory floor. He made his way through the foyer, past the parlor and dining room, to the back of the house where the kitchen was.

He could have sworn that her perfume lingered in every room of the manor. Even the hand towel that Missy placed on the table next to his wounded hand had smelled sweet, like Jamison.

"Hey, boy, what you doing in the main house?" the Colonel asked, who had stopped when he saw Missy standing over the sink, pumping water over Carrington's hands. Carrington inched over to Missy, not sure if he was trying to protect her or get farther away from the

Colonel.

Carrington stared at the ledge below the kitchen window, willing the Colonel to leave. When he didn't hear him move, Carrington glanced over his shoulder, surprised by the gleam in the Colonel's cloudy eyes.

"Sorry, sir. Split open my hand, cutting wood. Mr. Moses sent me to Missy to patch me back up." He turned back to the sink, hoping the Colonel would walk away.

"That so?" The Colonel sidled behind Carrington. Carrington could feel the heat of the Colonel's body as he angled over his shoulder, inspecting the blood in the sink. "Man, she's going to make a pansy out of you. Come with me, boy, I'll fix a little cut."

The Colonel strode to his study, brooking no argument from Carrington.

Carrington waited in front of the Colonel's oversized Victorian pedestal desk, watching him pour himself two fingers of Wild Turkey.

He had never been in the Colonel's study before. Now, he didn't all too much care for it; it was gloomily dark and too quiet. The study door shut as solid as a sarcophagus lid.

Carrington tried to be calm. Maybe it was the stress of being shut in with the Colonel that had him wanting to raise his hands to cover his ears, certain he could hear the snarls and screams whirling through the room, from the trophy whiskered faces on every wall surface, all glaring glassy-eyed back at him.

Carrington had never killed anything larger than a rabbit, and even that had been an accident. He and Jamison were throwing hatchets at a block of wood in the forest. If she hadn't pushed him, he'd have split the wood and won their little competition—but his hatchet flew way beyond the mark and into a thicket.

The scream had sounded like a little girl. Carrington had then found his hatchet cleaved through the rabbit's hind leg, behind its soft gray belly. The accident turned truly ugly when Jamison got jealous; she apparently thought he'd meant to do it, to show he was a better throw than she was. He crushed its skull with a rock to end its misery, leaving the hatchet behind.

Now, the Colonel struck a match in front of Carrington. A dim light flickered in the Colonel's hand as he lit the candle on the bar trolley. The pungent odor of nutmeg quickly filled the room, making Carrington feel slightly green. The rag in his palm was now soaked with blood. His belly roiled and convulsed, and saliva coursed his mouth. Being in close quarters with the Colonel added another layer of discomfort, but one that only made him more aware of Jamison, which amped up his desire for any kind of distraction.

The Colonel waved the match in the air and then turned to face Carrington. "Come over here, boy."

As Carrington stepped over to the trolley he had a sour taste on the back of his throat. He swallowed it down, and then cradled his wounded hand closer to his chest.

The Colonel lifted the candle to his nose and then took a whiff. He placed it back on the trolley. "The September rotation of alfalfa needs to be harvested soon. It's come to my attention that one of the baling machines needs new rubber belting." The Colonel grabbed Carrington's wrist. "Unwrap that."

The Colonel dug his fingers into Carrington's skin. Carrington involuntarily pulled away, but the Colonel didn't let go and instead dug his nails in deeper. Sweat poured from Carrington, as they engaged in a tug of war battle over Carrington's hand. When battle brought them chest-to-chest, Carrington relented.

He wiped his face with the backside of his better hand and then unwound the tourniquet. He wasn't surprised when the Colonel tightened his grip. Carrington didn't pull away this time, and instead he watched his hand get pale while the tips of his fingers turned cold. He splayed his fingers and then fisted his hand until it had turned numb; when he opened it again, his hand spasmed.

The Colonel sighed in disgust and then shook his head. "Since you seem to be unable to work like a proper man around here, I think I'll task you to drive to Ohio and find that belting."

Carrington's fingertips started to turn into a nearly cadaverous shade of blue. The Colonel kneaded his thumb into the center of Carrington's palm, forcing glistening blood from his wound. This time Carrington tried to pull his hand away as he felt blood rush to his head. His whole arm shook. The Colonel cocked an eyebrow at him before pressing harder, steadily gripping with his meaty corpulent fists as a python might vice its prey.

Carrington felt lightheaded and oddly detached, observing the blood drench his hand and then drip between his fingers. His brain pulsed with every sloppy beat of his heart, forcing blood through arteries so loud that they almost completely hushed the Colonel's voice.

"You'll leave in a few days," the Colonel said with only a hint of the exertion seeping into his tone. "It's a little over three hundred miles to Akron." And then, without letting up, the Colonel refilled his bourbon glass with the other hand. The spicy scent of nutmeg, mixed with the sweet odor of liquor, sent hot tears dribbling from the corners of Carrington's eyelids.

"Now, don't you make a sound, boy." The Colonel's voice was manic jubilation bordering on bloodlust, as he poured the bourbon into the bloody open flaps of Carrington's palm.

Fat tears spilled from the corners of Carrington's eyelids as the bourbon eddied around the raw edges of his skin. It seared inside his cut, and an instance of pain traveled from his arm to his heart, and then against his ribs. Blood drained from his face. Sweat seeped out from between his legs as he convulsed and shuddered, barely able to breathe.

The pain was quickly being overtaken by Carrington's growing fear of the Colonel, who seemed to display a maniacal pleasure watching him writhe.

Carrington cradled his arm after leaving the office, thinking about all of the times Jamison didn't want to talk about her father. But he didn't want to think about Jamison.

He tried to think of the cauterizing burn within his veins.

28.

Four days hobbled by, slowing even more when the Colonel realized that Carrington was keeping himself scarce. The Colonel pulled back the drapes. His eyes stung and watered in the direct sunlight. He looked up toward the barn and then over to the bunkhouse, wondering where Carrington was hiding.

His thoughts then drifted back to when he used to hide as a little boy; Haley James Duarte Davenport had been running and hiding, but no matter how hard he tried, his siblings had always found him. As the redundant fifth son, he'd had a lot of practice, and had spent a great deal of time hiding from his older brothers.

They were a mean and exacting bunch who liked to teach their youngest sibling how things worked.

One of his favorite escapes was to disappear for days in the hills and bow hunt. His brothers were simple riflemen, the end justifying the means, as they aimed and fired without any thought to the romance of the kill.

Haley, what his father called him, set his sights on a distant prey and he chased it, silently tracking, watching it live as he plotted its death.

He loved the thrill of the chase, and actually felt kinship with the smarter animals that were able to avoid the pain of his arrow. He looked up to them, which made him want to down them even more.

The hills were the perfect battleground for Haley to combat the demons which infiltrated his soul. He wasn't sure how they had found him. He was a good boy—went to church, tried hard in school, didn't talk back, and even said his nightly prayers.

His brothers beat him on the outside, while the demons chewed at him from the inside. Together, they burned away his goodness, filling him so full of hatred that he couldn't remember a time when his face didn't look like it was being internally devoured.

Riles Davenport, his father, worried about him as he struggled in school and had a hard time making friends. Riles directed his other sons to assist young Haley, but he refused their help. Each night, when the Davenport family held hands for dinner prayers along the dining table, Riles listed his hopes for his life, and those of his boys.

Haley struggled to be still and listen to his father's prayer as the man ticked off his dreams, enumerating his desires for each of his sons. Haley was ready to cry by the time his father got to him, last in line. His father seemed to pause, as if Tic number four had already filled his hopes.

But, Haley, as Tic number five was the reason their mother died.

Riles stared at his son on many occasions, probably wondering what it might have been like had Haley actually been the daughter they had wanted.

One night with a mouth full of food, Riles laid out the possible benefits to Haley, should he join the military. Riles believed that the army would make a man out of his youngest, give him some pride and direction—a reason for getting up in the morning.

But that was not possible until he turned of age in three more years. Over a thousand more nights to endure the hateful position of being Tic number five.

Haley had left by the time his family had woken up the next morning.

As the Civil War was already in the history books, he was early to enlist, but late to battle.

He cut his teeth chasing Indians off of their own lands.

He was underdeveloped and ruthless; yet, that combination within the chaos of battle became his strength; he was a strategist with plans that had always placed him in front and center of all campaigns. His first strategic move was to refer to himself as James, leaving the name Haley in the dark corner of his childhood.

As time progressed, he found a liking toward whiskey and how it could silence the demons, if only for a moment. Eventually, the liking turned into a habit, and then the habit became the demons in their new form. They took too many forms.

Now, no amount of whiskey would silence the taunting and goading demons after the Colonel had smelled the nervous sweat that gleamed on Carrington's neck—and when he felt the tightening of shock in the boy's body, after he poured the stinging liquor over that wound.

"Well," the Colonel spoke to himself, dragging the drapes shut again. He fell into his chair and plopped his boots on his desk. "Things are gonna change now, boy. You're gonna do what I say, 'cause I'm the boss here." He tipped his chair back and rubbed his palm along the rippled keloid scar on his thigh.

He lightened his touch, and his nipples tightened under his suede vest. With his other hand he pushed on his crotch while thrusting his hips.

"Got a few things for you to do, boy, before you hit the road for that belting." The Colonel's head lolled to the side as he looked at the eight-point whitetail on his wall.

29.

The Colonel made sure that Carrington's leave for Akron was delayed by handing Mr. Moses a list of last-minute chores.

Mr. Moses glanced up from the paper. It was probably the granite hard glare of the Colonel that stopped him from voicing his doubts.

The Colonel didn't have to be the expert tracker that he was to find Carrington; the truck didn't have headlights and there was only one obvious stop on way to Akron before dusk. As well, the tire tracks along the dirt road were easy enough to follow. The Colonel pulled his truck off of the road onto a small mining byway, quietly doubling back on foot with his pack strapped across his back.

The Colonel traversed the slope leading down to the valley where Carrington had set up camp. He watched Carrington lay out his sleeping roll in the long shadow at the base of a willow tree near the river. The high-pitched zing of the cicadas buzzed over the stream, almost matching the near deafening screeches of the Colonel's demons vying for attention.

The Colonel stayed low, behind a thick patch of shrubbery. He had spied on Carrington in the past, but never like this—out where no one could find them. His heart pummeled against his ribs when he saw Carrington unbutton his own shirt and then slip his pants down his bare legs. The boy was buck-naked under those pants. The Colonel moaned, chugging hot breaths past his slack lips. He angled a branch downward so that he could keep Carrington in view, as the boy eased himself into the water.

"Fuck'n shit!" Carrington yelled out, snatching his left hand out from the river.

With that a shiver of pleasure rippled through the Colonel. He heard the pain in Carrington's voice. His demons swallowed that pleasure and then demanded more—they craved Carrington to keep going, or else the Colonel would be left feeling nothing at all.

Nothing was what the Colonel had felt most of his life.

Carrington fell back against the rush of water, dipping his head into the stream's caress. His smooth belly rose and fell above the glassy surface, as his muscular shoulders reached toward the warmth of the setting sun.

From the vantage point, the Colonel managed to see a glimpse of Carrington's semi flaccid penis swaying to and fro in his movement. The Colonel then lifted a bottle to his mouth and then took a long drag of Wild Turkey. He watched the boy standing there in the river, raising his arms up to the sky.

The Colonel's eyes watered, strained with rapt attention as Carrington dragged his hands down his own wet body. The boy then threw back his head, moaning into the early evening air, stilling the cicadas.

The Colonel staggered forward to his knees, hidden in a thicket of black chokeberry and bladdernut shrubs. The veins in the Colonel's neck pulled as tight as steel cables, imagining Carrington's warm tongue in his own mouth. The Colonel pressed his palm against his crotch, and then reached an arm out as if to grab hold of the boy. He ached to taste those long fingers, and feel through his own calloused skin, that young body against his hand.

Pulling his rawhide glove from his pack, the Colonel unfastened his pants. He watched Carrington caress his own neck before his wounded hand reached lazily down his belly.

Carrington then climbed to shore, water dripping off of his slick skin. His black hair was plastered to his head, a few curls loose around his face. Carrington looked up toward the sky, before reaching between his legs to grab his thick, smooth shaft.

The Colonel mirrored Carrington like a three-legged dog, his gloved hand on his penis as he pulled it forward and then drew it back. He circled the tip, smearing his pre-cum along its head, and then shifted back onto his heels before reaching forward, as if to grip onto Carrington's strong shoulder. He remained staring in Carrington's direction, pumping his own penis harder, squeezing his aching balls, fantasizing about the image of the boy offering himself.

With his ungloved hand he scratched along his plump torso, pulling at his hair with one hand and yanking his dick with the other. A choked back grunt flew spittle from his mouth, and then he panted out with his tongue extended.

His release dribbled from his shaft over his gloved hand.

His demons got there first. Once again.

He pitched forward, biting his forearm—stifling a shameful sob.

The Colonel lay in the dirt, still sucking the skin of his arm between his teeth and lips. He glared at the mummified glove that fit the curl of his grip like a second skin. He then ripped it off of his hand, pelting it somewhere into the dark.

The Colonel bargained with his demons and endured—but he despised them when they broke free and trampled him on their way to grabbing what truly belonged to him: the moment just after orgasm, when he felt open and right. The mental and physical steeplechase that he endured to orgasm, in the first place, was fraught with inhumane and unfair obstacles; there had to be a chase and an unwilling submission for him to touch that one golden moment, when he felt whole. That's all he wanted.

He pulled from the haze, listening to Carrington groan out his daughter's name over and over. Deep down, his demons howled with laughter.

The Colonel reached for the Wild Turkey, and then guzzled it down.

30.

As the second son of an Irish-Catholic family, Jennings O'Rourke was destined to go the way of the cloth. Always having been told that he had a kind heart, which would make him a worthy priest and servant of God, he attended Bangor Theological Seminary in Maine at the age of sixteen, in the spring of 1914.

Jennings soon relied upon the ritual of rising each morning at 4AM to join the other neophytes for cockcrow prayers.

He embraced the coolness of the worn stone as he knelt beside the other fledgling disciples. His spirit was elevated by the sound of men's voices as they chanted their adoration to God. The early morning rays enchanted him as they filtered through the Stations of the Cross, illuminating the shadowed faces of the young priests. Jennings discreetly watched their lips move as they prayed before the body of Christ. While he tried to fit into the prescribed mold that the other seminary students took on like the mantle of Christ, it always felt false to him.

Jennings tried to balance the dogma of the church with what he knew of himself and the world, but found it to be almost impossible to reconcile.

Deep down he believed that he was made in the image of God, and by this extension he had been born perfect. He now was not certain of the purity of his flame, because he couldn't help but question his own perfection, and that of mankind.

If all of man was created as an extension of Him, how could they over the centuries kill so many under a banner glorifying God Almighty?

He didn't believe that man could still burn of the purest flame while killing, conquering, and decimating scores of humans simply because they thought differently.

Jennings now zig-zagged his finger over the page that he'd been trying to read, as his mind continued to wander.

He thought of the painting that hung in his uncle's church in Craigarogan: Rory O'Connor, High King of Ireland, the Red Knight of God—portrayed in the painting as charging with Christ's banner out of the chaos which he himself had created, worriedly looking back over his armored shoulder.

Jennings believed that more living minions of God should look over their shoulder; that led him to withdraw from Seminary School in 1915 and then transfer to Notre Dame University. He never looked back after he had heard a lecture by Julius Nieuwland, a Notre Dame professor of Chemistry and Botany. Jennings felt a sense of kinship with the scientist. He was an ordained Holy Cross priest able to reconcile his love of God with his curiosity about the natural world.

Jennings closed the catalogue in front of him; his mind had been too stuck in the past to make heads or tails of anything written on the page. He tossed it onto the shelf below the table and then grabbed the broom leaning against the bookcase behind the counter. He turned back to see the catalogue laying skewed on the shelf. He knelt down and repositioned it, using his hands as guides, making sure it was equidistance from the edge and the right corner.

The bell hanging over the door jingled. From his vantage point, he couldn't immediately see the person who entered his shop. The person hesitated upon entering—common for newcomers because the door was in the far left front corner, while his table was across the room in the far right, hidden by the three rows of dry good shelving units that displayed stock items—things he had made in his small factory in back.

Jennings straightened up and buttoned his jacket. He placed his hands on the counter, and then to seem a little taller he pressed down on the balls of his feet. The customer seemed to have an athletic gait to his step. Jennings recognized that light step to be reflective of the lightness of his spirit—unencumbered by worry. Maybe that was youth, but there was something grounded about him that was imminently pleasing and trustworthy.

Jennings' customers were usually men past their prime, and past caring about appearance. That saddened him, for men were made in the image of God, and it was a disgrace for those to not pay Him homage in the simplest form. It wasn't necessarily about how they looked, it was how they wore their lives—or better yet how they lost their radiant selves in the pursuit of life. They would trudge into his shop looking for a deal, or thinking that because Jennings wasn't some rubber titan they could take advantage of his naiveté. Jennings was smaller and younger than those accomplished in his trade, but he was not a pushover.

The young man stepped down the middle aisle, taking his time picking up display items, washers, erasers, bike tires, rubber straps of various dimensions and weight. Jennings watched him turn them over and then test their firmness in the palm of his hand. He stretched a length of banding, before holding it up to the light that streamed through the front window. When he turned to Jennings and was holding the four-inch banding taut overhead, he smiled with a vivacity that Jennings could feel. The young man lowered his arms as if apologizing for testing the durability of the products.

This gentleman, though naturally attractive through his virility, seemed different. Goodness shone from him, as if he appreciated life in both its simplest and most complex forms. There was something about his smile and how his eyes matched the jovial, yet slightly mischievous upturn of his lips.

Jennings looked down just to listen to the footfalls on the worn wooden floorboards. As the young man reached the main counter, Jennings felt blood rush to his cheeks. He looked up and the customer extended out his hand—an image reminiscent of God's hand reaching for Adam. A hand so expressive, it was as if he held the power to create with the stroke of his finger.

"Name's Carrington," he introduced, "Carrington Marcs."

Jennings dried his hand on his trousers before shaking Carrington's hand. "Jennings O'Rourke. What can I do for you?"

Jennings listened to Carrington detail his rubber belting needs, taking copious notes to ensure that the order would be correct. From time-to-time he would avert his eyes to save from giving away his excitement.

Jennings believed that people were brought together for reasons deeper than the obvious, and he had hoped that this meeting was, as such, an example of that divinity.

31.

At his desk the Colonel felt sweat trickling down his neck, soiling the standing band of his collar. His drapes were closed while the ceiling fan spun hypnotically, rippling the hot air against his already sodden clothes.

The bourbon was finished from his glass.

He was out of ice.

And he was in need of some air.

He grabbed his glass before heaving himself from his chair, and then headed for the door. He had a rare hankering for lemonade, so he made way to the kitchen. He slowed upon seeing outside of the window a cloud of dust moving up the front drive, sparing himself a trip to Missy's domain.

The Colonel planted himself in a rocker on the porch as he watched Carrington pull the handbrake on the truck.

The boy bound up the steps like a young mountain lion, full of energy and thoughtlessness. The Colonel felt his lip quiver in a snarly way.

The Colonel only watched Carrington's face as he spoke to him, uninterested in how the boy found the city. Dell Marcs jogged over to pull his son into a bear hug, releasing him, delivering a few pats on the back.

The lemonade was a short-lived novelty. The Colonel gave his face a slow-moving forceful scrub with his hands, tenderizing his cheeks down flat and testing the durability of his eyeballs. He needed a real drink after all.

But then he heard the boy mention a name that piqued his sensibilities.

The Colonel knew all of the big industry names, and hearing 'Jennings O'Rourke' being said had a rare sobering effect on him.

"O'Rourke, you say?" The Colonel put down his tumbler and scooted forward on his rocking chair. "Is he, by chance, related to the O'Rourke Shire's Farms?"

Carrington held his finger to the tip of his nose. "Right you are, Colonel. They have farms in many counties surrounding Jefferson where the Derby's held. I believe he said that their largest operation is in McCreary County, Kentucky, but they have farms in Tennessee, Indiana, Virginia—"

"Son, tell me something I don't know!" the Colonel bellowed, smacking his boot heels on the porch. "This place—" his hand swept through the air "—is called Davenport Holdings, case you forgot." The Colonel hauled himself from the chair and tipped unsteadily forward, his face pecking toward Carrington's like the early bird.

As the Colonel felt hot blood rush to his extremities, he called out louder. "I know my business," the Colonel said, "and I know who's in my business! Don't need you tellin' me nothing of the sort." He stumbled forward.

Carrington put his hands up, bumping backward into one of the rocking chairs on the porch's weathered boards.

Dell Marcs reached out to stay the chair. "Colonel Davenport, the boy didn't mean to be disrespectful."

Carrington looked from the Colonel to his father, nodding his head.

What did that look say, the Colonel wondered, that big eye look that passed between the two of them? Father and son. He pressed his hand to his chest, groaning out at a sudden pulse of heartburn. The Colonel flung the dregs from his glass onto the porch.

Who were they to judge the Colonel?

Dell added, "He's just a little tired from the drive back down."

"Yes sir, Father's right—I didn't mean any disrespect." Carrington looked back at his father, who then nodded for him to continue. Carrington again spoke up. "Jennings offered to drive the goods down," he said. "I didn't want to wait in Akron, when there's extra work around here that I could be doing."

The Colonel reached for the bell near his empty drink. Before he even had a chance to ring it, Mr. Wu opened the front door. "Wu, don't sneak up on me like that" the Colonel said, staring ahead with heavy eyes, paying the Chinaman no mind. "Get me another drink." The long-robed houseman rounded the gentlemen to retrieve the Colonel's tumbler.

"Yes, sir." He bowed.

The Colonel was certain that Chinaman was in cahoots with

Missy—slinkers, both of them silent as skinny cats.

"Anyway," Carrington continued after the door shut, "we'd need more hands in my absence was my thinking, so I rushed back." He shrugged at his father. "Listen, I made it to the city, I ordered the belting. It's going to be delivered by an O'Rourke family member to boot. That's gotta be a boon, right? I thought I had followed your orders to the letter, sir. I believe I..."

"Son," Dell Marcs interrupted, "why don't you go down to the house and change, then head on over to Willow Fields?" Carrington took off his hat and smacked it against his thigh. He gave a single shake of his head as he made his way down the stairs. He paused on the lowest step, waiting for his father to finish the thought. "Colonel wants to add another exercise ring there, needs to be cleared of stumps."

The Colonel scrubbed his hands over his own face again, and then patted his pockets, searching for his flask. Yeah, he thought to himself, I want another exercise ring—but, right now I want a drink.

"God damn it," the Colonel said when he remembered he'd left his flask on the bar trolley. He plunked back down in the rocker, picked up a half-smoked cigar from the ashtray, and then struck a match to his boot—all the while keeping Carrington in his sights. He flicked the lit match over the railing, nearly hitting Carrington on its path.

Carrington snuffed it under his boot before walking away.

The Colonel smashed his cigar in the ashtray and then banged his fist on the wall behind his chair.

"Mr. Wu! Bring me my drink!"

"Colonel," Dell Marcs piped up, "it could be a godsend to have young O'Rourke pay us a visit. We need to bring in some new bloodlines to strengthen our shares, and stake a position in the European market."

The Colonel looked over his left shoulder at the front door. He smacked the wall again. "Wu!"

The houseman glided out and onto the porch with a tray in hand. He stopped in front of the Colonel and bowed.

"Bout time, Wu," the Colonel said, biting at the slimy film that had stuck in crevasses of his lips.

Mr. Wu turned and then looked at Dell Marcs, offering him drink service.

"No thanks," Dell said.

Mr. Wu then turned back to the Colonel who had already finished a third of his new drink.

"Maybe we should have a welcome dinner for the boy," Dell said, "and see what he knows about his family's farms."

The Colonel sat back and rocked, strumming his fingers on the arm of the chair. His bourbon level had just reached the drawing point where the back of his eyes felt like they were being pulled down to his cheeks, and his cheeks drawn down to his throat.

He held his drink up to his nostrils, pulling a deep whiff.

The Colonel leaned forward, eyeing Carrington in the distance, who headed toward Willow Fields.

"Dell," the Colonel managed an amicable tone, "that *is* a capital idea."

He swallowed another gulp to be on the level.

32.

The Colonel prized his office. The walls were dark, wood furnishings substantial, and the velvet drapes were a purple so deep that they looked almost black. On the walls hung the heads of nearly every kill he'd ever accomplished. Every single one had a visceral effect on him.

His most prized possession though was a replica of Yellow Boy, a Sioux Indian. That puppet maker he'd met at the racetrack wasn't kidding when he had said he didn't make dolls; the Chief was no child's toy. The face was realistically carved with full wide lips, a long proud nose, and strangely piercing deep-set eyes. Real black hair was gathered behind the skull with a string of beaded hide. Around the Indian's forehead was an intricately beaded band of feathers. His chest was bare, the carved muscles appearing to ripple beneath the painted skin. The legs were partially covered by rawhide leggings and a loincloth, typical of the actual Sioux dress.

That was all very well and good, but what really made the Chief a king was what the Colonel did after the wooden Indian was uncrated.

The Colonel never missed an afternoon at the track. There was something about the guttural vibration of pounding hooves that grabbed the Colonel by the balls. That tight, solid feeling turned him on more than any kind of foreplay. A cigar held between his lips, a chilled whiskey glass sweating in hand, the Colonel pressed his body against the shuddering white rail, as tons of flesh thundered over hard packed dirt. The Colonel would close his eyes when the horses ran by, and then would open them only as the pounding quieted.

"*Merda!*" Signore Zappala shouted, tearing his race ticket to pieces.

"*Merda?*" The Colonel huffed out a plume from his cigar. "What kind of a word is that? Maerr-da," he asked, waving away the ticket scraps that swirled near his face. He leaned on the rail looking out over the track as the horses walked back to their gates. The Italian rested his elbows on the highest rung.

"It is shit. Shit is what I get for stopping in *buco di merda.*" His hand movements reminded the Colonel of Al Jolson in white gloves; all of his gestures were at chest level.

"*Bu-ca de mer-da?*" The Colonel repeated it as if fixing to memory.

"Shithole. This town is shiiiit-hole," said the little man. "This country *un buco di merda.*"

The Colonel pushed off the rail taking a forward step to the Italian.

"Well, I have to take offense to your statement, sir." The Colonel widened his stance and puffed out his chest. "This is a fine country, one that I fought for. Shot many an Indian to make way for civilization." The Colonel topped the little Italian by a head.

The Italian straightened up, turning to look up at the Colonel.

"Ah, mistake I am. You are?"

"Colonel Davenport." The Colonel straightened, topping him by a head plus a few eyebrows.

"Lieutenant Sebastiano Zappala, at your service." The mustachioed Italian bowed.

"At ease, Lieutenant." The Colonel's timbre was slightly amused. "Now, what brings you to this prosperous country?" The Colonel pulled the racing form from his breast pocket, circling his next bet.

"You have not heard of me?" Zappala asked.

Looking around, it seemed obvious to the Colonel that no one had heard of Signore Zappala.

"I am Sebastiano Zappala, master puppet maker." He clicked his heels together.

"I don't play with toys." The Colonel puffed air through his teeth.

"I no make *toys,*" said the man, waving away the idiocy like a bad smell. "I make life-size men, not *bambole.*"

Zappala had gained a few eyebrows on the Colonel.

The Colonel propped his hand on the railing shrinking against it, his eyes sanguine while his mouth slacked opened as if his jaw had come loose.

Before the final racehorses hit the backstretch, Signore Zappala was mentally designing a remarkable and unusual piece of art for the Colonel, one that had articulated arms, legs, hands and fingers.

That was twelve years ago. The Colonel had to wait a year for it to arrive in America, but since then it had given him over four thousand days of pleasurable escape.

33.

CeCe Jones was the only daughter born to Charles Carlton and Gardenia Jones. She was delicate and fair from the day she was born, but always slightly unsettled. Her parents dreaded the evenings when they would have to share duties to keep an eye on their daughter, who never seemed to settle into a deep sleep without a dropper of Laudanum under her tongue.

Charles enjoyed the attention he received when bringing little CeCe into town. He paraded her up and down the sidewalk as if he was showing off a prize horse.

People were in awe of CeCe's soft beauty, her golden hair like that of an angel. Her sleepy blue eyes were slightly out of focus, which made people believe that she was a deep thinker—when really she had trouble holding onto any thoughts at all. Charles called her his "little lucky charm," and let her sit on his lap whenever he played cards in the saloon. Occasionally, when he played late into the night, the two stayed together in one of the rooms above the dining hall.

As CeCe reached her awkward teens, her father stopped taking her to town, where he stayed most days selling horses from their ranch to the government, and then eventually straight to the cavalry, as they fought to secure the Plains and Western states for settlement. By then he shared his nights with a Miss Darlene Smith, who ran the profitable business above the poker tables—where the bourbon flowed and the life-altering cards were dealt nightly upon the table.

Charles Carlton Jones was a gambler at heart who loved playing the odds; it was his tradition to bet on both sides, figuring that he couldn't lose as long as he had the money, and was circumspect in his approach.

He was a man who sold horseflesh to both the northern cavalrymen through the government, as well as to the southern troops who had to buy their own.

It didn't bother him as long as he was selling to the highest bidder. With horses being so valuable in the Mexican-American War and in the War Between the States, his only problem was breeding them fast enough—and his only regret: not figuring out a way during the war to sell to both America and Mexico.

It was ironic that he only sired one daughter but bred thousands of horses, making him a player amongst men, a titan in business, and the envy of many whom had no idea he was a failure as a father and husband.

Charles regularly visited the bed of Miss Darlene. She welcomed him with open arms, and legs. In fact, he was with her when he found out that Gardenia had succumbed to the stress of their household, committing suicide by hanging herself in the wishing well. CeCe was now Charles' problem, one that he had planned to take care of in his own circumspect way.

After servicing Charles particularly well, Miss Darlene mentioned that she would love to do "the tour."

He turned her over and took her again—all the while considering what it would be like to take her however he pleased in all of the major European cities. He withdrew a large sum of money from his bank, sold off much of the farm equipment, leaving *Jones's Horses* a shell of a place.

All of this to set up his final poker game, inviting the Colonel who'd always been interested in his business.

He had met the Colonel many times at the tables and recognized one of his weaknesses, an overarching need to win.

That night the Colonel won not only the farm but the farmer's daughter, who he had yet to meet.

CeCe and the Colonel married in 1889, in a small quiet ceremony on the farm.

CeCe now sat in the kitchen on a stool with her hands folded in her lap and her ankles crossed. She rested on the brass railing that circumvented the oversized wooden table, which stood as the centerpiece of the work area. In front of her was a teacup filled with one of Missy's remedies. This was her kitchen, and had been her mother's before she died, but it had never been anything more than a room to her until Missy showed up with child, and without a husband.

CeCe never questioned the woman and didn't care how she had found them. She had just stood there next to Mr. Wu after he answered the door. CeCe remembered lagging behind the two of them as they then walked straight to the kitchen, him as narrow as a wheat stock in his long yellow tunic and black cotton shoes, and Missy barefooted with calico fabric wrapped higher than a beehive on her coffee-colored head.

Missy had that strange kind of connection to everything otherworldly—connections that CeCe couldn't make heads or tails over. In Sunday school, people like her were referenced as the salt of the earth, but CeCe knew she was even more than that: she was the pepper in the soil.

She suspected deep down that Missy was a witch.

CeCe now stared at Missy's fingers. They wrapped like gnarled branches around a green gray pestle, as she pulverized a deer antler. Smelling salts were on the menu today. Yesterday it had been poppies—baskets of dried poppies mixed with salt and wine, and then set aside to be siphoned out for whenever the agitation of sleeplessness had plagued CeCe.

From the moment she crossed under the Davenport Holding arch and floated down the long hallway to the kitchen, she'd been able to corral the Colonel's acerbic humors. That had made CeCe willing to worship at her table.

CeCe ventured into the kitchen more than ever now that they were expecting a guest. Salt and pepper, that's what she was here for: smelling salts and Laudanum.

CeCe's heart tumbled like a bent tire in her chest. Her hand shook as she sipped her 'tea.' The fact that the Colonel was willing to host a stranger filled CeCe with a new sort of dread; any change to the status quo, any disruption, set her heart racing and left her light-headed. In her state, she still knew enough that no good ever came from the Colonel and his big ideas.

"Drink up, Miss CeCe," Missy said in a way that made swallowing more difficult.

CeCe stood outside of the Colonel's door. Her belly was hot, while her skin felt thick. She willed herself to knock, but instead lifted her wrist to her nose and then took a deep, fortifying breath—perfume and smelling salt lingered in the fabric of her blouse where her hankie was hidden. A deeper breath then brought tears to her eyes, and steel to her spine.

She knocked on the door and then waited.

The door was cold against her ear. She heard the Colonel's chair scuttle across the floor, and then noises she couldn't recognize. He could be doing almost anything in there.

Most likely pouring himself another drink.

CeCe warmed her fist in her hand and then knocked again. When she didn't hear anything, she turned the knob and peeked around the door.

There, the Colonel paused with his tumbler at his mouth.

When their eyes met, she felt prickly sweat tickling her underarms. She pressed her arms to her sides and then took a few slight steps into his private space, avoiding any further eye-contact with him, nor the clay eyes of his stuffed trophies on the walls.

A thick sticky scent of nutmeg hung in the air from beeswax candles on the bar. They eternally seemed to flicker their display of shadows like dancing puppets, and from one moment to the next they gave each shape in the room an altered tone.

To CeCe's recollection, she had never seen that statue of the native chief be in one singular place. Right then it was conspicuously standing next to the Colonel's desk, as though serving him as a tactical commander. Illumination from each jerking candle flame made the chief's eyes project a kind of condemning stare, taking to note each of her missteps to consult upon the Colonel as soon as the closed door marked her exit from their realm.

"Colonel," CeCe ventured, "I understand that we are to have a guest very soon, and that you would like to host a welcome dinner in his honor?" The statement was more of a question, since it had been years since the Colonel had ever wanted to host any strangers at their home.

"Yes," the Colonel said, taking a sip of his drink. "I want you to arrange a dinner—a *fine* dinner. His people are well known around here. It was a real shock to their family when he dropped out of that church school. Don't matter to me. He's still horses even though he got himself a factory. I want them to hear how fine this meal was. Hire extra kitchen help for Missy, and a few extra girls to serve the meal."

CeCe pulled her hankie from her sleeve, and then fluttered it below her nose. She approached his desk as if she was testing the waters with the tip of her toe, while the rest of her hung back, wary of any kind of movement he might make.

The Colonel leaned back in his chair, elbows on the arms of it, his fingers intertwined. She never understood what he saw when he looked her up and down. She now tried to follow his gaze by glancing down, before noticing red splotches had sprouted across her chest and a small ring of sweat had formed under her arms, darkening the pale yellow fabric of her dress. She brought her hand to her heart, trying to calm its erratic beat, and then she dropped it after seeing how crepe-like and swollen her skin was around the band of her watch, which was sinking into the soft flesh of her wrist.

Just finish and leave, she thought to herself.

"...And, Colonel, would you like venison, pork... or turkey as a main course?"

The tea was already doing its work. CeCe steadied herself by holding onto the back of one of the two chairs in front of his desk. "Once you choose the main course... I can decide on the dish... the side dishes and get things organized for this... occasion," she heard herself say as she slipped onto the seat.

The Colonel stood up and then walked over to her chair. "CeCe, dear," he said, grabbing her upper arms and squeezing tight, rubbing his thumbs with precision over the burn scars hidden underneath her sleeve.

She couldn't even remember what she'd said that had riled him back then to the point of stubbing his cigar into her forearm.

"I said it would be a *fine* dinner." He inched closer, grinding the stubble of his beard against her cheek. "By fine dinner, I mean, I—want all—of—it—on the table." He pulled her up from her chair to hold her against his body. He spat the words into her ear with a venom she still didn't understand. "I want it *all* at once, CeCe dear." The Colonel then whispered each word and exaggerated each animal name as to become multisyllabic. "I want that buh-ck, I want that pi-guh, and I want that bir-duh presented for our guest's pleasure. I want every side dish that goes with it. Do I make myself clear?"

When he released her, she stumbled back against her chair.

CeCe's mouth opened, but she was unable to get her mind, tongue, and jaw to form any kind of response. She just managed a gurgled choking sound as she struggled for a deeper breath. She brought her hankie back to her nose. The ammonia burned a line straight from her nostril to the inner corner of her right eye.

She'd make sure he got what he asked for—all of it.

34.

All of Davenport Holdings was in a flurry of activity before the arrival of the belting and Mr. Jennings O'Rourke. Carrington worked feverishly to clear the willow field. His father and Mr. Moses, along with the day workers, hauled in the alfalfa and repaired all of the equipment so that everything was in proper working order.

CeCe Davenport along with Missy, and a few other hired women, cleaned, polished, mopped, and scrubbed every surface of every room in the house. The French doors on the upper veranda were opened to air out any lingering scents left by the deep cleaning. She even took it upon herself to clean every filthy ashtray.

Fresh floral arrangements were placed in crystal vases throughout the house. The piano was tuned and the carpets beaten; not a particle of dust lingered to mar the intricate weave of the Turkish rugs.

CeCe put her dust rag in her apron pocket before sitting down on one of the dining room chairs. She gazed along the exotic wood inlay of the cursive D and H in the center of the mahogany table. The last time she recalled having guests in her family home was when they opened it up for the wake of Carrington's mother. So many people came, and there was so much grief.

She narrowed her eyes at the Colonel's dining chair, recalling how he sat her down and then told her that she needed to be a good soldier, to step up and allow young Carrington to spend more time in the main house.

It surprised her that he even noticed the boy, since he had no time for his own child.

CeCe pushed herself up from the table and then eased over to Jamison's regular chair. She brushed her palms along the edge where she had watched Jamison transform from that little girl who would press her bony ribs to the edge of the table, caught up in whatever tale the Colonel was telling.

And then when Jamison matured, CeCe remembered all of the times Jamison had banged her fist against the table, clattering her plate, proclaiming something or another.

CeCe rested her cheek on the table and then closed her eyes, wishing she could go back in time—for so many reasons—but mainly to show that she was more than just Jamison's rattled, scatterbrained mother. All of the delicate and distorted emotional threads that CeCe had woven to define herself had at some point become her actuality, and ever since Jamison had left she had found herself fraying.

She sat up and propped her head in her hand, staring past the Colonel's chair.

There was an ashtray on the small fern table that she had missed.

All of the tender care that she showed him was a lie, but she was a soldier and would do all that she needed in order to play the queen to her king. With her eye on the cigar and the gray ash in the tray, CeCe rose from Jamison's seat and then calmly walked over to the little table. She picked up the single blade guillotine and then cut the cigar in half.

She liked the way that it had felt, so she did it again, and again—until the cigar was in little pieces.

With a smile, she moved the plant forward to hide the filth.

35.

Jennings felt a sense of relief when he turned off of South Broadway onto Red Mile in Lexington. His clan's Standardbred horses were the ones to bet on at the harness track; he used to watch the races with his cousins every time he visited McGrath's.

Now he just needed a place to clean himself up before he drove the last few miles to Davenport Holdings. Many of the hands at the track recognized the O'Rourke name, but weren't too familiar with his particular logo since it didn't feature any horses.

They didn't question him when he pulled up to bunkhouse B.

All of the cousins back then had known the bunkhouse was just one of many, but the boy cousins said it was *for boys only* and the girls had to stay out.

Jennings now took off his hat and wiped sweat from his brow. The August humidity made the cab of his secondhand Sterling truck feel like an aquarium now that he'd parked in the slim shade of the low building.

The smell was familiar: fresh moist dirt, sweet grass, and horses. He leaned over the steering wheel, and then stretched his arms and his back. It had been a long, tense drive.

The door creaked when he opened it. His knees didn't make an audible cry, but he still felt their rustiness when he stepped away from his truck to check on his load. He untied and then lifted the canvas that protected the belting; eight reels of belting lay in the bed, carefully looped and stacked four layers high. Seeing that the order was fine, he set about his next task. It was important that he would make a good impression when delivering the Davenports' order. He'd been taught that cleanliness was next to Godliness, so he turned on the hose bib to wash the dirt and grime from his truck.

The chill of pride's guilty shadow swept over him as he swiped the damp rag over the cross-shaped I in Eire, for *Eire Mowers and Belting Works*.

Did others suffer in that same way? He knew that he was an intelligent man, and honest; he'd almost become a priest, but was it normal to go through the day berating accomplishments just because hubris was one sin of seven?

Jennings fished his handkerchief from his pants pocket, wrapped it around his middle and pointer fingers, and then, like he used to do while practicing the blessing of communion, he solemnly polished the proud I with a down and across motion. After deeming the truck presentable, he grabbed his satchel and then walked to the bunkhouse to put on a fresh shirt and slacks.

On the road again, as he neared his destination, the sky lost its blue. Its clouds became devoid of movement as a gray pallor stretched overhead. He could feel a tempest mounting through the electric current in the air.

Just the same, a small storm gathered inside of Jennings' chest as he slowed his truck to the arch that heralded his arrival at Davenport Holdings. He leaned out the open window and then looked down the long road that led to a white Colonial Revival structure. Three spires rose out from a gray and steep slate roof.

The grass fields on both sides of the chalk-colored fence were even and flat. Everything seemed idyllic, but there was an uneasy quality to the weeping willow trees shading the road. Their heavy tendrils drooped with moss that looked hell-bent on suffocating the blue hydrangeas in their huge white ceramic planters.

Jennings exhaled, tightening his belly muscles in an attempt to still the churn of his stomach. He was anxious to see Carrington again—and was happy that the completed belting had allowed him to promptly make the journey.

36.

Jennings continued to drive along the road toward the house. He saw young colts in the ringed pasture to his right and then spotted Carrington on a striking black Morgan. It was a pleasure to watch a man and horse so attuned to each other; he'd never really cared for riding, but he appreciated a look of true transcendence. That's what he saw in Carrington as he rode closer.

Jennings waved at Carrington, slowing his truck to the pace of a slowly trotting horse.

"Jennings, old man," Carrington said, as he leaned down from his mount to give a hearty shake to Jennings' outstretched hand. "You're a sight for sore eyes, City Boy. I was wondering when you would get here."

Old man? Jennings turned away from Carrington while gripping the steering wheel. "Well, I didn't want to rush your order, Mr. Marcs, I took some extra time..."

"Mr. Marcs?" Carrington squawked. "Jennings, I'm kidding!" Carrington leaned over to smack Jennings on the shoulder. "I'm happy you're here so I can have a reason to take a break. Lord knows I've rubbed my hands raw keeping busy." Carrington turned to look up at the main house before turning back. "Now that you're here with the belting, we can let the machines do some of the work. Why don't you drive up to the house, and I'll follow alongside." Carrington, riding Cole, put his hand on the truck as it inched forward.

"Are all of your horses so well behaved?" Jennings put two hands on the wheel, in case he needed to steer clear away from a spooked horse.

"Well, if either myself or my father raised 'em—they are. We breed Saddlebreds, mostly. Jamison used to joke that I had an easier time relating to animals and nature than I do to people." Carrington's face suddenly faltered at that thought as he looked up at the house. "I think she had a point. I do feel better out here in the fields, and around animals; there's no pretense. They make their needs known—and their wants obvious." Carrington patted Cole's neck and the horse nodded, as if agreeing whole-heartedly with him.

"Jamison?" Jennings rested one arm along the open window and then leaned slightly closer to the door. He looked up at the second story where Carrington was focused.

"Yeah, she's the Colonel's daughter. I hope you'll meet her one day."

One day, in Jennings' mind indicated that he'd be asked back; that made his heart beat a little faster.

When they arrived to the house, Carrington dismounted and then tied Cole to the metal jockey as Jennings parked the truck. Carrington rubbed his blistered hands on his dungarees.

"Can I help you with your bags, Jennings?" Carrington gestured toward the house with his head. "I believe the Colonel and Miss CeCe have you in the main house."

Jennings shook his head. "I can manage. Thanks." Jennings reached into the cab, grabbing his satchel. "And where do you stay?" Jennings asked, looking around for other buildings.

"Oh, nah, my father and I have a place near the paddocks, over there." Carrington pointed somewhere to the right of a very large building, about a furlong away. "We have our privacy and the Davenports have theirs. Works well, since we need to be close to both the paddocks and the bunkhouse, where the seasonal men bed down during heavy working months." Carrington led Jennings over to the main house.

Before they even reached the bottom step the doors swung open and out strolled a man and woman followed by a flurry of bounding hounds, galloping down the stairs in a tangle of large paws and flapping tails.

"Bartholomew, Joseph—heel, down," Carrington said in a stern voice, while motioning his hand to the ground. Jennings almost laughed at the heartbroken looks in the dogs' eyes as they dropped to the gravel.

"Colonel Davenport, Miss CeCe, I would like you to meet Mr. Jennings O'Rourke of Eire Mowers and Belting Works," Carrington said.

The Colonel stepped down the broad white stairs with his hand outstretched and his cigar leaving a trail of smoke in his wake.

"Mr. O'Rourke, welcome to Davenport Holdings," the Colonel

said. Jennings had never heard a man speak so clearly while holding a cigar between his lips. "We appreciate that you've gone through such trouble to bring the belting directly to us. I hope that you can be spared for a few days so that we can repay your kindness."

Through the wisps of smoke Miss CeCe toed her way down the steps, reminding him of a debutant at her first cotillion; she was a bit unsteady, but then fully committed once she started down the steps.

"Yes, Mr. O'Rourke," she added. "I insist that you stay with us for a few days and unwind from your long journey." Even though she said it with a sweet southern belle lilt, her voice had a nervous edge that conditioned him to accept her offer.

Jennings hadn't actually considered how long he could stay; he'd been so focused on finishing the order and delivering it. But her tone combined with the pleading look in Carrington's eyes made it an easy decision; he'd get a chance to spend more time with Carrington, and possibly garner a few more orders if he stayed put.

Jennings bowed. "Yes. It would be my pleasure to spend a few days here on the farm with you all."

"Carrington, take his bag," the Colonel said. "Mr. Wu will show you to your room, Mr. O'Rourke." The Colonel flicked the ashes of his cigar into the potted roses next to the front door. He then disappeared back into the house.

Miss CeCe Davenport's hand was light on Jennings' arm as she led him up the stairs to his room on the third floor. Her touch was so timid that she seemed totally unaccustomed to it. Jennings bowed his head and kept his eye trained on her as they mounted the stairs; she rambled on about Mr. Wu, the houseman, and how he literally came with the house. Jennings looked behind him unable to hear any footfalls from the houseman, and then he realized how quiet Carrington was, as well. Both men seemed to tread thoughtfully in her presence.

Jennings sensed a bit more confidence from her when she stopped at a door. He presumed that the room was his because he could feel her excitement. She even flung it open with a flourish, but then she slunk back in that same way to which he could relate; pride's shadow had stolen the moment away from her.

Regardless of the room, he would show her that he thought it was perfect in every way.

Jennings stepped into what must have been the largest guest suite he had ever seen. Three sets of French doors across the room leading out to a covered sleeping porch. The hickory floor was inlaid in a chevron pattern. The dark mahogany bed featured bedposts that spiraled upward to pineapple finials on top. The blue damask silk bedding matched the deep purpled blue of the hydrangeas on the lawn.

What a far cry from his austere room in seminary.

At Notre Dame, Jennings had lived with his aunt and uncle who had furnished his room with old country rough-hewn wood furniture worn oily-smooth by generations.

He was unaccustomed to the luxury that was in front of him. As a sleeping provision, the floor seemed more in tune with his ascetic cot at seminary. Even though he could afford to purchase a feather bed and upholstered chairs for his dining table, he preferred a life that was reflective of spiritual wealth—which also gave him pause. Was he then guilty of boasting that he was better than others because of his selective austerity?

Carrington placed Jennings' satchel on the bench at the foot of the bed.

"The bathroom is down the hall on the left. You're the only one on this floor, so you'll have free rein of all the rooms up here," he said.

"Well, Mr. O'Rourke," CeCe said, "I pray that you'll be comfortable here in our humble home. If you need anything, please don't hesitate to ask Mr. Wu, or myself. Dinner is at eight sharp. The Colonel likes things done on time, so please be mindful."

She hesitated and then opened the drawer in the nightstand next to the bed. She pulled out the saffron-colored bible and then placed it next to the lamp. She looked at Jennings, her face as hopeful as a child presenting a stray kitten for her parents' approval.

She turned and then scurried from the room.

"Don't worry, it won't be that bad," Carrington said with a mischievous smile on his face. He smacked Jennings on the back. "Please forgive us, if we seem a bit awkward and rusty with all this. If it'll make you feel any better, I'll let you help me cut down the last tree in the willow field and clear the stumps tomorrow." Carrington looked him up and down as if manual labor was something Jennings had only read about in a book. "That'll have you begging to take advantage of our southern hospitality. Then the bath down the hall and the soft bed pillows'll definitely be calling your name."

After Carrington left the room, Jennings riffled through his bag and pulled out a wad of tissue paper. He sat on the side of the bed and then unwrapped the candle he always traveled with. He then placed it next to the yellow bible on the nightstand.

37.

The dinner conversation had already turned to horses before the first course had been served. Jennings learned that Davenport Holdings produced the finest American Saddlebreds in the world, and that it had provided both Grant and Lee with many of their storied mounts.

Jennings was surprised by that claim, considering the Colonel was probably still wearing knee pants during the Civil War. Jennings' own family raised a greater variety of breeds; he particularly liked crossbreeds. He appreciated the science of it almost as much as he marveled at the outcome—a new horse breed created by man.

"Speaking of crossbreeds," the Colonel said, "I'm sorry our daughter Jamison isn't here to meet you."

Carrington stopped in mid-chew at the Colonel's mentioning.

"She's a pretty filly, bit of a crossbreed herself," the Colonel said, flicking his ashes into the tray.

Carrington quietly lowered his silverware.

"That is to say…" the Colonel paused, taking short puffs of his cigar to stoke it up. "…That is to say, she's more than just a pretty filly—she's a smart one, that girl. University of Cincinnati. Aren't many women there… at the University, I mean. Named her Jamison, she's sorta grown into her name; a name's important. A man's name is *very* important. Signifies his strength and position in the world. *O'Rourke*, now that stands for something." The Colonel stopped, waiting for Jennings to add a little something to the conversation.

Jennings reached for his water goblet, and then took a long drink.

"She's strong, too. Matter of fact." The Colonel stopped talking in order to nod at CeCe. "CeCe, you fill in the parts, if I get this wrong."

CeCe's knife clattered onto her plate. It seemed to Jennings that Miss CeCe had no idea what the Colonel was about to say.

"I remember, for instance, the time when she beat Carrington, here, at wood chopping." The Colonel blew smoke in Carrington's direction. "Split a log into four pieces before Carrington got his in half." The Colonel leaned back in his seat and then puffed on his cigar, catching the eye of each person at the table before blowing smoke circles in the air. When they dissipated he leaned forward and then pointed at Jennings with his cigar. "You ought to meet her. She's something else. That right, Carrington?"

Carrington leaned forward and then he sat back, putting his silverware on the table. "Yes sir. Jamison *is* something rare." He kept an even tone.

"Speaking of family names," Jennings chimed, "I have a story about my own family, if you care to hear about it."

"Well, of course son, we'd love to hear your story. Right, CeCe?"

"Yes, well, I..." she started before looking across the table at her husband, and then back over at Jennings.

The Colonel just waved her words away. "Go on with your story, O'Rourke. I am truly curious." The Colonel angled his body toward Jennings, and CeCe closed her mouth.

"So, I'm going to tell you about my uncle McGrath, whose parents didn't hold to the O'Rourke tradition of settling in Gaelic-named countries..." Jennings shook his head, lightly pinching his lower lip between his fingers before smiling.

"Not Seamus McGrath—he wanted to do things his own way. He moved to America and laid down roots in Fayette County, Kentucky. They were quite poor, both of them working long hours in the fields. H.P., my uncle, was said to have been born while his overly large mother toiled in the fields one day." The Colonel perked up at the mention of H.P. McGrath. "He dropped clear out of her at the base of a giant oak tree where she stood. The tree was unique because it had been formed by the union of two seeds, from two different families of Irish oaks." Jennings held out his hands as if having a seed in each one. "When a violent storm shook the trees one day, they bulleted acorns to the ground. Now, this odd occurrence caused two seeds—one from each species—to pierce the ground at the same time, in the same exact spot." He dashed those invisible seeds at the table. "Those two seeds had grown together to form that amazing oak tree, where his mother found herself in her time of need. And then the 'little people'—winged leprechauns—appeared."

"Pfft," the Colonel groaned, waving away Jennings' tale. "Now you're just going on, O'Rourke. Here, I thought this was going to be somethin' historical, private tales from your family—not a little girl story," he said, falling back against his chair.

Jennings turned his head and then held up his long narrow hand, like Christ showing the evidence of his crucifixion.

"Just one moment, sir, this *is* the tale of my family—handed down over the generations."

Carrington hadn't moved, hadn't even appeared to have taken a breath, as he waited for Jennings to start up again. Miss CeCe was squishing left-over peas on her plate with the side of her knife, and then finally the Colonel shrugged, letting Jennings know that he could continue.

"So, they—the winged leprechauns—had heard her screams and decided that she had paid the price for her husband's foolish pride of defying their tradition of putting down roots in only Gaelic countries. They would now allow the young couple to prosper and grow as long as they stayed in this area, and built a farm around this magical Irish tree."

The Colonel threw down his napkin onto the table, shaking his head.

Jennings sharply waved his hand to dismiss the Colonel's disbelief. He spoke up louder and faster as if doubling down on the seriousness of his tale. "Now, now—she *listened*, and she *promised*, and, as a sign of her promise she named her son Hal Price—short for Hallelujah Price, appeasing the little people who had wiped her brow as she cradled her newborn son in her arms." Jennings took a gulp from his wine before leveling off his voice again. "H.P. McGrath was gifted with the luck of the Irish from that day forward and *did* go on to be quite a success, winning the first Kentucky Derby in 1875 with Aristides, ridden by Oliver Lewis." Jennings sat back and then punctuated his story with a confident sip from his goblet. Miss CeCe looked up from her plate at the mentioning of the Kentucky Derby, and he responded to her look by giving her a quick wink.

The Colonel leaned forward, his lips tight around his double Corona. He took a long drag of his cigar and then puffed the smoke from his mouth. He then shook the ashes onto the ceramic tray, before stuffing the cigar back into the lazy comma of his lips.

He chewed it as he spoke, making it bob up and down.

"Well, Mr. O'Rourke, I knew H.P. McGrath won the first Derby, but I had no idea that he had such a storied beginning. Thought he made his money during the gold rush in California. Had no idea that he had help from… fairies. Pour Mr. O'Rourke another glass of wine." The Colonel spoke to Carrington in a vexed tone as if Jennings' whole performance was a hideous waste of time.

Everyone waited while Carrington pushed back his chair and then walked over to the sideboard for the carafe of red wine. He stood next to Jennings.

"More wine, Mr. O'Rourke?" he asked with a bow, holding the carafe for Jennings' inspection. Carrington tilted his head toward Jennings and then smirked, cocking his eye as if telling him, I dare you to say no.

Jennings raised his glass and then continued talking while Carrington went around the table to fill the Colonel's.

"It is true, Colonel," said Jennings, "that not many outside our clan know the full story. You have to admit that if offered and possible, wouldn't you appreciate a little fairy would step in and change your future?"

The Colonel turned red in the face and started to choke; apparently, he had bitten straight through his cigar.

CeCe Davenport looked up from her peas.

Jennings' chair was caught on the rug, and then fell backward when he tried to stand up and help.

Carrington, who still had the wine carafe in his hand, grabbed the Colonel from behind. Carrington wrapped his arms under the Colonel's ribs and then abruptly pulled him up, which sent the offending glob flying from his mouth and sputters of red wine all over the front of his brown suit.

The Colonel sagged back into his chair, wheezing, his face purple and green like a rotting eggplant. The room was quiet except for the sound of the Colonel gulping and gasping.

He finally wiped his mouth with his napkin, and then only partially stood up as if a knotted-up chain had kept his lower half connected to his upper half. Everyone could see his discomfort as he forced himself to stand up straight. He then reached into the breast pocket of his jacket and pulled out another Corona. The Grandfather clock chimed in the foyer.

The Colonel bit the head off of the cigar and then spit it on the floor. The silver-plated match holder nearly tipped over at the strike of his match.

Even though they could all see his hand shaking, he took great care in rotating the cigar near the flame, drawing slow deliberate puffs.

He tossed the spent match onto the center of the ashtray.

"Goodnight," the Colonel said in an awkward conclusion to the meal. "We rise early here on the farm, Mr. O'Rourke. Breakfast set for 5:30AM. Goodnight," he repeated, before heading to his study. "Fairies for Chrissake," he muttered.

38.

Early the next morning, Carrington walked up to the main house to collect Jennings after breakfast. He was anxious to topple the last tree and finish the necessary preparation to ready Willow Fields for the imminent delivery of new horses. Jennings, CeCe, and the Colonel had been settled at the dining table.

"Good morning," Carrington gave a cheery welcome to Jennings. "Ready to put your back into some real man's work for a change?" he asked.

Jennings straightened in his seat at Carrington's challenge. "It may surprise you, Carrington, that even though I do spend a great deal of time at my desk and the factory floor, I as well keep in shape while fencing at my club. I'd be willing to take you on stroke-by-stroke to see who the better man is."

"Well now," the Colonel chimed in, "that is a competition I would like to put a wager on."

CeCe teetered a bit, her hankie pressed to her lips. "Now, Colonel, I'm not sure that is a smart idea. Mr. O'Rourke may have moved away from the path of the church, but it's still a bit inappropriate for you to place a bet upon his head."

The Colonel waved off his wife's concern. "Care to make a wager, gentlemen?" he asked.

"Well, what would the wager be, sir?" Carrington asked.

"Let me think." The Colonel then slapped his knee and said, "I've got it. If Carrington wins, I'll take him hunting with me. He can get first try at bringing down that ten-point buck, which has been the envy and desire of every young man in town. I believe there is a purse to be won. If Mr. O'Rourke wins, then I shall invest three hundred dollars in Eire Mowers and Belting Works."

Carrington had spoken to his father many times about the trophy buck competition set up by the young men in town. It included a handsome cash prize in addition to full payment for the taxidermy work, so the buck's antlers could be displayed for generations to come.

Carrington really didn't want to bring the great beast down, but he badly wanted the cash prize. Working on the farm didn't afford him the opportunity to put away any savings. Without savings he could not build his dream business, through which he hoped to secure his future with Jamison.

"What do you think about my wager gentlemen, any takers?" the Colonel asked.

Both men agreed before making their way down to Willow Fields.

39.

The humidity was so high that they were blanketed in moisture the instant they stepped outside. A few birds called lazily in the distance; there was stillness to the laden air, which promised a thunderstorm in the near future. They rode Gray Arabians to Willow Fields and then stopped at the tree in question. Carrington let his suspenders slip from his shoulders and then peeled off his shirt. Jennings did the same, but kept his head covered with his wide brim sisal hat; the sun would quickly burn his fair skin, although he frequently used the hat to swipe at the mosquitos that were buzzing around him.

The Colonel rode up on Ranger, his dappled Saddlebred. He waited under a nearby oak tree where the Gray Arabians were tethered.

Carrington poured a bit of fresh water from a jug onto the red soil, making a paste. He then rubbed the paste all over his face, arms, and shoulders.

"What are you doing?" Jennings asked.

"Keeping my skin protected. Mosquitos don't like the taste of the soil, so they stay clear away. You should put some on, too—wouldn't want to have an unfair advantage over ya." Carrington tried to wipe the paste on his own back.

Carrington handed Jennings an axe and then they started at it. One hit from the left while the other hit from the right. They began to find a rhythm, strike-to-strike, well-matched as they made their way toward the center.

The Colonel, out of sight of the competing men, watched from his perch under the ceiling of the oak, massaging his groin with both hands. He had played his game well, he thought to himself as he reached down to squeeze his tightened balls; he knew he would win either way.

With a crack, the men yelled "Timber!" and the tree arced to the ground, bouncing slightly, red soil puffing into the air as it landed with a thud. Carrington and Jennings started to laugh, to whoop it up and congratulate each other on a job well done. Carrington had struck the lowest blow on the stump, meaning that his final strike was the one that fell the tree.

Jennings held out his hand to Carrington. "Congratulations, old man. The best man won, and I'm happy for you."

"No hard feelings, Jennings?"

"None." He put down his axe and inspected his palms. "I have to admit, swinging the axe is much harder than fencing."

"Don't worry, Jennings, we can hit the pond after we finish pulling out the stump. We'll dig around it so I can get a rope under some of the roots, and then have Pilsner pull it out."

"Pilsner? I hope he's an enormous German giant who can make wishes come true."

"Like your ancestral fairies?" Carrington asked.

Jennings couldn't help but smile.

He took off his hat and wiped the sweat from his forehead. He glanced over at the Colonel, who was still in the shade of the tree. Jennings brandished his hat in salute and the Colonel gave a quick flick of the chin in response.

"Pilsner, my friend, is one of our Czech draft horses that's gonna do the majority of pulling the stump out of the ground," Carrington replied as Mr. Moses walked Pilsner toward them. Carrington waved at him before turning back to the stump. "Mr. Moses to the rescue, as usual. Jennings and I'll be finished here shortly."

Mr. Moses tied a thick rope to Pilsner's harness and walked the horse just forward of the stump, handing the reins to the Colonel who'd roused himself from his shady perch. The men worked together to tie the rope to various points on the tree roots. When the ropes were secured the Colonel took a switch, and with a practiced flick of his wrist he swatted the hindquarters of Pilsner, who slowly moved forward.

The sky had dulled to a darker gray during the afternoon, the gentle breeze dragging angry clouds toward the farm. The path they walked to the pond was lined with Kentucky blue grass and alfalfa, butterflies flitting among the flowers. Coffee trees with their hanging pods, and tulip trees with their otherworldly yellow and green spiked flowers were interspersed with graceful dogwoods. Under the trees were various shades and shapes of ferns, yellow and white daffodils, black-eyed Susans, and wild orchids. One giant coffee tree stood closest to the edge of the pond, and from one of its branches hung a long rope.

"This is our pool," Carrington said as he dropped his shirt on the ground and pulled off his dirty trousers, divesting his body of clothes. In one quick motion he then ran for the rope, swung himself over the pond, and then let go, disappearing into the clear bluish-green water.

Jennings watched his new friend swim underwater. He could see Carrington's legs and feet kick with a strong fluid power, which made it difficult for him to look away.

"Come on in—the water's great!" Carrington yelled.

Jennings let his shirt also fall to the ground and then carefully removed his pants, leaving his drawers on. He scurried to the rope, grabbed hold and then swung himself over and into the water. When he surfaced, he looked up to see Carrington at the rope again before letting go with a holler and a cannonball.

The sight of Carrington's naked body swinging toward him made Jennings' stomach tighten and his groin ache. It was both a wonderful and a horrible feeling. He prayed for God to deliver him greater strength so he could resist his urges, and not embarrass himself or his friend.

Growing up, Jennings had avoided temptation by staying away from socializing. He prayed nightly, asking the Lord for guidance, wondering what he was to do with himself.

Jennings' resolve had failed him when Carrington walked into Eire Mowers that day. He felt elation at the very sight of him, and that he was somehow in the presence of God because Carrington was so painfully beautiful, graceful, strong, and decent.

When Carrington swam over to Jennings, Jennings swam to shore before walking over to the waiting rope swing. He felt that as long as he could keep some distance, he could maintain control of his urges. He splashed into the water as Carrington watched.

Then it was Carrington's turn. It didn't help Jennings' resolve to watch Carrington in his naked glory swing toward him on his way into the water. All Jennings wanted at that moment was for Carrington to misjudge the distance and fall into him. His last defense was to silently recite backwards Pater Noster in Latin; *Maloa nos libera sed. Tentationem in inducas nos ne et...*

Carrington lazily dog paddled toward the shore, eased himself out of the water and then onto the grassy bank. He rested on his elbows, one leg bent and the other outstretched along the ground. He rocked his bent knee from side-to-side without the least bit of self-consciousness.

"I love this place," he said. "It brings me such happiness to be here. Love the smells and the sounds. Love how the light trickles through the leaves as the wind blows. I even love it here during a downpour, when the sound of the rain pelting the tree canopy is deafening—so loud you have to shout to be heard."

Jennings was still reciting Pater Noster as he turned to look at his friend, thinking that he had gained control of himself. Though his concentration broke again as he looked upon Carrington's figure, his legs and what was between them.

Afraid to exit the water, he tried to focus on what Carrington was saying, but couldn't hear over the sound of his own heartbeat, and the incessant ringing of his ears as the blood rushed to his head.

He took a deep breath, reciting more of it: *...qui es in coelis; sanctificatur nomen tumm...* and then he stepped out of the water to join Carrington at the pond's edge.

Jennings lay on the ground beside Carrington. He was finally able to regain control in this prostrate position.

It reminded him of being in church, reciting morning prayers. A calm washed over him before he turned his head to Carrington, who was now talking about things he planned to create, having found so much inspiration from this particular spot over the years.

Jennings didn't ask any questions; he was content to listen to the sound of Carrington's voice, and watch his lips move, and the pulse of his neck rhythmic to his breathing. The effort of their earlier task, combined with the soupy heat of the day made Jennings' eyes heavy, drawing him into slumber on the grassy bank.

Jennings awoke with a start; a clap of thunder vibrated through the air as lightning emblazoned the sky. At some point Carrington must have fallen asleep too, because they were both in the same mixture of startle and semi-lucidity. The rain pelted the canopy with noise louder than Jennings' factory floor. They grabbed their clothes and sprinted through the wet bluegrass and the red clay soil, which made them slip and slide as they darted off to the manor.

40.

Missy was in the kitchen with her twin daughters, Midnight and Moonlight. She had been raised not to expect too much from life; her glory would come, according to her mother, when she was held in the bosom of the Lord.

Missy didn't wait for the Lord to hold her; however, she'd been held in the strong embrace of a man passing through her town buying horses.

He was a white stallion of a man who shined just like she believed Jesus would. His blue eyes were bright and soothing, his manner calm and understanding as if he had a second sense of this dark filly's skittish nature.

Compromised and, again according to her mother, unfit to sit at the feet of the Lord, she made her way to the address that the man had left with her. By the time she arrived at the Lexington farm she was in serious need.

Miss CeCe took her in immediately, sensing that they could help each other.

Missy had taken over the kitchen, which pleased the Colonel, whose gut was apoplectic because of his wife's poorly prepared meals. In return, Missy was given a roof over her head and a bed to rest in as her own belly grew large.

Little Missy had a hard birth with the twins. Missy, barely weighing ninety pounds soaking wet and standing four foot three inches, wanted nothing more than to bring her children into the world. Midnight and Moonlight seemed to have different feelings, though—as they didn't want to budge, content to be in her womb.

As they grew up they seemed able to read each other's thoughts—the mystical trait that's particular to twins. Missy loved her dark beauties, with their unusual bright blue eyes.

Tonight the girls were helping her prepare the evening dinner.

While Missy chopped parsley to put into the cold cream of parsnip soup, Midnight painted another layer of her mammy's bluegrass honey onto the smoked pork roast. Moonlight sat at the large worn wooden worktable, rubbing the haunches of the family's two Otterhounds, Bartholomew and Joseph, as their tails dusted the floor in anticipation of food scraps.

The dogs froze for a few moments before they lifted their heads and bolted out of the kitchen toward the grand entry. At that very instant the front doors flew open, partly due to the howling wind and partly because of the wet hands of Carrington and Jennings as they bounded inside to escape the punishing spears of rain.

The men were as out of control as the dogs, as they found it impossible to stay upright once their mud-covered shoes touched the polished hardwood floor. All collided in a heap of arms, legs, paws, and wagging tails as the dogs sniffed the drenched men avoiding the broken vase and the scattered daisy's knocked off the entry pedestal when the door swung open. It was such a commotion that even the Colonel came from his study to see what was going on.

The storm infused the entry area with sparks of heat at every clash of thunder and finger of lightning. Everyone rode that electrical current in their own way—the young men laughing harder than they normally would and the usually silent dogs more frenetic and boisterous, barking at the ghostly specters brought forth by the shifting atmosphere.

Moonlight could see what the dogs saw, but she couldn't say a word, having never been able to speak. She just looked from the spectacle of the men and animals, to her sister, and then to the Colonel who stood at the door to his study.

"Down boys, down!" Carrington tried to sit up and restrain the big bundles of fur.

Jennings was still laughing as he rose to his feet. "Oh my goodness, please forgive us," he spoke out to the watching Colonel. "What a sight we must present!" He cackled out. "We got caught in the storm and ran for dear life back to the house. I'm terribly sorry for the disruption, sir."

At that moment the lights flickered on and off, and then remained off, which left them all in semi-darkness. The Colonel stepped forward, the wind brightening the tip of his cigar that hung from his lips.

"Not to worry, boys. Just a little rain, a little smudge on the floor. Mr. Wu, help Missy clean this up so she can get back to making our dinner. Mr. O'Rourke—little water never hurt nobody. We're used to this weather on the farm."

Mr. Wu spoke up. "Perhaps Mr. O'Rourke, sir, you would like to soak in a hot bath? I will have Midnight bring up hot water so you might bathe before dinner." With a slight bow he retreated from the room. Midnight followed him into the kitchen to heat the water.

The Colonel closed his study door, walked directly to the bar service, and then uncorked another bottle of bourbon. As the lights flickered he threw back a full tumbler of the warm liquid.

He knew he shouldn't, but he poured another, and then tossed that one back as well. As his stomach grew warm from his preferred elixir, he turned toward the Chief and gave him a long unfocused stare.

His mind was twisted by the vision of the two wet men on the floor while the hounds licked and nudged them. The heat from the Colonel's belly traveled down to his crotch.

Peering at the Chief, the Colonel approached him to lick the wooden lips, pressing his body against the hard smooth texture of the Chief's sculptured chest. He stifled a moan, feeling himself grow hard as he pressed his length to the Chief's hide loincloth.

He deftly pulled pins from the Chief's arms so that he was held tightly within an embrace. The Colonel wrapped his leg around the back of the savage's thigh, which stood stock still—poised to take the inevitable beating. The Colonel rammed his tongue into the Chief's mouth as his hands traveled down to cup the expertly carved ass of the Indian.

Sweat began to trickle down the Colonel's belly, dampening his shirt and causing his nipples to grow hard from the friction. He continued to fantasize about a tangle of men and beasts on the floor of the entryway, and then he remembered the proud savage who he had chased for days through the Black Hills during the Sioux War in 1876.

His own thigh still held the ghost pain of the arrow that had struck him. He bit down on the full broad lower lip of the Chief, which wasn't enough to erase the images that burned in his head.

His hands shaking, the Colonel unlocked a drawer hidden in his desk. He unfolded the retrieved oilcloth before burying his nose into the dark hair that resided within it.

Holding it with both hands, he licked the patches of skin that held the black hair in place.

He could still picture that Indian trying to get away. Having been pierced through the left shoulder, the Indian clawed his way higher on the boulders, turning one last time to look at the white man who had nailed him in the back.

He had then slid out of sight.

Even after so many years, the eventual sound of the Indian hitting the dirt continued to resonate in the back of the Colonel's mind. When the Colonel reached the red man he was bleeding out. The Colonel snapped the arrow from his back before he raped the dying man—paying him homage for a valiant chase.

The Colonel now collected his bow and arrow from its spot near the bar. He tossed the scalp into the air and took aim. Even in drunkenness the Colonel managed to pierce it through, pinning it to the wall. The savage once again at his mercy.

The chill he felt from the memory now turned into ecstasy as he relived in his mind that exquisite kill—arrow after arrow, until he came. The lightning continued to flash outside, casting fearsome shadows on the walls, the curious and ever observant silent specters.

41.

Along the upper section of the Colonel's morning *Kentucky Post* were sentences of patchy blurs of black, white, and gray. He could feel the definition of his own thumbprints like dry sandpaper, wearing thin circles along the crisp newsprint.

The Colonel pushed his glasses higher on the bridge of his nose and looked down at his coffee. It had turned tepid, diminished in its allure.

He gazed through the doorframe leading out to the foyer toward the main doors of the house. In his head echoed the juicy bubbly swish of his own saliva, as he jabbed his tongue like a toothpick along the chipped side of his eyetooth. He glared at the dust motes, floating flagrant and aimlessly through the windows in the beams of morning light.

Carrington was late for breakfast.

Something clattered to the floor in the kitchen and the Colonel smirked. He could practically feel the trembling in Missy's hum as she rushed about the kitchen, completing his last-minute task.

She was a smart one, he'd hand her that. He'd never admit it, but she made him feel more than a little uneasy—like he couldn't hide from her.

Like she had some damned second sight, something more informative than intuition. He was certain her twins had it too. Especially the one who couldn't talk, Moonlight. Thank God *she* was a mute. That one moved like a ghost in the house, and caught him doing things she ought not see.

His tongue finally coaxed free the shred of sweet ham stuck between his teeth. He sluiced it along the roof of his mouth and then smacked his lips together like a toothless old codger working chew over to his cheek. He could imagine Missy's daughters watching their mammy with their wide dark blue eyes, as she scuttled about in the next room.

The familiar cadence of bowls and utensils clanking and scraping along the rough-hewn table was replaced with the sound of wax paper tearing and creasing, of food being wrapped and bundled for a journey. He was sure those daughters' eyes were full of suspicion, but they would not be around for what he had planned.

Today was the day he'd take Carrington hunting.

The groan of the porch had already told the Colonel that Carrington had arrived, before the door whooshed open and then smacked shut.

The Colonel tossed his newspaper onto the table and then sat back, crossing his arms over his chest. He could feel his heartbeat beneath his right hand, strong and racing.

"Morning, Colonel," Carrington said. "Sorry I'm late. I had some extra chores to finish, with my father being away and all."

Carrington breezed into the dining room, bringing with him a guileless vitality that seared the Colonel's blood like boiling coffee. He headed straight for the sideboard. The pewter lids clanked against the platter when he lifted the first cover. The sounds of Carrington's pleasured inhale floated back to the Colonel, making his oilcloth hunting pants feel a little tighter.

"Mmm, ham this morning," Carrington said. "I love Missy's ham—always reminds me of how my mom used to make it." Carrington took his plate heaped with ham, eggs, fried green tomatoes, and sweet slippery pawpaws to the seat next to the Colonel, who was enthroned at the head of the table. "So, what's on the schedule for today, sir?"

The Colonel watched Carrington cut his meat, holding the knife and fork as if he were about to paint a picture.

Such expressive hands.

Carrington lowered his fork and knife, resting them on the painted lip of his dish, when he noticed the lost look in the Colonel's eyes. "Sir, can I get you some more coffee?"

The Colonel's head lolled a bit as he shifted his gaze to Carrington, like it was a stopper not properly seated in the neck of a bottle. With a quick jerk of his chin he sat back planting his elbows on the arms of his chair, and then steepled his fingers until crescent moons of red appeared below each white nail tip.

"Carrington, I think it's about time for us to go hunting. It's mid-October, boy. Bucks will shed in a couple of months, and we want to bag that prize beast before it loses its rack."

The only sound to be heard in the house was that of Carrington squirming in his seat. He carefully wiped his mouth with a cloth napkin.

"I do agree, sir," Carrington said.

The Colonel relaxed against his seat and tossed his napkin on the table, secure in his knowledge that what he wanted more than anything was now *fait accompli.*

"Doubt you want to wait another year and possibly miss out, just 'cause some other young man in town makes the kill first," the Colonel said.

Carrington nodded in agreement, but wouldn't look the Colonel in the eyes.

"Yes, that's true—but shouldn't we wait until my father returns? I mean, if we're gone and…" The Colonel leaned closer, halting Carrington's words as surely as if he had put a gag in the boy's mouth.

"Mr. Moses is here, and Missy," the Colonel said, "and I don't think it will take me too long to find that buck."

Carrington pulled back when he got a whiff of the bourbon that held up the Colonel's words.

"If you say so, sir." Carrington threaded his napkin between his fingers. "I'll be ready whenever you say the word."

"That'll be fine. Get your gear together, but keep it light." The Colonel crossed his arms over his belly, cradling his chin with his right hand. His index finger moved like a metronome scratching the scraggly low turf of his unshaven jowl. "Extra weight slows us down and makes us noisier—easier to detect. Element of surprise is key to hunting, boy."

The Colonel's elbows rested on the table, his right hand squeezing the fisted left. Carrington's attention went from the napkin he was twisting in his lap to the Colonel.

The Colonel was already getting up from his chair. "Meet me out front in an hour," he said.

"Yes sir. Thank you sir, I'll be ready." Carrington watched the Colonel make his way to the stairs before stopping short. He turned back to catch Carrington's stare.

"I always like a good fight. Makes me relish the win more. Remember that, boy." The Colonel stepped back onto the landing, one hand on the carved hickory newel post in the shape of a horsehead.

"Set a goal, make a plan, be patient—then fight for what you want. Gain without struggle teaches you nothing. All this," the Colonel swept his hands around the foyer, "I've worked *hard* for this. Broke my first tooth in a struggle. Builds character. So, it's time to toughen you up, boy."

The Colonel stood on the bottom step of the staircase and listened to Carrington make his way down the porch; the boy didn't bound down the stairs, his boots plunked down on each step and there was a hesitation, like an old swayback nag picking her way down a rocky slope. The Colonel then heard creaking upstairs. He saw CeCe heading down the stairs with the Chinaman at her heels. The Colonel smacked the horsehead finial before retreating to his office.

Once inside, he cracked his neck side-to-side and then let his head fall back against the door. He looked at his hunting trophies; the moose head above the fireplace, the bucks and deer, two mountain lions, and the nine-foot black bear stuffed with his paws up arching over his desk. And then there was Yellow Boy to the right of his office door, strategically placed so that the Colonel could see him from his desk and sofa. A man needed a den, a space to be a man. Even though he was the Colonel, and marked his territory with cigars, ashtrays, and empty crystal tumblers, the air in most of the house still reeked of that woman.

He turned his ear to the door while looking Yellow Boy in the eyes. CeCe was on the other side. He could smell her, feel her nerves jangling through the wood grain, making the back of his head itch. His plan had been to gather his gear and be ready when Carrington arrived, but now because of her he was staring at Yellow Boy—feeling his demons make breakfast out of his soul.

He swiped his hand across his mouth. A gooey crust had already settled into the corners of his lips but his mouth felt as dry as ashes. He was thirsty—thirsty with a want that shook awake his demons like the ammonia under his wife's nose. His stomach began to percolate. He zeroed in on the bar, and his flask that he had filled but planned on leaving behind.

He felt the door shift when she pressed against it, nosing in on him. He had a mind to pound the door back, just to hear her yelp. After she finally left, he continued staring at the flask.

42.

Carrington's horse, Cole, danced uneasily under him as he waited for the Colonel near the broad steps that lined the front porch. A phantom gust of wind creaked the empty rocking chairs on the veranda. Carrington's case of unease seemed to weigh the both of them down like saddlebags filled with lead.

It was unusual to leave Mr. Moses in charge of the farm; Missy would be fine in the house—but the sizable estate required more than was fair to ask of even a big black bear of man like Mr. Moses.

The door flung open, the frame gobbled up by the visage of the Colonel decked out in his split back oilskin duster. It reached midway down his Chippewa snake boots. Soiled gloves hung like clenched fists from his pant waist.

Carrington gnawed at the soft flesh of his cheeks as the Colonel marched onto the landing.

Miss CeCe made a showy fuss, patting down the Colonel's shoulders and arms as if she had made the coat herself and was checking for fit and give. He swatted her away like he was trying to kill a mosquito.

Poor thing, she was always moving at a discordant speed, like she had one foot in the here and now while the other was tiptoeing around the terrain of another life.

Then, like a burnished musket ball, Missy dashed past them both making it impossible for Carrington to do anything other than smile. He thought of her as the wind, always felt her presence. Carrington dismounted from Cole to help Missy with her bundles.

"Honeybee," she said, "this is for you and the Colonel. Some warm food to keep the cold out and your strength up during the first leg of your journey. After that, God and Miss Jessica—God rest her soul—will protect you on your way." Missy said this with tears brimming in her blue eyes. Her smooth, dry hands cupped the sides of his face.

Carrington closed his eyes, calmed by the heat of her palms. Her delicate fingers traced his eyebrows and the bow of his upper lip, leaving a scented trail of sweet orange, basil, and bergamot. He mouthed the hoodoo prayer which she murmured at his ear, the one she taught him when he was little.

Carrington put the bounty into his saddlebag and then looked back at the property. He gave thanks to God for Missy—so indebted he was to this tough little woman who called him her honeybee.

She had quietly stepped into the role of his mother, after his had been killed many years before.

Missy's lustrous skin was like a layer of chocolate caramel over finely sculpted bones, her head covered in an ever-changing assortment of multi-colored kerchiefs that added at least six inches to her tiny frame.

He leaned down and kissed the top of her head.

"Don't you worry about me, Missy. I'll return before you know it with the biggest buck ya ever did see." He brightened up. "Might even start a trophy room of my own!"

Carrington remounted Cole and then settled. Missy made her way toward Cole's face, wrapping strands of his mane three times around her pointer finger, whispering into his alert ears what Carrington had figured was another prayer.

"It's time, boy. Let's go," the Colonel said, staring at Missy who stared right back.

Carrington waved to Miss CeCe, who stood on the porch waiting for Missy to join her, and then he fell into line behind the Colonel who was now mounted on his horse, Ranger. They headed down the blue hydrangea-lined path of Davenport Drive.

It took them about forty-five minutes to get off of the lands of Davenport Holdings.

Neither man spoke as they made their way up through the low brush to the taller trees, which were a wash of reds, golden oranges, and dull greens.

The crunch of the horses' hooves over a fall carpet of leaves was only accompanied by the occasional bird calling, squirrels scattering out of the way, and the crisp clamor of the rustling leaves.

"You know, Kentucky was full of Indians. We had the Shawnee—the biggest tribe spread over most of this great state. Then we had the Yuchi, and next to them, the Cherokee." The Colonel lifted the stirrup, and then rattled his boot. "The Chickasaw were in the toe of the state. Great hunters. But they all got moved in the 1800s. I fought the Sioux in the Dakotas."

Carrington's mind drifted as the Colonel started talking about how Sioux went on vision quests to get closer to the Great Spirit.

Carrington couldn't stop thinking about Jamison.

He imagined her with those leaves surrounding the curves of her body, how she might wriggle if a leaf or two traveled over her naked flesh.

At that, he leaned forward in his saddle, pressing his balls against the hard leather.

To show he could support her, he was now hunting with her father to kill a majestic buck for some prize money. Carrington thought back to the last time he saw Jamison—when he hung the crystal necklace around her, the glistening driblets of perspiration that rolled from her hairline to darken the white collar of her dress. Her neck was a creamy canvas, which he wanted to dust with kisses, nibbling into reds, or even sucking into purple.

"Boy, you even listening to me?" The Colonel rested his left forearm on the horn of his saddle, as if it were the arm of an upholstered chair; he gestured with flings of his wrist. "Now, I like the quiet as much as the next man, but when I'm trying to teach you something I suggest you pay attention, son."

Carrington itched his hat against his forehead, and then spoke over his shoulder. "Sorry, sir, just enjoying the trees—and the colors, and sounds. Guess I sorta drifted. I've always liked it out here. Mind just seems to wander away." Carrington's voice trailed off as if his mind were drifting along with it.

"It's okay, boy. I was the same way when I was your age. Spent more time out hunting than I did with my brothers on my father's farm. I liked being alone in nature." The Colonel followed Carrington's skyward gaze through the branches of a massive golden oak. "Like that tree there. Could be the World Tree, the one I was telling you about. I'll say it again, 'cause I don't think you heard me. The Sioux believe the Great Spirit, Wakan Tanka, manifests in everything—the sun, the moon, stars, the earth—everything lives under the shade of the World Tree." The Colonel caught one of the falling leaves as they rode by. He held it up. "It has so much to offer should you actually see its magnificence."

Carrington could feel the forest air fill his mouth as he listened.

"Some people ride through here and don't see a thing. Not only do I see, but I feel, too." The Colonel sat back in his saddle and let the horse rock his stocky body side-to-side, the reins lazy in his left hand.

As much as Carrington wanted to accept the Colonel's words at face value, as he would from any other man, hearing the Colonel share his perspective turned Carrington a little inside-out. It didn't fit right, like the Colonel was trying on 'open' and 'relaxed' like it was a two-piece suit. Maybe it was just because he hadn't before been out alone with the Colonel, that he missed his real affinity for nature.

"Yes sir. I guess I was just lost in that majesty," Carrington offered. "Often lose myself sitting under the catalpa tree by the pond, thinking similar thoughts." Carrington sat a little higher in his saddle, wondering if maybe this would work out for the better. Maybe they would forge a stronger bond because of this hunting trip.

"I appreciate your ability to see things differently, Carrington. Truly do. Always thought there was something different about you. I encourage your curious nature, and as long as you do your daily work I see no conflict with you possessing a fertile imagination." The Colonel smoothed his gloves around his wrists, tightening the drawstrings. "Always had an imagination, myself."

Carrington nodded his head as if he always suspected it.

"When I was your age I was scouting Indians, clearing the plains for settlers. Didn't have much time to develop it as much as yours, but it's there. Sometimes my mind thinks of things that make me actually stop and wonder."

"Well, I guess there you go then. So does mine, sir. Sometimes things I think of make me shake my head at…"

"The audacity, yeah?" the Colonel asked. "Audacity of the thought makes me wonder. Makes me turn full circle and look around with that imaginative thought needling in my head. Am I right?" The Colonel flicked off an insect from his temple.

"Sometimes you just got to go with the thought, sir," Carrington said. "Can't always pick it apart or reason with it. Sometimes there just ain't any reason for a creative urge. I feel like there's something inside of me trying to get my attention, and I'm happier for it when I give over to it. Like I was doing what was in my nature, but for some reason before I was aware of the urge, I was working against it." Carrington's horse stumbled over a tree root. "*Whoa*, careful there, Cole."

The Colonel pulled on his own reins, lining up Ranger neck-to-neck with Cole.

"That is a very astute observation," the Colonel said.

Normally, Carrington would trail behind the Colonel, giving him his due—but so far the Colonel either rode next to him, or let him go ahead when the space was too narrow for two riders.

It just didn't feel right having the Colonel at his back.

Before long, the low brush was shaded by tightly packed groups of trees jutting from soft rivers of earth, and through cracks in sandstone boulders which formed the Appalachians.

Once in the woods the Colonel occasionally dismounted to check tracks, broken branches, and to sniff the earth near various piles of scat; does were in heat, bucks nearby.

The Colonel made a big show of letting Carrington know they were on the trail of that trophy buck. He pointed out the deep scrape lines consistent with a mature male. The color rose in his face when he stopped by a fat pine rubbed creamy from the rack of a ten or twelve pointer. The Colonel dismounted and then kneeled down near a divot in the soil.

"Get down here, boy. Smell this." The Colonel sat back on his haunches, watching Carrington swing his leg over the cantle of his saddle.

Cole snorted and bobbed his head, before chewing at his bit.

Carrington crouched alongside the Colonel.

"See this," the Colonel said. "This here is an impressive buck scrape. See how deep it is?" The Colonel measured the depth by sticking the toe of his boot into the scrape. "He's been scraping, putting down his mark every fifty yards or so." The Colonel made a chopping motion in the air to emphasize the regular intervals. "It's his perimeter, keeps the other bucks out. Especially when the scent of his urine is this strong."

He held up a handful of earth and some shreds of bark.

"This," he said, "smell it."

Carrington dropped his nose closer to the Colonel's hands.

"Has the added scent of musk," the Colonel said. "Tarsal gland. He's saying to all the other bucks, it's his territory. Buck in full rut will rut himself to exhaustion. Won't even eat. Only one thing on his mind. One thing."

"Yes sir." Carrington already knew about the single-minded behavior of bucks during rut. All the guys his age joked about it when they got together. "Well," he ventured, "I guess it's a blessing then that the season only lasts a few months—then things will settle back down again." Carrington stood up, ready to step away when he felt the Colonel's hand on his boot.

"Hold up, son. Gonna rub this on your boots so your aroma will be more enticing. Attract more estrous does."

Carrington wasn't sure what to make of the sight—the Colonel kneeling down at this boots, smushing dirt clotted with deer urine onto the scuffed leather. He'd never seen it done before—and he couldn't remember ever seeing the Colonel kneel before any person. From the sound of his voice and the tight curve of his shoulders, it seemed as though the Colonel wasn't real sure what reception his action would garner.

It was as if he waited to be kicked.

43.

At the end of that first night they put down camp beside a fast moving muddy stream, edged by just enough rock-less flat ground to handle their bedrolls. Carrington had seen a number of spots he would've chosen instead, but he deferred to the Colonel's experience.

"Want the other leg, Colonel?" Carrington asked, pointing at the fried chicken poking up from beneath a breast.

"Naw, you have the rest of it. I'm done with chicken. Guts are gurgling." The Colonel heaved the carcass of his poultry into the river.

Carrington grabbed the other leg.

"After you're done, best go wash in the stream," the Colonel said. "Fried chicken's no aphrodisiac to a doe, *or* a buck."

Carrington slowed his chewing.

"Need to blend in if we want to bring it down," the Colonel said. "We need to be like them." The Colonel dragged the back of his bare hand across his mouth. He then fished out a narrow embossed silver canister from the inside pocket of his coat, before popping the lid and pulling out a silver toothpick. He jabbed his teeth and sucked the debris from the tip of the pick. "Need to be like that big buck—understand the romantic urges that narrow his focus, so he is unaware of what's to happen." The Colonel scoured and sucked at his front teeth, making his lips pucker like a baby at the nipple.

Carrington never thought much one way or another of washing in the river. It was just what they did to keep their scent in check. Like other things Carrington did, he followed through because it was expected of him.

It's what all the young men in town talked about—killing that buck and hanging its head over their fireplaces.

Some even boasted they'd mount it over their beds, like a sign of their virility. That was the last thing he wanted hanging over his head each night. He'd rather have Jamison over him, with her long hair blocking out everything other than her eyes staring at his.

He sucked the air through his teeth.

The Colonel got up and then took off his coat, snapping its length over his bedroll. He unbuckled his belt and then yanked out his shirttail, pulling his buttoned shirt over his head.

His union suit looked new. Even the buttons shined opalescent.

He bent at the waist to unlace his boots, which he placed next to his bedroll. He stepped on top of his coat, slipped off his pants followed by his socks, and then he shuffled back into his boots and walked down to the river.

The newness of the Colonel's underwear made him look as though he were wrapped in cold lard. Carrington's own long johns were full of stains and mended holes.

Carrington decided to head to the bushes and then relieve himself while the Colonel was washing up. If there was a buck nearby when the Colonel splashed around in the stream, he had certainly sent it packing. Carrington moved downstream of their campsite and then washed up—just his hands and face.

When he returned, the Colonel and his clothes were gone. Carrington stretched out under the cover of stars, placed his hat over his head and then pulled his blanket under his chin.

He then continued to think about Jamison.

The Colonel listened to the bucks circling higher on the hill. They were trailing the does, which were moving along lower on the incline.

From where he sat he could see down into the campsite, where Carrington took on the posture of sleep. He knew the boy wasn't actually sleeping because he kept lifting the hat from his eyes.

A doe hopped over the bushes a few yards above the Colonel's perch. A buck then crashed through the shrubs in pursuit, undaunted by a hefty branch caught in its rack.

In spite of nature's dance, the Colonel remained staring down at their camp.

Carrington turned onto his side and his hat rolled off of his face. In the moonlight his hair looked obsidian; it was so black that the skin of his face looked translucent, like milk-white marble.

A few geese took flight past the stream, like black shadows against the orange brown of the sunset. He was unsure of why it reminded him of CeCe. When he saw those geese his mind immediately involved itself with her.

He remembered when the two of them had first married and she insisted that he take her buck hunting. CeCe couldn't tell the difference between a duck squawking or a goose honking; lost on her were the guttural burping of bucks, or the softer estrous bleats of the doe.

"A-a-a-ah," the Colonel now whispered as if he were a doe. "A-a-a-ah." He murmured it on his way back to his sliver of sleeping space before lying down. He turned toward Carrington who had one arm curled under his head, and from what he could tell by the drape of the blanket, the other arm was between his legs.

He wondered how warm it was between those thighs—and if there was a little dampness, a little trickle of sweat meandering through the dark hairs on his legs.

When Carrington woke at dawn, the damp cold made him think that ice chips flowed through his veins instead of warm blood. There was a dense crystalline frost knitted into the sticks and over the sparse grass, which poked up around their bedrolls.

Carrington opened one eye, the one closest to the ground, to see if the Colonel was awake. The Colonel was curled up, strangely mirroring the shape Carrington was unraveling from.

Cole and Ranger were tethered and calm.

Not wanting to wake the Colonel, Carrington eased off of his spread and then inspected the crisp dew to find the darkest spots—the path that would make the least amount of sound when he stepped away to relieve himself.

Carrington made his way to a cropping of mountain laurel and elderberry.

The morning sounds were sweet; the rays from the sunrise reached long through the tree branches, sending a tittering of birds over the low rumbling of the stream.

Carrington buttoned up his fly and turned his head when he heard the unmistakable grunt of a nearby buck, signaling that does were not far away.

The Colonel watched Carrington walk away from the camp. The boy didn't just walk—he slinked with the grace of a young panther.

It was in every movement he made—effortless power in the simple roll of his shoulder, the sway of his ribs as each leg reached forward. The Colonel wanted to harness that effortlessness.

He wanted to hold it, and crush it with the strength he still possessed—and then he let his imagination take it from there. The Colonel closed his eyes; his lips went slack at the thought of it all.

His right hand fell to his back pocket. Even though the flask wasn't there, the outline of it was so pronounced that it jutted out almost in full shape.

He made his way over to his saddle and unlatched the buckle.

His mouth watered when he felt the pattern embossed on the metal. He unscrewed the silver lid and then let his lips form around the metallic neck, before tipping it back.

His tongue prickled tight, sweating out his saliva.

He swished it around his mouth and then swallowed the amber liquid, masticating the residue around his teeth.

Nothing wrong with a little bourbon before the hunt.

He was just knotting the laces on his boot when Carrington sauntered back into camp.

"Morning Colonel," Carrington said, untying Cole and Ranger before leading them away from the stream. "Heard the bucks a little while back."

Carrington adjusted Cole's saddle blanket, and then lifted the saddle onto his back.

The Colonel felt the bourbon firing up. A haze of acceptance washed over his soul. He could almost feel his demons in that haze—freeing themselves, stepping all over him with cloven hooves. He felt his lip spasm as if an invisible mustache was being pulled.

"I feel like today is your lucky day," the Colonel muttered. "The day you bag that buck." He rolled his shoulders, his jaw jutting off kilter. He turned his head like a blind man trying to see with his ears. "Yes sir-ree, hot on its trail," he muttered again.

44.

They moved up higher on the mountain, slightly above the rut line that the Colonel had been following the previous day.

At one point he stopped and put his hand up to still Carrington and Cole.

He then pointed into the distance, where Carrington saw the ten-point standing majestically atop a hill on the other side of the stream.

A doe grazed nearby as the buck approached. He courted her by licking around her tail. Erect, he tried to hop on her back, but she sloughed him off again and again, making him bellow.

Finally he connected, holding her still, his forelegs dangling over her sides.

Something about the sight always made the Colonel hard. Hunting was his nature; killing was the vice he used to face his demons. He worshiped the aggressiveness, the way the doe ran, and how the buck chased—the single-mindedness of that intent was base evolution.

It thrilled him.

The sound of the skirmish, the heavy colliding, and the erotic pumping of the dominant male had made the Colonel so ready to fuck that he felt like his whole body was an aching dick. Even if it turned into a fight, he'd make sure to hold on tight enough so that every pore was open and every inch of his skin would receive what he needed—what his demons demanded.

The Colonel slid his bow from the pouch hanging from his saddle. He handed it to Carrington without a sound.

"This is it, son," he breathed. "Your moment." The Colonel squared his body to Carrington, who was looking at the buck and doe on the clearing. "Take aim while he's at it."

Carrington reached for the bow and then nocked the arrow. He raised it and extended his arm, but didn't pull back.

The Colonel pulled Ranger alongside Cole, so he didn't have to raise his voice.

"Go on, son," he whispered. "He won't notice you coming."

"Should I wait? What if I hit the doe?" Carrington's words barely scraped past his dry, tight throat.

"If you kill the doe, you load up again."

Carrington lowered the bow, unseating the arrow.

The Colonel tracked the buck with a watery gaze, his voice barely above a mumble. "Look at 'em, six of the little rodents," he said. "They're just hanging around, waiting, teasing—pretending they don't want what they want."

The Colonel twisted in his seat, his chin dropped low in his collar. He then narrowed his eyes at Carrington.

There was a look of revulsion and embarrassment still hanging like dirty laundry from the lines stretched across Carrington's forehead. Every demon inside of the Colonel reared up and howled, their sounds and beckons shrill enough to eviscerate the last pocket of human tenderness he had claimed.

The Colonel rose up in his seat, squeezing his saddle between his legs as if he might cut Ranger in half from his effort.

"Don't you look at me that way," he said. "Don't you dare judge me. You want to win, don't you?" He rose a few inches higher, pushed his boots into the stirrups as Ranger danced beneath him, tossing his head up and down.

"I'm not judging you, sir," Carrington said. "I'm just not… that good a shot. Don't want to hurt the doe."

"Hurt the doe? Forget the doe," said the Colonel, flinging his hand through the air dismissively.

The Colonel likened does to a bunch of ugly things, with their heads down eating their fill while their tails were up like a waving flag, stinking up the air and making those bucks crazy.

Females, the biggest bunch of schemers there was.

The Colonel grabbed the bow from Carrington's slack grip, and with frightening speed he nocked an arrow across its beam. He then laid waste to two does, both of them crumbling to the ground before Carrington had a chance to react.

Carrington then reached for the bow, almost falling from his saddle.

"Colonel," he yelled, "Don't kill 'em. We're here for the buck."
The Colonel lowered his bow after connecting an arrow to a third doe. The doe trembled and then collapsed.

The Colonel then cracked his neck side-to-side.

"You're right, boy." The veins on the Colonel's neck seized up, like he was gritting his teeth to keep from screaming out.

He casually handed back the bow.

"Take aim," he said. "Buck still ain't aware, not too sure how much longer that doe will last." The doe arched her back, her long neck rocking up and down as she pushed herself back. "Look at her, can she raise her tail any higher?" He smirked then spit. "Ut! Her legs are about to fold. Go on, boy."

Carrington's arms shook as he raised the bow and sighted the beast in the clearing across the stream. He struggled to look past the knoll dotted with dead does. The Colonel curled his fingers around Carrington's shoulder and then leaned in as if he were trying to help Carrington line up the shot.

He eased his face just behind Carrington.

His nose was a breath away from that perfect shell of an ear, surrounded by those lanky black curls, the tips shiny with sweat.

The smell of Carrington filled his nostrils.

The Colonel could have nibbled along Carrington's strong neck, nuzzled his jaw—and if Carrington turned he could kiss him.

He instead dug his fingers into Carrington's shoulder. "If you want that money, you better fucking kill that buck. Make it a clean kill," he whispered, "or I will castrate your beloved Cole."

Carrington swung around and butted heads with the Colonel. "What are you talking about!" he yelled. "That's insane—you're not going to touch Cole!" Carrington backed Cole away from Ranger. "He's my horse and you have no right to threaten me by hurting him. I've had enough of this." Carrington threw the bow and arrow into the bramble bushes. "Get what I need some other way." Carrington maneuvered Cole around the shrubs, heading back the way they came.

"That a fact?" the Colonel said.

The Colonel smoothed his rawhide gloves up to his wrists.

Cole found his footing and then began a careful trot through the low bushes.

The Colonel reached for the rope on his horn, whirled it overhead, fiercely whipping his wrist until he threw the lasso around Carrington's trunk and then pulled him off his mount.

Cole sidestepped away, his ears alert, eyes filled with fear.

Carrington wriggled on the ground attempting to get free of the rope, while Cole danced away trying to keep from stepping on him.

The Colonel jumped off of Ranger in mid lope, pulling sharp on the lasso as he hustled toward Carrington who'd struggled to get onto his feet.

The Colonel backhanded Carrington across the face, sending him sprawled sideways onto the dirt, and then he jumped onto Carrington, pinning him down on his back.

"Boy," he yelled, "you feel better between my thighs than my saddle ever will."

"Get off me! Let me go!" Carrington jerked his hips in an attempt to throw the Colonel off.

"Have to work harder than that, boy. Told you I like a fight." He held down Carrington's shoulders and leaned in, rubbing his nose and cheek in Carrington's dripping hair. "Builds character," he jeered. The Colonel lay down on Carrington and hooked his feet around the boy's calves, his arms curled around his neck.

"Thrash harder, boy. Can you feel me? You feel me growing?" The Colonel ground his hardness into the bucking hips of Carrington.

"God, get the fuck off me," Carrington screamed. "Please, I'm begging you, Christ sake!" He thrashed around. "Snap the fuck out of it."

The veins and tendons in Carrington's neck were like mountain ranges with rivers of sweat cutting a dirty path between them.

"Can beg all you want, but I'm not gonna stop. I want you, pretty boy." The Colonel set his forearms on both sides of Carrington's head and then threaded his fingers through his hair. He cocked his head, analyzing the boy like a piece of art. "I've wanted you for a long time. Matter fact, ever since your daddy came looking for work. But I'm no monster. I waited till the fight was *even*."

The Colonel eased up onto his knees, waist still planted down onto Carrington's stomach. "So, fight me, boy. Fight me!"

Carrington's knee managed to connect into the Colonel's back, and that one strike connected surprisingly hard. The Colonel fell head-first into Carrington's forehead, breaking his nose on impact. It was somehow the perfect sequence: the placement of the Colonel's position on Carrington's body, the placement of Carrington's strike on the Colonel's back, and the perfect momentum of the Colonel pitching forward to clash into that hard, unforgiving surface on Carrington's head. The fortune barely registered in Carrington's mind, because now he could only wish that the strike had miraculously killed him.

Blood spurted everywhere.

Choking and out of breath, the Colonel's mouth opened wide, his eyes saturated by a welling of tears—yet he let out a cackle of laughs and then a shrill sound that sent the birds flying from their trees. Eventually, the loudest sound in the clearing was of their exasperation.

He leered over Carrington and let his blood drizzle down onto the boy's skin. Then he leaned down and licked Carrington's face, and continued to smear blood onto him. "Open your eyes, boy," he said. When Carrington held them shut, the Colonel slapped one cheek and backhanded the other.

"Please, don't." Carrington blinked away the tears that had gathered in the corners of his eyes. "Just let me go, I won't tell anyone."

"Think I'm worried about that? C'mon boy, get up and fight me."

Carrington's body went lax, all of his energy captured in a stare of pure hatred up at the Colonel.

"You don't fight me," the Colonel said, "then I'm gonna fuck you; actually, I'm gonna fuck you either way—but you just might best me if you fight." The Colonel let out a gooey belch, orts and dregs from the demons chewing through his gut.

"Look," the Colonel said, "I'm a fair man." He thumped his knuckles against his chest as he leaned over Carrington's shoulder, aiming to speak into his ear. "I like a chase. I'll let you get up."

The Colonel leaned so far over to the right that he landed on the ground next to Carrington.

Carrington clambered to his knees, about to stand, when the Colonel charged at him, laying Carrington flat out. He pulled up Carrington's hips before shoving his face into the dirt.

With his free hand the Colonel undid his own pants and then pulled out his dick, while the boy continued his futile struggle on the ground.

Pebbles scraped and pocked the flesh of Carrington's face as he twisted to see what the Colonel was doing.

"Oh God, oh..." Carrington wriggled and jutted, scrambling, kneeing away and pitching forward, before losing his balance. His shoulder smashed back into the earth.

"Mmhm, that's it, squirm harder. Fight to get your ass out of here." The Colonel pulled tighter on the rope and then harder on his cock with his other hand—Carrington still trying to get free. "That's enough struggle, boy." The Colonel pushed Carrington's face back into the dirt and then yanked down Carrington's dungarees. He shredded the worn fabric of Carrington's long johns.

The Colonel paused to feel Carrington slap against him. He relished the heat of exertion as Carrington's thighs battered his own, the wiry hairs of his muscled legs felt deliciously rough against him.

Carrington's scream silenced all sounds in the forest and ignited the Colonel even more.

He pumped into Carrington like a dominant bull. Their blood mixed with sweat, it all fueled him. He was taking what was his.

Carrington felt like he was underwater. His head was swallowed up by the deafening pulse of the artery close to his eardrum, as if he heard his own heartbeat. It fired through his veins into his brain.

Carrington opened his mouth, and he wouldn't have known he made a sound had his body not vibrated by it. His muscles strained thin and tense, surged in waves like he was a huge metal sheet snapping and twisting in a hurricane.

Cole's ears were pinned back as he ground his teeth into his bit. He stomped his front legs, kicking up clots of dirt. Cole bolted over to the men, before rearing up. As he lowered himself, he kicked the Colonel off of Carrington, landing with a thud several feet away.

Carrington collapsed over.

He had no idea how long he lay still, but he could sense Cole prancing nearby. He opened his eyes to watch Cole rear up inches from the Colonel, who let out a guttural sound—a grotesque, almost roar, with the inflection of gargling blood.

The Colonel lurched to his feet, buckling his belt as he staggered to Ranger who stood legs splayed and ears pointing forward. Carrington could feel the rope completely loosened around his trunk.

The sun glinted off of the hunting knife which the Colonel grabbed from his saddle.

Carrington's mind fell silent as he felt his own body pitching forward, leaping toward the Colonel as the mad son of a bitch was about to thrust the blade into Cole's neck. Carrington grabbed the Colonel's wrist and yanked it back, sending them both tumbling to the ground.

The Colonel landed on top of Carrington and they rolled like logs in a fast running river, until Carrington was favorably on top. For a moment they had actually lain still, the fight gone from them both.

Panting, Carrington felt the pressure building under his ribs. He eased up and then looked down at the Colonel, whose gloved hand still clutched the hilt of his hunting knife. The angle of the hilt looked like the blade had gone straight into the Colonel's body, and then had sliced up toward his ribs.

Blood cascaded from the wound, soaking clear down to the Colonel's belt. Carrington hoped it was deep enough, but the Colonel was still breathing when Carrington scrambled back to his feet.

The Colonel rumbled a hoarse *phaaawww* sound, followed by a choked back aching sound of laughter amidst the pain.

Carrington staggered as he watched the Colonel seize up and twist around, struggling to wrench the knife from his wound.

Saturated with blood and soiled with bodily fluids, the Colonel got to his knees. His eyes, bloodshot, continued to focus on Carrington.

Just like a woman in those pornographic Kinetoscope movies, the Colonel's mouth opened, his free hand pushed back his hair as if in sexual ecstasy. He lifted his side that had the knife plunged into it like he was offering his breast.

"Built you some character... Didn't I, boy?" the Colonel wheezed out, his skin as sallow as candle wax, highlighting the broken red veins around his nose and cheeks. He doubled over, but kept his heated gaze on Carrington, before yanking out the knife to send his body into convulsions.

The autumn leaves swished and shimmered like fire against an angelic blue sky. Birds called out to each other. Nature was still going on about its business, unperturbed.

Section 3: Jamison

45.

The sensation of days, nights, and the in-betweens, were all in-betweens to Jamison. All dull and chilly, like being underwater in a winter pond. She wanted to open her eyes.

Where was she? Her panic continued to ramp up as she was unable to open her eyes. She felt enormous pain in the smallest of movements. And she couldn't even speak. It was too difficult to make even the quietest of noises.

So she listened. She tried to use whatever senses she could, much in the very same way she had done with her writerly practice—before those four quick knocks at the door.

Telegram.

She recalled the same wooden voice of the boy behind her door, and with that she supposed this very well could be death—experiencing a strange awareness in the dark, and feeling everything that life had left her in that last moment.

Pain—and thrill. The satisfaction of actually facing him—the Colonel. If only she could smile.

But she knew she wasn't dead.

With the panic she'd felt before, so too did it suggest a heartbeat.

She became aware of her own breathing, shallow but there.

And she could smell a familiar scent. Something cool and dry touched her forehead. Regardless of the pain, Jamison managed a deeper breath. Flowers. Tuberose. Jamison wanted to curl around the body of the Countess who had taken a seat on the bed.

"Jamison, *moya dorogaya devushka.*" The Countess leaned closer to Jamison's face. "My dear girl, *moya dorogaya devushka,* I'm so sorry… *tak zhal.* We have you. Jon and I. You are safe—*bezopasno,* safe."

The words were soothing—even so, she felt her mouth begin to tremble and her eyes sting with tears.

"Shh, *moya dorogaya devushka,*" the Countess cooed to her ear. Jamison willed her hand to move. And then she felt the Countess. Warm. Soft. Living. It spoke to Jamison more than anything else, that she was alive.

Outside the bedroom door, Jon stood there holding up a meal tray—ready to knock and be let in. He'd heard the shower going, and it took everything not to situate himself by the two-way mirror. He supposed it was as good a test as any to recognize when voyeurism had its place. In contest with his arousal, this was a rare time when he was able to win out.

Jon knocked on the bedroom door with his free hand, and was invited in by Bepa.

"Good morning, Jamison, Bepa," he greeted. "I had Amelia make breakfast. Maybe you would like a little something?" Jon put the tray on the corner of the bed. He couldn't help but let his eyes roam from the V of Jamison's dewy, flushed skin, where her robe opened to reveal her neck up to her face. After the glance he searched for any tells on her face, but she seemed mostly stoic when regarding his presence in the room. "Please, allow me," Jon said.

He scooped his arm under Jamison's legs while the Countess supported her at the shoulder, and then they gently sat her up. A bead of sweat rolled down the side of Jamison's neck from the effort.

Jamison swallowed, squeezing her eyes shut.

Jon pulled over a chair to the bed before sitting down. The Countess held a glass of water up to Jamison's lips.

"I'm so sorry… such a bother," Jamison said. Another tear hung on her lower lashes. "I've… hurt… I've never needed any—" she croaked, her voice barely a whisper when her breath hitched in her throat.

Jamison wiped her eyes before seizing up in pain. Her broken ribs must have been electrocuting all of her senses, as the tears streamed down.

The Countess rushed to her side. "Chérie, don't worry," she consoled. "Just relax, just breathe. We will take care of you."

"Jamison," the composure in Jon's voice wavered, even sounded a bit foreign to himself. "I'm going to mix you up your pain medication while Bepa helps you eat." He backed away from the bed and then glanced around the room. "Bepa, do you have the packet?"

The Countess pointed to the desk.

"Bepa?" Jamison repeated.

The Countess smiled. "Bepa is short for Veronika in Russian. It would be silly for Jon Derrick to call me Countess all day, don't you think?"

She cut Jamison's fruit into small pieces and then began to feed her.

"I know you are not used to being taken care of, chérie. Thank you, Jon Derrick." She took the glass from Jon. "I imagine you haven't been hand-fed since you were a baby, but raising your arm even slightly causes you pain." She held the glass to Jamison's lips, making sure she drank all of the medicine. "Jon Derrick, can you make something to hold her ribs in place more firmly than these wraps?" she asked, dabbing Jamison's chin.

Jon eased himself from the wall.

"I was actually thinking the same thing. I'd like to try something out. If you'll excuse me..."

Jon took to his office and looked through his cabinets to where he kept rubber samples of some products his company made. He began to construct what he thought might bring Jamison some relief. He laid out rubber sheeting on his desk, and then drew a subtle arch on the surface, about twenty inches long and five inches high. Then he drew a V four inches in from both ends. He cut out the shape and punched holes along the V's edges, as well as along the ends. He threaded rubber cording through the edges, cinching them together, creating a seam. He then found some ribbon and cut a long length, about two feet long. Satisfied, he returned to Jamison's room and quietly tapped on the door. About two hours had passed since he had left, so he felt certain that Jamison was asleep.

The Countess opened the door and then tiptoed out of the darkened room.

"I want to show you what I made for Jamison. I hope it helps her have less pain when she moves. It's like a mini corset, which she laces up the front so that she can do it herself after you... leave."

Jon handed Bepa the corset. She didn't take it from him right away, nor did he let go. Instead, they held the black material between them. Jon clenched it beneath his fingers as he stared at her and then glanced at the door. He knew she could see his fear. Bepa was the only one with whom he could naturally express those emotions.

She patted his hand and then he let go. He turned his back to the Countess to look at Jamison. "It should help hold her ribs in place, but also allow her to move a bit freer and breathe easier." He slightly turned back to her. "What do you think, Bepa?"

"A stroke of genius, Jon Derrick. I think it should work quite well," she said, trying it around her own lower ribs.

Jon rested his hands on her shoulders. She looked up and then placed her hands on top of his. "Bepa, you go rest now. I'll handle it from here. I'll wake you later so that you can help her put it on."

After lighting logs in the fireplace, Jon sat in the chair vacated by the Countess. He got up two more times to rebuild the fire.

Jamison's rest continued to be deep. Her dreams shifted away from any connection to her memories, toward a reality where she had come apart, had no recognizable body to claim. And yet every bit of her had a knowing, and an energy—and a need to become something other than what it was.

Water outlined her body, lapping over her ankles, her belly, and her throat.

She was weightless on the surface; from below her the pond grass tickled her legs and back. The air felt warmer, like the sun was about to break through the defense of the gathering noxious smoke.

She heard the coo of a dove higher than the clouds, higher than the sun. It swooped through a hole in the sky screaming down like a meteor, setting off trails of infinite colors that bloomed out like a combustion of the brightest rainbows.

Burning dust then singed her skin. She tried to splash water to stop the pain, but her hands turned into thirsty pigs, nosing down deeper into the pond. Voraciously they drank, sinking lower, squealing louder, stretching her arms to the point of ripping from her shoulders until she reached the bottom, straining back upon a sodden cigar butt as large as a chest of drawers. The center of her cracked open and the corpulent pigs pulled her farther apart. That gray dove caught fire and then turned as black as coal. It landed on her, securing its talons around her exposed, shredded rib—its wings as heavy as lead, battering down at her face—its shiny beak tearing at the red meat of her heart.

Jon heard the sound of Jamison struggling in a tangle of sheets. He dropped the fire poker he was using to stoke the flames, and dashed over to her bedside. He grabbed her flailing arms and then held them carefully to her sides.

"Jamison, I'm here." Jon let go of one of her hands, and then smoothed the hair from her face. He ran the back of his hand along her neck to feel her racing pulse. "Come on now, sweetheart, wake up." She seemed to calm as she felt the heat of his gentle hand upon her skin. He took a slight joy that his touch positively affected her.

She opened her eyes.

"Hi," he said, still stroking her neck. Jamison stared at his hand on her. She wriggled like old bait on a hook, trying to move away. His heart sped up again as he pulled his hand away, before stepping back.

"I... won't ever hurt you, Jamison," he said. "Please don't be afraid."

They stared at each other, and then she softened against the pillows. His shoulders relaxed. "Let me get Bepa," he said. "She has something that might make you feel more comfortable."

He shortly returned with the Countess. She was dressed in her night wrap, her hair braided down her back.

"How are you feeling, chérie?" the Countess asked, pulling Jamison's nightgown higher about her shoulders. Jamison shuddered as if she had been crying.

"Not well. I think I frightened him." Jamison's face was etched with equal parts pain and worry.

"Don't be silly; it takes a lot to scare Jon Derrick." The Countess gave Jon a look which seemed to ask him to reaffirm. He managed a slight arch of his eyebrow. "Jon Derrick made you something that we think will help you move a bit more, with less pain."

The Countess unfolded the black cincher. Taking off her robe, she used herself as a model.

"It wraps around the back, and ties here in the front." She stretched and arched her back in demonstration. "It is more secure than the cloth bandage that the doctor used, and it gives more consistent, ah… how do you say?"

"Pressure," Jon said.

Jamison frowned at the sight of it around the Countess's waist.

"Chérie, just try it," the Countess said. "You may be surprised at the comfort. Jon Derrick is very creative with his solutions, particularly in rubber." She winked at Jon.

"I'll leave you two alone," Jon said. "Let me know when she has it on, or if I need to make any adjustments. I'll wait outside the door."

Jon had never spent as much time in his hallways; he could only hear the Countess coaching Jamison, encouraging her to stand up.

The two-way mirror would've shown him everything.

The door finally opened and the Countess said, "You can come in now."

Jamison stood in her white lace nightgown with the rubber cincher in place, just as Jon envisioned it should be, the red ribbon laced up the front like a Christmas gift.

"It fits quite well. You always find creative answers to a practical problem." She turned to Jamison. "Don't let anyone tell you that rubber production is boring, chérie. Jon Derrick can make anything with rubber." The Countess retied her robe.

"How do you feel?" Jon asked Jamison. "Can you move easier, and with less pain?"

"I do… I feel more relaxed—less strained when I breathe and move." She looked around the room as if thinking of something else to say. "Maybe I should call you 'professor' or 'doctor' instead of Mr. Roe?"

Some tightness around Jon's shoulders relaxed with her comment. "Jamison, you can call me Jon," he said, and then Jamison blushed.

The Countess smiled at Jon. "Now, if you will excuse me, I'm going back to bed." She gently kissed Jamison on the forehead.

The changing of the guard in Jamison's room had marked the hours of the week. When the Countess was in, Jon worked in his office and rested. When Jon was in, the Countess rested and readied her trunks for her own departure on Saturday.

46.

Jamison heard three soft taps on her door. She knew it was the Countess coming to say goodbye. She didn't want the Countess to go, but then the human part of her wanted to know what it would feel like to be in the residence alone with Jon.

In the fog of her current situation, she found that she could almost imagine it—but until it actually happened she couldn't be sure. The Countess wasn't a chaperone; she didn't need to be present for Jon to behave. If anything, Jon was rather like a buffer between the two of them. The fact that Jon and the Countess were readily on hand was a reminder that she was recuperating from a beating that nearly ended her life.

The relationship Jamison had with them changed into something new. They used to brazenly provoke sensual thoughts within her, but now they were so concerned and gentle with their more clinical touches.

As soon as the Countess swept into the room, Jamison's lip strangely began to quiver. She touched her fingers to her lip and chin, feeling them move but unable to stop it.

The Countess canted her head, her eyebrow raised in question until Jamison lowered her hand. Taking a deep breath, the Countess began to twist her emerald ring around her finger. "Chérie, I've come to say au revoir. My bags are in the car, and the driver is waiting." She shook her head. "I'm sorry that I waited until the last minute. I don't want to drag this out, or else... I just won't go." She settled on the edge of the bed, the scent of tuberose caressing the whole room.

Jamison tried to push herself up against the headboard.

"Chérie, let me help you." The Countess turned to kneel on the bed so that she could reach around Jamison and pull her higher up. To help, Jamison dug her heels into the mattress. When the Countess sat back again Jamison was out of breath. She glanced at the Countess who had her hand resting on her own chest, apparently out of breath as well. As the cool mid-day sun cast a dulling light along the carpet, Jamison watched the Countess breathe, how her chest began to slow, and how the room got quieter as her hand came to rest upon her own lap.

She stared with more consideration at the Countess who was twirling her ring again. She felt her face begin to fold into regret. At that moment it dawned on her that Bepa was her first real female friend—and beyond that she was an exceptional human being. The Countess was so giving. She genuinely listened. She always gave Jamison time to find her train of thought and let her speak without interruption. She made Jamison feel like what she had to say actually mattered to her.

How was it possible that just moments before, she had wanted the Countess to leave?

The Countess clasped her hands and then raised her eyebrows in a hopeful manner. "Jamison, chérie…" Jamison's quivering lip gave way to sobs that erupted harsh and achy.

"I—I'm so sorry I'm crying, I didn't think…" Jamison covered her face with her hands, shaking her head. "I didn't think this would be…" Her words tumbled over tortured breaths. "I'm going to miss you." Jamison gave up trying to hold back. She sobbed and dropped her hand from her face.

The Countess embraced Jamison. "*Moya milaya*, my sweet girl." The Countess kissed Jamison's hair. "I *will* see you again, and I always do what I say. I am true to those I care for. You are part of our family."

Jamison took a deeper breath and then pulled away, wanting to see the Countess, to make sure that her face spoke the same as her words. Jamison nodded in agreement, but her throat felt like it was blocked.

The Countess wiped Jamison's tears from her cheeks and then sat back. "I want you to know a few things about Jon—before I go." She considered.

Jamison's eyes widened as she pressed her body against the headboard.

"Chérie, Jon is a good man, a very good man," she said.

Bepa probably considered memories that Jamison would never be privy to.

"My advice to you, my dear… is to be you. Don't try to be anything other than you." Bepa lay her palm over the nape of

Jamison's neck. "You caught his attention and you've kept it. Be strong, *moya milaya*, but be aware. Know that Jon is a complex man. He can be distant, and, at times, judgmental—but it's precisely those qualities that make him successful." The Countess pinched her lip between her fingers and then raised her eyes back up to Jamison's.

Jamison's heart beat even faster, wondering what the Countess wasn't saying.

The Countess looked around the room before staring at the shut door that led out to the hallway. "His assessments aren't quick, but, generally, they're spot on—and not something for you to concern yourself with. Be patient with him. I know he will be patient with you." The Countess kissed Jamison's forehead and then stood from the bed.

She walked to the door and then turned.

Jamison swallowed hard, as more tears spilled from her eyes. She couldn't speak as the Countess stared at her. It was as if Jamison was trying to put this last moment to memory.

"There's perhaps one thing more. I know not what happened that day to put you in this shape... That man, your father did this—this I know. But… what caused him to?"

Jamison stared down at her knees under the bedcovers.

"I…" She considered the long explanation, but then simply looked up at Bepa and said, "I just didn't run this time." She nearly laughed about it, but strangely could only keep herself from crying. Jamison would never know what her face actually expressed.

The Countess brought her hands up to her own face, and then dragged them down. She gave one last glance at Jamison, showing her a tearful smile. Instead of saying anything else, she reached behind and opened the door.

She dipped her chin, and left the room.

47.

Jamison stood outside the marble lip of the immense shower; there was an elegance to the dual glass doors edged with copper, as well as the shiny copper handles to adjust the temperature. She was stymied by the desire to wash her hair, because she couldn't quite reach her arms overhead. The steam filled the enclosed space as she undid the ties of her rubber support and then dropped her lace nightgown from her shoulders. The mist billowed out as she opened the shower door, sending a rush of moist air over her skin. The goose bumps made her feel more naked; she shuddered before stepping into the stream.

The bar of soap carried the Countess's scent.

She began to ache between her legs as she remembered the Countess's touch upon her breasts, how she delicately ran her fingers over Jamison's nipples. She visualized the Countess's fingers and lips exploring her sex, triggering a jolt and surge in that same area, pitching her forward.

She lost her breath as her ribs gave that terrible stabbing pain, tearing away her fantasy—now an image of her father repeatedly kicking her with his boot.

The side of her face twitched and tightened. The Colonel. Where was he now? How was her mother? She futilely hoped that once her body healed so too would the vile memory.

She lathered up the soap and spread bubbles in an attempt to hide the discoloration. She shut off the water and then slumped onto the tile floor.

None of this was supposed to happen. She was supposed to assist her suffragette mentor and learn how to stand on her own two feet as a fully actualized woman. She never envisioned making love with another woman, or getting beaten by her father, or sitting naked and battered on the floor of a shower of a man she hardly knew.

But there she was.

She leaned her head on the enclosure. The skin at her temple felt hot. She could feel the stiff tip of the thread poking up near her eyebrow. She'd never had stitches before.

But she managed a grin. That kind of defiance felt good.

The muscles around her ribs seized up again when she pushed open the shower door. Perspiration erupted along her hairline as she crawled from the shower to the chair where she'd dropped her nightgown. She braced herself on the seat, and then pulled herself up until she was half leaning against the wall. She tried to make her way back into the bedroom, and then managed to put back on her nightgown.

She held the wide black rubber strip to her belly. The ribbons ran down the front of her nightgown like streams of blood; she flicked a strand with her finger, just to make sure.

The fireplace had a dying flame.

She knew Jon was on the other side of the door, waiting in the hall. She placed his creation on the bed before padding closer to the door and turning the knob.

When she peeked out, Jon stood up from the spindle-back chair.

He had a slight guiltiness to his face. She'd caught him sitting like one of those men her mother warned her to stay away from—the shifty ones who picked their teeth with their bare fingers. He looked a bit manic as he rubbed his finger along the face of his watch.

"Mr. Roe—I mean, Jon," she stammered, "I was coming out to find you."

"Oh," he said, placing the chair back against the wall.

As Jon stepped forward he said, "I heard the shower, so I thought I would sit here, in case you needed anything. I was concerned that you might slip and fall."

Jon hadn't been anything but kind to her, but now she'd have a hard time fighting back if he did cross any lines.

But maybe it was better not to feign strength. Maybe showing fragility would make him honor-bound to assist her without thinking he had the upper hand.

Her shoulders dropped when she again looked down at her feet. "I can't reach behind me to put on the cincher. It makes me feel so much better when I have it on. I was wondering if you could help me with it."

"Of course," Jon said. He stayed rooted in place as Jamison returned to the bedroom.

"Mr. Roe?" Jamison spoke over her shoulder, calling for him to enter.

He walked into the room as if he'd never done it before, and then picked up the cincher from the bed. "I… think it would be best if you stayed like that, facing me," he said.

Jamison leaned back, and then looked up at him.

She squeezed her eyes shut, tensing the area around her stitches to distract herself with pain, instead of focusing on the peculiar heat she felt as he moved his fingers over her belly. The cincher was pressing against her back, her linen nightgown sandwiched in between her warm skin and the thin black pliable rubber.

She opened her eyes to see his white dress shirt, as pristine as fresh snow.

His movements seemed deferential. Jon measured the ribbon and then threaded it through until his hands were just below the swell of her breasts. She tried to calm her racing heart.

He tied the bow before turning away.

It seemed to Jamison that this ordeal might be as much of a trial for Jon as it was for herself.

With the support of the cincher at her waist, Jamison bent forward trying to bring her hair closer to her hands, so that she could tug at strands of hair trapped underneath the bandages. She groaned in discomfort, but also in embarrassment, feeling her limp dirty hair between her fingers.

Jon's eyes remained on her as she attempted to straighten up. By the knowing smile on his face, it seemed he could see the grimace behind her own tight smile.

"Jon," Jamison said, picking at the bodice of her nightgown, attempting to loosen the fabric from being so form-fitted at her breasts. "Could you help me with one more thing this morning? I'd like to wash my hair, but, as you can see…" She grimaced while raising her arms.

Jon pinched the space on his forehead between his eyebrows and then nodded solemnly. "Of course." He walked over to the en-suite bath. Jamison stood at the side of the bed, waiting for the sound of the water.

She listened for quite a while before Jon leaned back into the room. "Would you mind if I removed my shirt? I don't want to get it wet." Jon reached for his collar stud.

Jamison focused on the wall just to the right of his shoulder, afraid that if she looked directly into his eyes she wouldn't be able to speak.

"Of course, go right ahead," she said, rolling her hand in mid-air. "I'm from the South. Men work shirtless all throughout the summertime." She couldn't help but blush at her lie. The truth was that Mr. Moses would never let the workers strip their shirts off, as they plowed the fields or exercised the horses.

The bathroom looked entirely different now that Jon was standing next to the sink in his trousers and undershirt, holding a stool in front of himself like a lion tamer. The steam didn't billow over the top of the shower door as it had before; it slunk and traipsed, teased around the thin fabric of his clothing.

Jon ducked around the water spray to place the stool in the shower. He then motioned for her to sit.

"Wouldn't it be easier if I got in while the water was off?" she asked. "I'm sure it's hot enough."

"You're right. What was I thinking? Hold on, let me adjust the stream and…" He shut it off and then stared at Jamison with a look that begged for her support. "I'll be as gentle as possible," he said, gripping her elbows to assist her onto the stool. "I need to remove the bandages so that I can get to your hair." He carefully peeled the gauze wrapped around her head. She winced when he tugged at a section stuck to the dried blood at her temple.

"Sorry," he said, "I bet that stung a bit. Let me know if you're ever uncomfortable, okay?"

Her breath caught in her throat.

Of course she was uncomfortable. She was in a shower with a man. It would have even been uncomfortable for her to be in a shower with Carrington. Of course this was off the pale for her.

Jon took hold of the handheld nozzle and then turned on the water, testing the temperature with his hand. "How does this feel?" he asked, spraying a light stream onto her palm.

She watched droplets of water ricochet off of the tiled floor and onto the hem of her nightgown.

"Feels… nice," she said.

Jon wetted a washcloth and then placed it over her head, bringing it down along her hairline. He then brought the nozzle closer to her scalp while holding the back of her neck, letting the water stream through her hair. As she relaxed, she noticed how gently his fingers cradled her neck. He turned off the water and then lathered shampoo before washing her head.

"That smells incredible, what's in it?" she asked. "Missy makes our shampoo using lavender flowers… This isn't lavender."

Jon cleared his throat. "Ishmael makes it from soapnuts and hibiscus flowers." Jon stilled his hands on the crown of her head. "I was fine with bar soap until he left a vial of this liquid on my dresser." Jon's two baby fingers swept suds from her temple back into her hair. "It does something more than bar soap, doesn't it?" He started at her forehead before working up to the crown, massaging deeply as he went. His fingers danced little circles all over the top of her head.

Jamison glanced at the muscles rippling beneath his undershirt, then to where his shirt met the stiff belt circling his waist, a slight bulge along the side of his left trouser leg.

Jon began to lightly massage her nape. She closed her eyes. With his thumbs he followed strands of knotted muscles up her neck to her hairline, one by one. Jamison's lips parted as her tongue rested just outside of her mouth. While he caressed her neck, the white fabric of his undershirt turned more translucent.

He pressed her earlobes between his fingers; the pressure heated her skin, making the wet fabric over her breasts feel frigid. She was tempted to peek at him; she knew that he could clearly see her nipples, but she didn't want to stop him from looking. Like those other times, it made her feel curiously powerful.

"How are you doing?" he asked, shifting closer. "You okay?" He cradled the base of her head in his palm, kneading her neck before running his fingers along her shoulders. "…Care to share?"

She tilted back her head, feeling the tug of her hair. "I don't think so, Jon." She hid her smile. "I think I'll just *be*—if you don't mind."

Jon released her coil of hair from his hand.

He reached for the nozzle again, carefully rinsing Jamison's head.

48.

Jon wrapped a warm towel around Jamison's head and then helped her from the shower stall over to the sofa in front of the fireplace. The fire had burned down to embers, so he stoked it back to life.

Jamison watched Jon maneuver around the hearth. He had slipped his shirt back on, foregoing the collar and cuff studs. He had beautiful fingers, but she found herself oddly mesmerized by his bare feet. His skin was tan, his ankles were narrow, and she could see the tendons flexing as he kneeled.

"Almost done, just one more step," he said walking over to the dresser. He showed her the hairbrush. "May I?"

When Jamison nodded he carefully unwrapped the towel from her head. "How does your head feel? Any pain near your stitches?"

"Not really," she said, carefully walking her fingers around the swollen parts of her face. "Today is the first day that I haven't had a headache, or been aware of that awful pinching in the corner of my eye."

"Good," he said. "The doctor will come next week to remove your stitches." He stared back at her. "The bruising on your face is almost gone, as well." He traced his finger along the pattern on the silver brush handle.

Jon clenched the head of the brush in his hand. The bristles poked like quills through the spaces between his fingers.

The fire crackled and the logs shifted into a new position.

How empty the château seemed.

"I think you should know," Jon said, "that I told your father I would kill him if he ever left his farm again."

The clear sound of the grandfather clock began to match the low-level throbbing around Jamison's temples.

"I'm not sure what I'll do," she said. Jamison put her cool hands on the sides of her face.

Jon narrowed his eyes at her, giving her the feeling that he would not let her comment slip by without elaboration.

"I came to Lucerne to assist a writer who happened to graduate from my prep school in Lexington. I lost my position because of my father." She folded her hands in her lap.

"What do you mean?"

Jamison shook her head. "Doesn't matter, anymore. They're gone and I'm here, still in Lucerne, trying to get my life in order."

Jon grazed his thumb over the quills of the brush as if considering which of his many questions to ask first. "I want to know more about you." He walked over to her. "Tell me about… growing up on the farm, about the Colonel and your mother." Jon took a section of her hair into his hand, and then starting at the bottom he began to brush out the tangles.

Jamison stared at the fireplace. From a wormhole in the log, sap sizzled and dripped onto the stones under the flames.

"I don't know where to begin." She scrunched up the fabric of her robe over her legs. "I'm ashamed of my father… embarrassed by all that's happened."

She smoothed her hands over the crinkled linen and said, "I barely know you and the Countess, and…" Jamison lifted one hand to rub her forehead, "I think, sometimes, I'm going a bit crazy, behaving in ways—doing things that I didn't even know people did. Not sure I know who I am." She looked over at him through her fingers.

Jon lowered her hand from her face. "You're still young. It's not uncommon to be confused at different times in our lives."

Jamison's mouth pulled tight, and her words came out hard-clipped and raw. "I haven't been able to leave it behind. From Kentucky, to Ohio, to Switzerland, I'm dragging a suitcase full of confusion. I've struggled since… forever. I've never figured out how to make my parents happy—mainly the Colonel. It's been a… moving target, measuring up to what *he* wanted." Jamison pressed her lips together, stopping herself from admitting any more.

"Come now, Jamison. How could you not measure up? Just look at you."

She shook her head. "You know, he gave me that name… set me up for failure."

"Jamison, son of James. That it?" he asked, skirting around the coffee table to sit down next to her.

"The Colonel's foreman, Mr. Moses, set me straight once. 'No use wasting God's time, praying to be nothing other than what you are.'"

Jamison rested her cheek on her knees. "What did old black Moses really know about anything, anyway?"

Jon crossed his arms over his chest. "Well, he seems wise enough. He might have been giving you a bit of advice."

"Maybe that's advice best saved for someone else. At this point what I have is a whole bunch of nothing because I already failed to measure up. I refused to go along with the Colonel's scheme. Look where that's gotten me." She turned away.

Jon lifted his finger to her jaw, encouraging her to look at him.

"What was the scheme?"

Jamison glanced down her nose at his hand and then turned her head, breaking contact. "You won't judge me, will you?" Jamison tightened up, steeling herself. He had on the same distant look when he spoke about being unable to turn back time.

"Life is too short to be something that some other person wants you to be." Jon sat back against the sofa. "Believe me."

Jamison nestled against the sofa arm and bounced her knee. "We are seeing eye to eye on that one, that's for sure." Jamison shook her head and bounced her knee faster.

He stilled her leg with his hand and then he stretched across the sofa, grabbing a fur blanket from the other end.

He draped it over her before settling his arm along the sofa's back. Jamison pulled it higher.

"What plan did the Colonel have for you?" he asked again.

She took a deep breath and sighed. "He showed up with Jennings, as you saw... part of his most recent plan." She spoke to the fire. "He calls us his little soldiers—and if we don't go along with his plan, we get punished."

"Punished? Is—this..." He pointed at her wounds "...punishment for something that you didn't do?"

She tucked the blanket around her body. "I was to use all my feminine powers to persuade Jennings into marriage," she said crossing her arms.

As Jon then shook his head, Jamison could see the disbelief in his face. As if it was ridiculous to think she could seduce anyone.

She shoved the blanket off and snatched up the pen from the coffee table. "Don't judge me, Jon. You have no right," she said using the pen like a rapier.

Jon stood. "No. Listen, Jamison… I am not judging you. I want to understand you. I'm… I'm seeing who you are, up close. I'm watching you be fierce and I'm watching you be soft. I'm seeing your want," he said quietly.

She dropped the pen next to the books on the coffee table, and then settled back to the sofa arm. "My want? Jamison Jones Davenport has brought me way more pain than just all of this." She quickly pointed up and down at her wounds. "What you said that you see in me might be there, but whoever I was before the Colonel beat me up… it needs to go. I want to leave her behind and see who I can become. To just get away from this lie that's held me back."

He smiled in a way that showed his relief and then sat down. "Now, that makes perfect sense," he said. "Are you suggesting a name change? What would your name be?"

"A name change? I actually wasn't sure what I was referring to, but now that you mention it, maybe that's precisely what I need." The first thing that came to Jamison's mind was the last time she saw Carrington—the day of her nineteenth birthday, when he hung the crystal necklace around her neck.

"Well," she said, "I was given a beautiful gift once that meant so much to me. It's kept me strong, and it gives me hope that I'll be happy." Jamison patted her chest and then looked down, pulling open the top of her robe. "Where's my necklace—I've lost it!" She leapt from the sofa, again stabbed by a jolt of pain. Jon jumped up to steady her.

"Relax—I have your necklace. The cord was ruined, so I changed it. Wait here," he said.

"Wait here?" she said, beginning to pace after he left the room. Jamison critically eyed her bedroom; the fancy silk of her bed, the marble fireplace with its huge inset mirror above, and the fur, mink no less—all of it expensive.

She settled back onto the sofa and rested her head on a pillow. "Jamison," she spoke aloud, "how are you going to know what's worth keeping?"

Jon seemed to have some definite opinions; perhaps he saw something in her that was just as unique? Maybe she didn't want to ditch all of what she was.

He returned with her necklace in hand, letting it swing from side-to-side. She drew it closer.

"I hope it doesn't bother you too much that I changed out that flimsy thread," he said.

She looked at the new black cord. It was rubber. It looked like a string of licorice.

Carrington's face came to mind—the kaleidoscope of shimmery blues in his eyes, and that soft smile when he placed the necklace around her neck. "No—no, I don't mind." She could feel her cheeks heat up as she considered how that cord was one more tie to Carrington that would be gone forever. She wanted to cry, but instead just felt a soulless, empty mood.

Jon settled back onto the sofa.

He sat patiently, holding her hairbrush in his hands, appearing almost boyish, plucking a strand of her hair from the bristles. He wound it around his little finger just below the nail. "Please," he gave a gesture to continue with what she'd started telling him.

Jamison squeezed the crystal in her palm.

"Crystal—Crystal Jones... That's who I'd like to be." She held her necklace up to the light of the flames. "No more Jamison, and no more Davenport," she stated, feeling rightness swell within her. "Jones was my mother's..." she thought about her mother's current situation and stared blankly at the fireplace.

Jon unwound the string of hair from his finger; the blue-white of his fingertip turned back to a healthier pink. He placed the neatly rolled hair in his pant pocket, reassuring her with a smile—making no effort to hide the moment he stashed it.

"Crystal Jones," he said. "I like the sound of that. Whenever you're ready, I'll have one of my attorneys start the process to legally change your name."

She assumed it would take a series of telegrams and a drag-out fight with the Colonel and her mother. Difficult, like everything else had ever been.

"You're an adult, Jamison," he seemed to answer the look she gave. "You can do as you please. You don't need permission from anyone."

“Well then,” she said, placing her hand over her heart, “call me Crystal.”

49.

After Jon said goodnight she lay back down on the sofa, snuggled the mink blanket up to her chin, rubbing it along her face. One direction was soft, the other bristling against her skin.

After a while she folded the fur side away; the pretty chocolate colored satin wasn't distracting enough to hide the low stench of an animal pelt.

She lifted the crystal away from her chest, rolled it between her fingers, studying its sides. As she stared at it she envisioned Carrington again, remembering how he looked when they got back from their pond, when the Colonel yelled at him for lollygagging with her. He was frustrated, she'd been cruel, and that fit of anger swept around them like a dust devil.

"Carrington," she said quietly, holding the crystal in the cradle of her hands. "I've been wearing this necklace for four years. They were four of the most difficult years of my life. Nothing has turned out like I thought." She shook her head. "Absolutely nothing." She again mouthed the word 'nothing' to herself while the flames wriggled and spread over the logs, eating away at the dry bark. She blew a strand of hair off her face and then pushed the fur to the floor.

She needed to strike a balance between her past and who she would become with this new name.

And that's what she had now: a new name and no plan beyond the shelter of a stranger's roof—a man who had the ability and power to send her parents away. Jon had *capital*. That was a word her father would use.

The Colonel had been willing use his own capital to help her too, until he wasn't.

She pressed the crystal to the stitches above her brow, the black rubber cording dropped in front of her eye. She examined it and then rolled it between her fingers—thin, yet dense—pliable, yet resilient to her pinch and tug. If she had a mind to, and used more effort, she could probably stretch it to the breaking point.

She looped the cord around her fingers like a slingshot, sighting targets around the room. She took aim at the painting of the demure woman toeing the water. Then, at the vase of flowers on the nightstand.

Peonies.

Didn't Jon say they represented transformation?

Her mother seemed quite impressed with them, said they must have cost a fortune—but what was money to Jon?

Her value to him certainly had little to do with her pocketbook. If he hadn't invited her to that dinner party…

No.

She'd been so stupidly reactive the whole time.

She tightened her grip on that makeshift slingshot and re-aimed at the painted woman whose posture seemed utterly unstable, yet somehow compelling.

"Pow," she quietly spoke. She unwound the cord and fixed the necklace back in place.

She braced her arm against her ribs to lean forward and pick up the leather-bound book and pen from the coffee table. She pressed her palm to the book's spine and forced the pages open.

She uncapped the pen and tapped it against her chin.

It's not what you're born with; it's what you choose to hold onto. Carrington's face again came to mind. She turned the page and started again.

Dear Carrington,

It's not what you're born with, it's what you choose to hold onto. That's what I've been thinking about.

I don't know where you are. I don't how you are. And I don't know how you could have been away each time I came home from college. I will admit that it hurt. Truth be told, it hurt so much I dreaded coming back, because I knew in my heart you wouldn't be there. I never got a straight answer from anyone—not even your father.

You never answered my letters, nor did I ever get one from you, so maybe you decided I wasn't worth keeping. But I want you to know that I've always kept you close to my heart. I'm wearing the crystal necklace you gave me. I always wear it.

I don't know what happened between us, but I've grown enough to understand that when things happen, we change in response. I've changed, or maybe I'm just in the midst of changing. It's not easy figuring out what to leave behind. We can't throw everything away. Especially not the decent sides, the sweet memories and hope. We can't lose hope. Please hold on to it. I am.

I am making a future for myself. I guess I had a plan before all of this. Have you heard the saying "Man plans, God laughs?"

I'm scared that I may never see you again, so I need to put it in writing, like a contractual letter that you may never get stating clearly that I choose you.

I love you. I always will.

J.

She ripped that page out of the book and folded it in half. Tomorrow she'd find an envelope, and maybe someday Carrington would find her.

She then began writing her book like she always intended to. The words didn't spill out. They tumbled rough, scraping around stubborn memories like an angry farrier with a hoof pick.

The grandfather clock was about to mark the beginning of a new day, so she doubled her effort.

She'd be damned to let that get in her way.

50.

Carrington's body felt like a carcass laid out and ready to be feasted on by the ants and flies. The chill seeped through his skin down to his bones, as he focused on one cloud drifting beyond the hill strewn with dead does. The pain went beyond physical—his soul was battered.

Cole nickered and bobbed his head, scratching at the ground.

"Cole," Carrington called out in a rasp; his trusted horse's name sounded like a whispered prayer. He said it again, over and over, as he dragged himself across the brittle leaves over to his horse.

He finally pulled himself up and onto the saddle. Too tender to sit, he just pushed his boots against the tread of his stirrups and then turned Cole away from the scene. By cover of darkness, Carrington rode in the direction of the farm—half blind of his surroundings.

He raised his head when he noticed that Cole had stopped.

Carrington had to have passed out.

Cole dipped his head down to drink from the pond Carrington knew as his own.

In the moonlight, Carrington could see the rope swing hanging over the water. It looked different.

Innocent, narrow, and waiting. But, he imagined the jute threads cutting into the skin of his neck. He imagined the water filling his boots, them slipping from his relaxed feet as his eyes lost sight of the middle of the pond, where he had always found with Jamison a solitary joy.

All he would have to do is walk Cole into the pond, tie the rope around his own neck and then slide from Cole's back to hang, to die in the one spot where he'd felt closest to her.

Cole would find his way back to the farm.

They'd find his body.

Eventually, she would forget; if she hadn't already.

Cole rounded, nudging his withers into Carrington's face. Carrington fell from his horse, knocking the wind from his lungs. His labored breath turned into sobs that rolled him as tight as a sowbug.

He sobbed into the dirt. The dirt covered his mouth, his tongue—he breathed it in. He fisted more into his mouth. He smeared it over his face. Filth burned from his ass up to his eyes. He felt stained inside and out, marked in a way that could never be washed.

The grit and sand that dropped into his eyes felt as sharp as chips of glass. Through the tears and dirt, he saw Cole nodding toward the shore.

Carrington again locked his eyes on the slender rope tied to the gnarled catalpa branch overhanging the pond.

Cole walked back to the water, splayed his front legs and then lowered his head for a drink. As Carrington dragged himself to the water's edge, Cole bobbed his head and snorted.

Once Carrington's fingers touched the water, he felt revitalized all the way from his hands and arms to his shoulders and belly. He willingly slid like a salamander into the icy water. His legs were useless as he clawed at the slick lichen that carpeted the rocks, trying to return to the surface. He screamed out into the water that swallowed him. He thrashed and kicked until his body finally floated to the surface of the pond.

There, the rope swayed above him. He looked beyond the rope, through the branches to the stars blinking above. He didn't want to pollute their sanctuary of sacred memories by defiling it with his corpse. He pulled off his boots and tossed them to land. He ripped from his body what was left of his long johns, and then he crawled ashore.

He left Cole at the pond and made his way through the darkness along the familiar path home. He then stood at the barn and listened. The building he shared with his father was to his left. The lights were off. He looked up at the sky to see that the moon was positioned at a late dusk; his father would be asleep. Luckily, his room had two doors, one that allowed him to come and go without going through the house.

Carrington didn't dare light the lamp. He slumped down onto his bed, considering the threadbare quilt as something he would miss; his mother made it for him.

But he couldn't take it—they'd know he'd been back.

He needed to take the essentials, and yet for the life of him he couldn't work out just what those were.

God, he just wanted to rest.

And then his hands fell upon his bare legs. He made his way over to the dresser, trying not to think about how sick he felt, and then he pulled on the first pair of pants he touched. The second pair he then rolled up and put on the dresser. He opened another drawer and slipped on a long sleeve undershirt, and then a sweater. He knew he needed to be more cautious with the top drawer—it was warped. He tugged it open just enough to reach his arm between the dresser and the drawer, before grabbing a pair of socks and underwear, placing them next to the pants. He threaded his arm into the drawer again, reaching back to the corner where he had kept his drawings of Jamison—the wooden box that held his drawing pencils and sharpening knife. It stood sentry, blocking unworthy attention. He knew by touch the shape of the painted lettering on the oblong container, and where the *C* of the logo had been dented by his nail, turning the curved edge into a flower.

He heard something skidding along the floor in the living room. He cocked his head as his arm stilled in the narrow mouth of the drawer. His heartbeat dashed between his ears. Someone was up. Even when straining to listen, he couldn't hear much over the pulse of his heart.

He eased his hand out, and then as he shut the drawer there was the same sensation he had felt when shoveling dirt upon his mother's grave. He had to leave Jamison behind.

Nimble footsteps moved toward the front door.

It didn't sound like his father.

He moved light on his feet over to his closet and then grabbed the leather satchel and coat that his father had given him. He checked the front pocket to find his savings still there. He then put his Sunday shoes in the bag, and then quietly walked back to the dresser for the other things. As he dropped the few belongings into his satchel, he leaned toward the front door, straining to figure out who the hell was out there.

Carrington backed off, keeping his eyes pinned to his bedroom door, which led to the main room of their home. He felt for the doorknob.

The house was quiet. It made him heartsick to picture his father in the morning as he always was: standing at the kitchen sink, sipping the dregs of his coffee, calling out over his shoulder to Carrington that it was time to get a move on. He could imagine the inevitable catch in his father's voice, day after day, remembering each morning that Carrington wasn't around to hear him. His dad had already weathered the loss of his wife, and now he would be without a son. Carrington wasn't dead, but neither was he living; he felt somewhere between, as he left behind the only home he'd ever known.

Acknowledgments

It took me half a century to decide I'd become a writer. This was after a fortune teller read my palm, suggesting I try my hand at a novel. She seemed enthusiastically sweet—and perhaps slightly mad from that assertion. At first, I disregarded it because letters and numbers only ratcheted my dyslexia into a deep-seated dread, the same heart pounding discomfort I'd feel every time when entering a multi-floor building: I'd never find my way out.

But the strangest thing happened one night of December that year. I was at Lake Tahoe with my three kids, while my husband was at home recuperating from surgery (don't ask)—and I experienced a dream that changed me. Maybe the cause of my dream that night was the subtle shift of familial energy, or my battered self-esteem; whatever it was, it woke within me a fighter. I always had vibrant nocturnal reveries, like a mishmash of Fellini, Coen Brothers, del Toro, Lynch, and Disney, where I'd wake up remembering scents and flavors, feeling myself dreaming while watching my body tremble from the action in my head.

That night in Tahoe I dreamt of two women making love on the threadbare carpet of a steamship stateroom. I can still see snapshot images of them, the light sheen of sweat on their luminescent skin, the delicate lace of their wrinkled petticoats; they were beautiful and otherworldly.

The dream lingered even as I drove my brood back home—the whole time thinking: I should write a book.

I sat down to write on the evening of January 3rd, and then by March 18th I had written over 340,000 words. That initial spurt of creative insanity gave me renewed strength and determination to live as I saw fit.

When I started writing, I wasn't sure where I would end up. I had no expectations for the final outcome; like a child, I tumbled freely. I changed direction many times and grew with each subsequent version, until I realized how this story reflected my own movement to claim agency over my situation.

This book series would not be possible if my life were anything other than what it is—a messy work in progress. And that work isn't done in a vacuum. I need to thank the Universe for the trials that have formed me, and those who guided me along the way.

Notably, I need to thank my sister, DeDe Silver Beheshti, who has read this story and every iteration leading up to it, always offering salient advice, a glass of wine, and a safe place to fall apart without a shred of judgment. She is my most fervent cheerleader.

As well, my editors. Stacey Donovan was my first. She asked the important question, "Dana, do you really want to write pornography?" Even over the phone I could hear her eyebrow eking into her hairline (Yes, those pages still exist. Join my mailing list for sections that didn't make it.). From pornography to erotica, I then met my current editor Ange Baker, whose patience, humor, diligence, and firm coffee-fueled nudges had led me to literary fiction.

And finally, I'd like to thank my family, Robert, Claire, Jacob, and Jacqueline—my gratitude for your patience and support cannot be overstated. I'm not sure that writing a book would ever be described as easy, but being a wife and mother required a delicate balance to be struck between familial duty and my desire to emerge as a freestanding agent. They're used to my creative vigor in short bursts, but this project lasted years—and with luck, will continue to be the focus of my creative energies in the future. I hope that this ongoing process has taught them that being passionate about a project is a *raison d'être*. The irony being that the last place I would have looked to find my salvation was in the discipline that gave me the greatest fear.

About The Author

D.K. Silver is the author of *The Weight of Flowers*, the first in a genre-bending saga. The series explores themes of sexual exploitation and dalliance, greed in its many guises, and the quest for self-worth.

D.K. Silver is fearless in her determination to explore taboos, using her gifts to relentlessly dig below the surface. As a costume designer, she's been trained to visually reveal a character's truer nature. As a writer she takes it to another level, passionate to unmask the deliciously decadent, the deviant, and the downright misguided aspects of our collective humanness. Her stories are paced like a slow-motion car crash that's difficult to look away from.

When not at her kitchen table in Carmel-By-The-Sea writing her next project, Signal Hill, you'll find her teaching yoga or walking the beach. She often divides her time between her own thoughts and the clamoring of characters who vie for her attention. She celebrates long, well-penned sentences with cooking and gardening, and irons her sheets for meditation. On Sundays, you'll find her letting go on a World Ecstatic Dance Zoom site.

Now that you've reached the end, I encourage you to leave a review on **Amazon**, **Goodreads,** or your favorite book sites. I'd absolutely love it if you could share your experience.

Alternatively, if you have read my book as a Kindle eBook you could leave a rating. That is just one simple click, indicating how many stars of five you think the book deserves.

In gratitude,

S. K. Silver

The Weight Of Flowers is the first of a four book series. If Carrington, Crystal, and Jon's story has your heart racing and your curiosity piqued, turn the page to get a sneak peek at *Forcing Shoots*, the second book in the series due out Fall of 2023.

Forcing Shoots

Carrington

1.

The wind kicked up at Lexington station, shrouding a train's engine in steam from the smokebox chimney. Carrington nestled closer to a post holding up one of the foul weather tin overhangs in the boarding area. As the steam rose and revealed the blue-black hulk of the train, Carrington pushed his knuckles against his Adam's apple until his tongue felt like a fist in his throat.

He strained to see beneath his cap's bill, at the figures milling about the platform.

Carrington was certain he would be found out.

He could still feel the Colonel's hand around his throat.

The long shrill of a whistle pierced through Carrington's thoughts, jolting his head against the post. His ears rang as he slumped forward, bringing his full weight from his hands onto his thighs. His head had been throbbing, and he struggled to catch his breath.

Carrington stared below the body of the train, at the dark wooden ties between the gleaming rails—counting each one, as he made his way.

The engine sighed, forcing a cloud of steam over the platform.

He hoped the Colonel was dead.

Beyond the train engine was a track leading Carrington away from everything he'd ever known.

Once more, the whistle's shrill.

"All aboard!" called the conductor, and Carrington felt the heaviness within his own chest—uncertainty with every step forward. It looked like a jail on wheels.

He gave the ticket with a trembling hand.

Up two metal steps and then three strides landed Carrington in the narrow corridor between the two rows of seats, more severe in angle than park benches. He walked through the car until he found seat 3. Luckily, it was one of the few singles. He wouldn't have to share his space.

Carrington hauled his bag onto the puny rack above his bench. He attempted to seat it more securely, as he peered out the window at the near empty platform. The station agent looked bored, as he checked his pocket watch, before blowing his whistle.

The carriage lurched forward, and then a violent tug whiplashed Carrington into his seat, toppling his bag into the aisle. The wad of cash he'd tucked into his bag's front pocket had slipped out onto the floor. He hunkered down, snuck a glance over his shoulder at the other passengers, while snatching up his savings back into the bag. His heart continued its heavy pulse as the train staggered from the station, the deafening hoot of the train wailed out like a demon.

The agent slid his watch back into a vest pocket, before turning to drag a handcart through the office doors.

Outside, the platform disappeared as the train picked up speed and eased to the left.

How long would it be before anyone took notice? He didn't even know how long they were to be set out on that hunting trip.

Missy would likely be the first to know something was up. He could picture her standing in the middle of the long front road with her arms crossed under her bosoms, her head canted at an angle, covered in a beehive of calico.

What if the Colonel wasn't dead?

What would be his story?

Carrington squeezed his eyes until they ached. A flash of senses hit him—the Colonel's bourbon breath, the sound of his own long johns getting pulled and torn, the dirt, blood, and grass on his tongue and lips, as he'd screamed into the ground. He clenched his teeth, until the upward part of his jaw ached enough to dull the thoughts.

The first day became the first night, and then the sun rose at the train's back, casting faint shadows on the huddled figures in the seat ahead of him—mostly indistinguishable lumps of humanity, save for a lady's hat here and there.

He passed his days and nights staying in that damned seat. His back was stiff, and his rump felt like a cold stone. Sometimes, he'd catch a whiff of himself, reminiscent of shit mucked from the barn stalls at Davenport.

The train thundered westward. His thoughts skimmed his consciousness as swiftly as the wheels skimmed the tracks—nothing stuck.

Carrington would only leave his seat to use the restroom or eat a simple meal from the food cart. When he finally stepped outside of the train as it ran along the tracks, he was reminded of riding Cole and that farewell moment; his fingers rubbed Cole's silky ears and he held the broad face between his hands, staring into eyes that were kind and forgiving. "This isn't forever, boy. I'll be back for you, I promise. I got a list of everything that belongs to me—you're number two." Carrington smiled when Cole shook his head, protesting that Jamison's name was above his, but she'd always be his number one.

www.ingramcontent.com/pod-product-compliance
Lightning Source LLC
Chambersburg PA
CBHW020936310726
48980CB00007B/796/J
* 9 7 8 0 5 7 8 3 7 5 5 0 2 *